Jennifer Probst brings the "nonstop sexual tension" (Laura Kaye) that lights up her *New York Times* and *USA Today* bestsellers to a dazzling new series of a matchmaking agency where love's magic is at work!

SEARCHING FOR PERFECT

"Entertaining and engaging and real. . . . Jennifer Probst is a romance writing superstar. . . . [A] fantastic series."
—*Bella's Little Book Blog*

"A wonderfully moving, deeply emotional, steamy, sexy, fantastic story of hope, healing, and love. 5 huge loving stars!"
—*Sizzling Book Club*

SEARCHING FOR SOMEDAY

"A sophisticated, sexy romance . . . witty, passionate."
—*RT Book Reviews*

"Refreshing."
—*Publishers Weekly*

"Full of emotion and heart. . . . 5 stars!"
—*Sizzling Book Club*

"Delightfully romantic and fun. . . . One of the best contemporary authors!"
—*Under the Covers*

"Offers both heat and heart."
—*Booklist Online*

ALSO BY JENNIFER PROBST

THE MARRIAGE TO A BILLIONAIRE SERIES

The Marriage Bargain
The Marriage Trap
The Marriage Mistake
The Marriage Merger

THE SEARCHING FOR SERIES

Searching for Someday
Searching for Perfect

the marriage trap

JENNIFER PROBST

POCKET BOOKS

New York   London   Toronto   Sydney   New Delhi

Pocket Books
An Imprint of Simon & Schuster, Inc.
1230 Avenue of the Americas
New York, NY 10020

This book is a work of fiction. Any references to historical events, real people, or real places are used fictitiously. Other names, characters, places, and events are products of the author's imagination, and any resemblance to actual events or places or persons, living or dead, is entirely coincidental.

This Pocket Books paperback edition May 2015

POCKET and colophon are registered trademarks of Simon & Schuster, Inc.

For information about special discounts for bulk purchases, please contact Simon & Schuster Special Sales at 1-866-506-1949 or business@simonandschuster.com.

The Simon & Schuster Speakers Bureau can bring authors to your live event. For more information or to book an event, contact the Simon & Schuster Speakers Bureau at 1-866-248-3049 or visit our website at www.simonspeakers.com.

Manufactured in the United States of America

10 9 8 7 6 5 4 3 2 1

ISBN 978-1-5011-0409-1
ISBN 978-1-4767-1754-8 (ebook)

To my husband.

I guess love spells work after all, and there are happily ever afters. Thanks for being with me through every crazy, chaotic moment. Thanks for keeping me halfway sane, being a fantastic father, and most of all, for cooking dinner. I love you.

And to my fabulous, wonderful, amazing editors, Liz Pelletier and Libby Murphy. This simply would not have happened without you.

the marriage trap

Chapter One

Maggie Ryan tilted the margarita glass to her lips and took a long swallow. Tartness collided with the salt, exploded on her tongue, and burned through her blood. Unfortunately, not fast enough. She still had a shred of sanity left to question her actions.

The violet fabric-covered book beckoned and mocked. She picked it up again, leafed through the pages, and threw it back on the contemporary glass table. Ridiculous. *Love spells*, for God's sake. She refused to stoop to such a low. Of course, when her best friend, Alexa, cast her own spell, she'd been supportive and cheered her actions to find her soul mate.

But this was completely different.

Maggie cursed under her breath and stared out the

window. A sliver of moonlight leaked through the cracks of the organic bamboo blinds. Another evening gone. Another disastrous date. The demons threatened, and there was no one here to fight them back until dawn.

Why did she never feel a connection? This last one had been charming, intelligent, and easygoing. She expected a sexual buzz when they finally touched—or at least a lousy shiver of promise. Instead, she got zilch. Zippo. Numb from the waist down. Just a dull ache of emptiness and a longing for . . . more.

Despair toppled over her like a cresting wave. The familiar edge of panic clawed her gut, but she fought back and managed to surface. Screw this. She refused to have an attack on her own turf. Maggie grabbed the raw irritation like a life vest and breathed deeply and evenly.

Stupid attacks. She hated pills and refused to take them, positive the episodes would go away by her own sheer force of will. Probably an early midlife crisis. After all, her life was almost perfect.

She had everything most people dreamed about. She photographed gorgeous male models in underwear and traveled the world. She adored her trendy condo with no upkeep. The kitchen boasted stainless steel appliances and gleaming ceramic tile. The modern espresso maker and margarita machine confirmed her fun, *Sex and the City* status. Plush white carpets and matching leather furniture boasted no children and bespoke sheer style. She did what she wanted, when she wanted, and made no damn apologies to anyone. She was attractive, financially comfortable, and healthy, aside from the occasional panic attacks. And yet, the question nibbled on the edge of her brain with an irritating persistence, growing a bit more with each passing day.

Is this it?

Maggie stood and yanked on a silky red robe, then stuffed her feet into her matching fuzzy slippers with devil horns sprouting from the top of the foot. She was drunk enough, and no one would ever know. Maybe the exercise would calm her nerves.

She grabbed the piece of ledger paper and made a list of all the qualities she craved in a man.

Built the small fire.

Recited the mantra.

Gleeful cackles echoed in her brain at the act of insanity, but she shoved them back with another sip of tequila and watched the paper burn.

After all, she had nothing left to lose.

• • •

The sun looked pissed off.

Michael Conte stood outside by the waterfront property and watched the perfect disc struggle to top the mountain peaks. A fiery mingling of burnt orange and scarlet red rose, emanating sparks of fury, killing the remaining dark. He watched the king of the morning proudly celebrate the temporary win and for a brief moment wondered if he'd ever feel like that again.

Alive.

He shook his head and mocked his own thoughts. He had nothing to complain about. His life was just about perfect. The waterfront project neared completion, and the launch of his family's first U.S. bakery would seize the place by storm. He hoped.

Michael gazed out over the water and took note of the renovations. Once a broken-down, crime-ridden marina, the Hudson Valley property revealed a Cinderella transformation, and he'd been a part of it. Between himself and the other two investors, they'd sunk a lot of money into the dream and Michael believed in the team's success. Paved-stone pathways now snaked around rosebushes and the boats finally returned—majestic schooners and the famed ferryboat that gave children rides.

Next to his bakery, a spa and Japanese restaurant courted an eclectic set of customers. Opening day was only a few weeks away after a long year of construction and sweat and blood.

And La Dolce Famiglia would finally take her home in New York.

Satisfaction rippled through him, along with a strange emptiness. What was wrong with him lately? He slept less, and the occasional woman he allowed himself to enjoy only left him feeling more restless when morning rose. On the surface, he had everything a man dreamed of. Wealth. A career he loved. Family, friends, and decent health. And pretty much his pick of any woman he craved. The Italian in his soul cried out for something deeper than sex, but he didn't know if it truly existed.

At least, not for him. As if something deep inside was broken.

Disgusted with his inner whining, he turned and strode down the sidewalk. His cell phone beeped, and he slid it out of his cashmere coat, glancing at the number.

Crap.

He paused for a moment. Then with a sigh of resignation, he punched the button.

"Yes, Venezia? What is it this time?"

"Michael, I'm in trouble." Rapid-fire Italian attacked his ears.

Michael concentrated on her tirade of words, desperate to make sense between gulps of sobbing breaths. "Did you say you're getting married?"

"Weren't you listening, Michael?" She quickly switched to English. "You must help me!"

"Go slowly. Deep breaths, then tell me the whole story."

"Mama won't let me get married!" she burst out. "And it's all your fault. You know Dominick and I have been together for years, and I've been hoping and praying he'd pop the question and he finally did. Oh, Michael, he brought me to the Piazza Vecchia and got down on his knee and the ring is beautiful, just beautiful! Of course, I said yes, and then we rushed to Mama to tell the whole family, and—"

"Wait a minute. Dominick never called me to ask permission for your hand in marriage." Irritation pricked at him. "Why didn't I know of this?"

His sister gave a long sigh. "You have got to be kidding me! That custom is ancient, and you're not even here, and everyone knows we were getting married; it was just a matter of time. Anyway, none of this matters because I'm going to be an old maid and I'll lose Dominick forever. He'll never wait for me and it's all your fault!"

His head throbbed in time to Venezia's whines. "How is this my fault?"

"Mama told me I can't get married until you're married. Remember that ridiculous tradition Papa believed in?"

Dread slithered up his spine and coiled in his gut. Impossible. The old family tradition had no place in today's society. Sure, the legacy of the oldest son marrying first was prominent in Bergamo, and as the senior count he was looked upon as the leader, but they were long past the days of a required marriage. "I'm sure there was a miscommunication," he said smoothly. "I'll straighten this out."

"She told Dominick I can wear the ring, but there will be no wedding until you marry. Then Dominick got upset and said he doesn't know how long he can wait before he starts his life with me, and Mama got mad and called him disrespectful, and we had a big fight and now my life is over, all over! How can she do this to me?"

Gasping sobs broke out over the receiver.

Michael closed his eyes. The dull throb in his temples grew to monstrous proportions.

He slashed through Venezia's wails with an impatience he didn't try to hide. "Calm down," he ordered. She immediately quieted, used to his authority in the household. "Everyone knows you and Dominick are meant to be together. I don't want you to worry. I will talk to Mama today."

His sister gulped. "What if you can't? What if she disowns me if I marry Dominick without her approval? I'll lose everything. But how can I give up the man I love?"

His heart stopped, then sped up. For God's sake, that was a snake pit he refused to jump in. An intense family drama would force him to fly back home, and with his mother's heart problems, he worried about her health. His two other sisters, Julietta and Carina, may not be able to handle Venezia's distress on their own. First, he needed to get his sister under control. He clenched his fingers around the phone. "You will not do anything until I speak with her. Do you understand, Venezia? I will take care of it. Just tell Dominick to hold on until I get this settled."

"Okay." Her voice shook, and Michael knew that within his sister's normal flair for drama she loved her fiancé and wanted to start her life with him. At twenty-six, she was already older than most of her friends who'd married, and she was finally going to settle down with a man he approved of.

He quickly ended the call and strode to his car. He'd get back to the office and think this through. What if he really needed to get married to fix this mess? His palms grew damp at the thought and he fought the instinct to wipe them down on his perfectly pressed slacks. With work eating up every spare hour, he'd put finding his soul mate at the bottom of his list. Of course, he already knew what qualities he needed in his future wife. Someone easygoing, sweet tempered, and fun. Intelligent. Loyal. Someone who wanted to raise children, make a home, but independent enough to have her own career. Someone to fit perfectly into his family.

He slid into the Alfa Romeo's sleek interior and pressed the button for the engine. The main issue flashed in vivid neon before his vision. What if he didn't have time to find his perfect wife? Could he find a woman for a practical arrangement to satisfy his mother and allow Venezia to marry the love of her life? And if so, where in Dante's Hell would he find her?

His phone beeped and interrupted his thoughts. One glance confirmed Dominick refused to wait to be soothed and was about to fight for his sister's hand in marriage.

His head pounded as he reached for the phone.

It was going to be a long day.

Chapter Two

"Here, take the baby."

Maggie automatically caught the infant as her brother pushed the wriggling handful into her arms and hurried off. Typical. She'd seen his savvy game of pass the baby before and refused to be the chump. Usually it was because her niece had—

"Oh, gross!"

The heavy odor of poop assaulted her nostrils. Her niece grinned proudly as pools of saliva dripped down her chin and trickled onto Maggie's silk slacks. Lily's diaper sagged with God-knows-what mess, and her three strands of hair stuck straight up like Alfalfa gone horribly wrong.

"Sorry, Lily, Aunt Maggie doesn't do diapers. When you get older I'll teach you how to ride a motorcycle, score a hot guy for the prom, and buy your first fake ID. Till then, I'm out."

Lily crammed her fist in her toothless mouth and gnawed in delight.

Maggie held back a laugh. She glanced quickly around to see if a relative hung by so she could do a quick swap, but most of the party guests were crowded in the kitchen and dining room near the buffet. With a sigh, she rose from the couch, swung Lily on her hip, and almost crashed into the one man who irritated her the most.

Michael Conte.

He grabbed her with firm hands before she even swayed. The heat of the contact sizzled like oil on a hot skillet, but she kept her face expressionless, determined that he never know how he affected her. He'd practically stolen her BFF, insinuating himself into Alexa's family with an easy charm that pissed her off. Since her brother designed the project at the waterfront, Michael was now invited to functions where business and pleasure combined into family events. She bumped into him everywhere, bringing back memories of that disastrous blind date and a prickle of humiliation.

"Are you okay, *cara*?"

The caressing tone of his voice stroked her belly like a velvet fist. Lily broke into a gummy smile and practically sighed. And who wouldn't? Michael was simply gorgeous.

She took apart his appearance with a ruthlessness that

made her one of the most sought-after photographers in the fashion industry. Long, jet-black hair pulled back from his face and tied at his nape. His face was an odd combination of grace and strength, with a high arched brow, slashed cheekbones, and a strong chin. His nose sloped with a slight crookedness that enhanced his charm. His skin was a warm olive that bespoke of his Italian heritage.

But what killed her were his eyes.

Dark and soulful, almond-shaped, and set off by a set of lush eyelashes. Always filled with a wicked sense of humor and a raw passion that glimmered right beneath his polished surface.

Crankiness stirred. Why did he bother her? Her work required her to handle half-naked men who were even better looking. Like chiseled marble statues, she rarely got zinged by an electrical current when moving naked limbs into a pose. She had dated a few models, and always retained an air of distance, enjoying their company, then moving on without a glance back. But Michael affected her by igniting a basic feminine need she'd never encountered before.

She pushed away the disturbing thought and bumped Lily higher on her hip. She made sure to keep her tone cool. "Hello, Count. What brings you?"

His lower lip twitched. "I'd never miss Alexa's birthday party."

"No, of course not. You don't seem to miss many events that revolve around Alexa, do you?"

His eyebrow lifted. "Are you questioning my motives, *cara*?"

Maggie hated his husky accent that curled like smoke and wrapped heated wisps around her senses. But she hated his body more. Solid muscles filled out his supple leather Armani jacket. He wore a royal-blue button-down shirt, jeans, and Paciotti crocodile black boots. Besides killer style, he exuded a masculine power that pressed down upon her, combined with a deadly charm. He pretended not to have a care in the world, but Maggie glimpsed the sharp intelligence hidden behind that facade, glinting in the depth of inky black eyes.

After all, she hid the same things.

Maggie threw him the same charming smile she'd perfected in her own way. "Of course not. Just making a comment on the close personal relationship you seem to have with my brother's wife."

Michael chuckled and tickled Lily under the chin. The baby actually laughed. Even her niece was a traitor when it came to him. "Ah, but Alexa and I are friends, no? And without your brother, my bakery would never have gotten off the ground. He's done an amazing job with the architectural design."

She grunted. "Convenient, isn't it?"

As if knowing he irritated her, he leaned forward. She caught the scent of rich coffee, clean soap, and a hint of Christian Dior cologne. Her gaze helplessly focused on those full, sculpted lips that promised sex and sin. "Do you have something to say to me, Maggie?" he asked in a low drawl. "I remember from our dinner date you are usually more . . . blunt."

Damn him. She fought the heat that rose to her cheeks and narrowed her eyes in warning. "And I remember you're usually more . . . honest."

He drew back and gave her the space. "Yes, perhaps we both made a mistake that night."

She refused to answer. Instead, she lifted Lily and placed her in his arms. He held her with such tenderness and ease that she regretted her decision immediately. "I have to go find Alexa. Lily has a dirty diaper. Would you do us a favor and change her, please?" She smiled sweetly. "After all, you're practically family. You know where the nursery is."

And with a turn on her stiletto heel, she walked away.

. . .

Maggie made her way through the richly decorated Tuscan kitchen, focused on getting a glass of wine. Why couldn't anyone else see that the man was after her best friend? Her brother used to hate him, but now Nick invited him to family events and gave him every opportunity to be with his wife. The few times she mentioned it to Alexa, she laughed it off, citing no sexual chemistry.

Bullshit.

She knew Alexa never imagined the possibility because she was so in love with Nick and believed the best in people. Maggie trusted Alexa.

She just didn't trust the charming Italian who'd wormed his way into their family.

She'd researched him for the past year, positive she'd discover a damning weakness in case she needed to blackmail him to stay away from Alexa and her brother.

She'd come up empty each time, except for one blaring item.

The women.

Michael was a well-known womanizer. She'd bet in Italy that females had lusted after him, and that hadn't changed in New York. He was one of the most eligible bachelors in the Hudson Valley. Never a harsh comment regarding his behavior could be unearthed, even from the gossip columns. Yet, one fact remained.

He never got serious.

His longest relationship in the past year was two weeks. Maggie smothered a humorless laugh. In a way, she felt as if she'd met herself, only in male form. She could only come up with one solid reason for why he wouldn't commit.

Alexa.

He was so in love with Alexa that he refused to give himself completely to another. Thank God he hadn't taken her up on her proposition for another date. The memory still embarrassed her. She'd never been rejected by a man before, especially one she initially wanted.

Maggie poured herself a glass of cabernet, then wandered through the elegant dining room. She noticed the removal of certain antiques and sharp edges, the beginning of baby proofing in her brother's mansion.

Alexa swooped down on her with a plate filled with food. "Why aren't you eating? I need support. I'm trying to lose the baby weight but these appetizers are too good."

Maggie grinned at her best friend. "You look fantastic. God, your boobs are huge. I'm so frickin' jealous." The black dress emphasized her curvy figure with the scooped neckline and knee-high length.

Alexa stuck out her tongue. "The benefits of breast-feeding. Let's hope I don't leak and ruin my sexy effect. Where's Lily?"

Maggie fought a satisfied smirk. "With Michael. He's changing her diaper."

Alexa groaned. "Why did you do that to him? You're always giving him a hard time. I have to go help." She put down her plate of food, but Maggie grabbed her arm.

"Oh, all right, I'll go check on him. I'm sure he gave Lily to your mom. He's not stupid, Al, and he's a man. Men don't change diapers."

"Nick does."

Maggie rolled her eyes. "Rarely. He gave Lily to me because he knew she pooped."

Alexa glared at her husband from across the room. "Why am I surprised? The other night he asked me to hold her for just a minute and when I went to look for him, he'd gone out. Out of the actual house. In his car. I mean, are you kidding me?"

Maggie nodded. "I'll schedule a shopping trip with you soon and we'll make him pay. Literally."

Alexa laughed. "Go save Michael. And be nice to him, for God's sake. I don't know what's up with you two. It's been almost a year since you went out on that blind date. Did something else happen you didn't tell me about?"

Maggie shrugged. "Nope. I told you, I think he's secretly in love with you. But no one believes me."

"This again?" Alexa shook her head. "Maggs, we're just friends. He's like family. Trust me, even Nick came around—there's nothing between Michael and me. Never was."

"Right." Maggie looked at her friend, whom she loved like her sister. Alexa never knew how beautiful she really was, on the inside and outside. Nick finally won her heart, and Maggie never wanted them to forget how important they were to each other. They'd fought a hard journey but she'd never seen a happier couple. Her brother finally discovered his happily ever after. He hadn't let their screwed-up family life affect his future, and she was proud of him for taking the leap.

At least one person in the family found peace.

Maggie hugged her. "Enjoy your food, birthday girl, and don't worry. I'll go rescue him." She took her time, expecting to find Michael nursing a Scotch, child-free. She climbed the winding staircase and padded quietly down the hall. A low laugh, then humming drifted in the air. She peeked her head around and took in the sight before her.

Michael held Lily in his arms as he rocked her. He crooned a lullaby in Italian, and Maggie realized it was "Twinkle, Twinkle Little Star." Lily gazed up at him with sheer adoration, gurgling in time to the melody. The nursery added to the almost mystical quality of the scene, with large moons and stars painted on the ceiling, and bright yellow paint splashing the walls like the sun.

Her heart stopped. A fierce longing shook through her core, and Maggie half closed her eyes in a battle to push away the emotional storm. He'd shed his jacket, which hung neatly on the back of a chair. Lily wore a different dress of yellow roses, her dainty tights and matching yellow shoes pristine and cleaned of drool. The scent of vanilla hung in the air.

She swallowed hard and clenched her fists.

He looked up.

Their gazes met and locked. For a moment, a raw, lustful chemistry shot between them. Then it was gone, and Maggie wondered if she'd just imagined the look of want on his face. "What are you doing?" she asked sharply.

He cocked his head at her accusation. "Singing."

She sighed with impatience and motioned toward the changing table. "I mean, the diaper. You changed her? And why is she wearing that?"

He looked amused. "Of course I changed her, just as you asked, *cara*. Her dress was dirty, so I picked out a new one. Why do you look so surprised?"

"Figured you were raised with that old-fashioned attitude. You know, men are leaders and don't cook, clean, or do diapers."

Michael threw back his head and roared with laughter. Lily blinked, then babbled in response. "You haven't met my mother. I grew up with three younger sisters. When a diaper needed changing it was my responsibility, and there was no game of pass-the-baby. I tried that once and paid dearly."

"Oh." She leaned against the white bureau. "Is your family back in Italy?"

"Yes. The original La Dolce Famiglia started in Bergamo, where we live. Then we expanded into Milan and have been quite successful. I decided to continue the tradition in America, and my sister runs the home base."

"What about your dad?"

Naked emotion passed over his carved features. "My father passed on a few years ago."

"I'm sorry," she said softly. "It sounds like you have a close family."

"*Si*. I miss him every day." He studied her with curiosity. "And what about you? I guess you never had to change a diaper?"

She smiled and ignored the emptiness. "I had it made. Nick was older, so I had no younger siblings to worry about. Never had to lift a finger because we lived in a mansion with a maid, a cook, and a nanny. I was spoiled rotten."

A short silence descended. She shifted uncomfortably as he made no move to disguise his pointed gaze as he searched her face, looking for something she couldn't understand. Finally, he spoke. "No, *cara*. I think you had it harder than most of us."

She refused to answer, hating the way he tried to get under her skin and figure things out. As if he already suspected more lurked beneath the surface. "Think what you like," she said casually. "But stop calling me sweetheart."

He responded with a wicked wink as he took in her form-fitting metallic top. As if he played with the idea of tugging down her shirt and bending his head to suck on her nipples. On cue, her breasts swelled in fierce demand, ready to play. Why did he affect her so intensely?

"Fine, *la mia tigrotta*." His rich, lilting tone stripped her naked and wrapped her in crushed velvet.

Maggie inwardly cursed. "Very funny."

He lifted a brow. "It is not meant to be funny. You reminded me of a little tiger the first moment we met."

She refused to get in an argument about something so ridiculous. Maggie waved off his endearment and headed toward the door. "We better get out there. Alexa was look-ing for Lily."

He followed with Lily tucked neatly in his arms and ran straight into Alexa's mother.

"Maggie, darling, I've been looking for you!" Maria McKenzie kissed both cheeks and gazed at her with a warmth that always tripped up her heart. "Here is my beautiful granddaughter. Come here, my darling." She took Lily and bestowed more kisses on Michael. "I heard she needed changing but it seems you make a good team."

Why did the entire family hold the misconception they'd be perfect together? Maggie held back a sigh while Michael laughed. "Ah, Mrs. McKenzie, you know how wonderful Maggie is about taking care of her niece. I only sat back and watched."

Guilt snagged her hard. She smiled but shot him a dirty look. Why did he always seem to come out the good guy?

"I'm having a small dinner for everyone this Friday and insist you both join me," Maria announced.

Those family dinners used to belong to only Maggie, Alexa, and Nick. She almost sagged with relief when she remembered her schedule. "I'm sorry, Mrs. McKenzie, I'll be flying to Milan this week. I leave in two days for a photo shoot."

"Then I will reschedule for when you arrive back home. Now, let me take this little one back out to the party, and I will see you later."

Alexa's mom disappeared down the hallway, and Maggie suddenly noticed Michael's strange expression. "You're flying to Milan? For how long?"

She shrugged. "Probably a week. I'll take some time to make new contacts, do some shopping."

"Hmmm." Somehow, the uncommitted sound seemed ominous. He looked at her as if studying her in a new light for the first time, probing her face, then dropping to her body, as if searching under her fashionable outfit for something more.

"Dude, why are you looking at me like that?" She shifted her feet as a tingly warmth heated between her thighs. No way was she going there. If there were one man in the world she'd never sleep with if the zombies took over the earth and they were the only ones left to procreate, it was Michael Conte.

"I may have a proposition for you," he murmured.

She pushed away the memory of their first meeting and forced a smirk. "Sorry, babe. That ship has sailed and left port."

She refused to look back as she walked away.

• • •

Michael sipped his cognac and watched as the party winded down. Luscious chocolate chip cannoli cake and pots of strong coffee were served, and a relaxed atmosphere rippled through the rooms as family and friends began making their good-byes.

Tension swirled in his gut and fought with the lovely fire of the alcohol. This time he was in trouble. Big trouble. After the phone call with Venezia and Dominick, he decided to confront his mother with a well-placed battle plan.

Michael knew sticking with the family tradition was impossible. He also realized his mother believed strongly in rules and rarely broke them. He had decided on an alternate plan that seemed brilliant. He'd throw her a story about a steady girlfriend, with a wedding in the firm future, and even promise a visit. Then he'd calmly insist Venezia marry first because of her history with Dominick, and he would cite Papa's heavenly blessing. Maybe he'd tell her he saw it in a dream, something to soothe her doubts.

Until his other sister Julietta blew his story to rubble with a simple statement.

His mind drifted to their brief conversation.

"Michael, I don't know what you heard, but to use one of your American phrases, the shit is about to hit the fan." Never emotional or pulled into drama, Julietta always acted with a clear plan, which made her the perfect person to run La Dolce Famiglia. "Mama promised Papa on his deathbed she'd continue the traditions of the family. Unfortunately, that included having you marry first, no matter how ridiculous it sounds."

"I'm sure I can talk her out of it," Michael said, ignoring the doubts slithering like snakes in his head.

"Not gonna happen. I think Venezia is planning to elope. If she does, disaster will be an understatement. We'll be at war with Dominick's family, and Mama threatened to disown her. Carina is going through a hard time right now, and she's been crying nonstop thinking her family is falling apart. Mama called the doctor and told him she was having a heart attack, but he diagnosed her with a bad case of indigestion and sent her to bed. *Dios*, please tell me you're seeing someone serious and can take care of this situation? Damn patriarchal society. I cannot believe Papa bought this crap."

The truth slammed through him. He'd never win on a deathbed promise. His father lured him into the trap, and his own mother shut the cage door behind him. He needed a wife and he needed her fast if he was going to clean up this mess. At least, a temporary wife.

What options did he have? His mind worked with brutal efficiency until the only solution lay before him. Convince his mother he was legally married, get Venezia to rush the wedding, and then a few months later break the sad news that his marriage didn't work out. He'd deal with the consequences. Right now, he needed to fix this. After all, fixing family dramas was his job.

"I'll be married by the end of the week," he said.

His sister's sharp indrawn breath cut through the phone.

"Tell Venezia not to do anything rash. I'll call Mama and tell her the news later."

"Are you serious? Are you really getting married, or is this a scam?"

Michael closed his eyes. In order to make the plan work, everyone needed to believe it was real. Starting with Julietta. "I have been seeing someone, and was just waiting to make it official. She doesn't like a fuss and doesn't want a real wedding, though, so we'll probably hit the justice of the peace and then I'll break the news to everyone."

"Are you telling me the truth, Michael? Listen, this may be a mess but there's no reason to rush marriage just to calm down Venezia. You don't have to fix everything all the time."

"Yes, I do," he said quietly. The heaviness of responsibility fell over him and smothered his breath. He accepted the weight without question and moved forward. "I'll give you the details after I talk to my fiancée."

"Mama will insist on meeting her. She's not going to take your word."

His sister's words locked the door on the cage with a final click.

"I know. I'll arrange a visit home toward the end of the summer."

"What? Who is she? What's her name?"

"I have to go. I'll call you back later."

He disconnected the call.

The situation swirled with limited possibilities and too little time. He decided to look for one of those elite escort services that hired out companions for big events. Perhaps, with some luck, he'd find one willing to pretend to be his wife. Of course, delaying the meeting with his mother would take careful planning, and with the opening of the waterfront, he may be diagnosed with an ulcer by the end of the week.

Unless . . .

His gaze cut through the crowd and locked with a pair of cat-green eyes. A flare of lust lit low in his gut in automatic response to the challenge. She arched one perfect brow and tossed her head in dismissal, turning her back on him. He smothered a laugh. The woman was a prickly mass of sex and sarcasm. If there was a rose beneath, she surrounded herself with a thicket of thorns to warn any prince on horseback to stay way back.

Maggie Ryan was perfect for the job.

What if he bit the bullet — was that the American expression? — and got the whole charade over with immediately? What were the odds of another woman he knew traveling to Milan for a week? He trusted her. At least, a tiny bit. If she agreed, he'd be able to rush the encounter, plead work as an excuse to leave early, and allow Venezia to marry this summer. Maggie's dislike for him was an asset — she wouldn't get any romantic, moony ideas when she met his family and pretended to be a part of it. Of course, his mama would freak at his choice, probably expecting more of a traditional, nonthreatening spouse. Still, he'd make it work.

If she agreed.

He'd dated many beautiful women, but Maggie held a mysterious quality that hit a man like a sucker punch. Her cinnamon-colored hair shimmered in the light, a straight, silky mass that fell over her cheek and hit her shoulder in a fashionable cut. Her bangs only accented exotically tilted eyes, reminding him of the endless misty green of the Tuscan fields, sucking a man in and allowing him to get lost in the fog. Her features were sharp and clear: a strong tilted jaw, high cheekbones, and elegant nose. The stretchy fabric of her top revealed well-defined shoulders and high, perky breasts. The pewter silk of her trousers glistened as she walked and showed off a perfectly curved rear and long legs that forced a man to imagine them wrapped around his waist. Her scent was a mix of earthy undertones of sandalwood and amber, sneaking into a man's nostrils and promising him a trip to heaven on earth.

She was no shrinking violet. Her attitude was kick-ass and woman, hear me roar. She walked and breathed and spoke pure sex, and any male in her nearby area scented it. Michael watched as she threw her head back and laughed. Her face reflected an open happiness he rarely caught— only around Alexa or her brother. Even on their first date, a heavy wall of armor barricaded her from any real emotions, evident in her quick wit, sexy smolder, and distant gaze.

She was exactly what she wanted to be without apology. Michael admired and appreciated such women, as they were too far and few between. But something about Maggie pulled him to look closer and scratch beneath the surface. Some lingering pain and need glimmered deep within those green eyes, daring a man to slay the dragon and claim her.

His sudden thought startled him. He mocked the ridiculous image, but his pants still tightened around his erection. God, that's all he needed—some misrepresented damsel-in-distress fantasy. He'd never be a prince and didn't want the job. Especially against a woman who'd probably steal his horse and rescue herself.

Still, for a while, he needed her. He just had to convince her to take the part.

"Hmm, I wonder what put that expression on your face. Or rather, who."

He looked up from his chair and met a pair of laughing blue eyes. His heart warmed at Alexa's smile, and he stood up to give her a brief hug. "*Buon giorno, signora bella.* Did you enjoy your party?"

Corkscrew curls slipped out of her ponytail and lay against her cheek. Happiness radiated around her figure. "Loved it. I told Nick I didn't want a party, but you know how he gets."

"That's the reason he's good at his job."

She rolled her eyes. "Yeah, good for business but a pain in the ass at home." She grinned naughtily. "Sometimes."

Michael laughed. "What do you Americans like to say? TMI—too much info?" Color flushed her cheeks and he tugged on one of her curls. "Sorry, I couldn't resist. I got you a present."

She frowned. "Michael, the cake was enough. You almost killed me it was so delicious."

"It's a small one. You have meant a lot to me this past year, and I love seeing you happy." He pulled a tiny box from his jacket pocket. "Open."

She sighed and looked half-torn. Curiosity won out and she unwrapped the gift. The simple baby booty charm with a gleaming emerald stone lay on the fluffy cotton. She sucked in her breath and pleasure filled him at her expression.

"It's Lily's birthstone," he said. "Nick told me he bought you a new gold chain, so this would go perfectly with it. Do you like?"

Alexa bit her lower lip and she blinked. "I love it," she said huskily. She leaned forward and kissed his cheek, and he clasped her hands within his. "It's perfect. Thank you."

"*Prego, cara.*"

A strong wave of admiration and love washed over him. The moment he'd met her at a business dinner, he knew she was an exceptional woman. Fortunately, since he discovered her marriage, there was never any sexual chemistry between them. Nick was the other half of her heart. But Michael believed he and Alexa were old soul mates— meant to be good friends but never lovers. Nick initially resented their friendship but even he had become both a friend and a business partner. When Lily was born, Michael enjoyed the status of honorary uncle, which soothed the occasional burst of homesickness for his own family.

Maggie, however, disapproved.

Suddenly, she materialized by their side, as if able to sniff out whenever Alexa neared him. She raked him with a sharp look. "Presents, Al?" she asked. "How thoughtful."

Her tone dripped with icicles and he caught an immediate chill. Her protectiveness and loyalty toward Alexa always fascinated him. How could someone who had the potential to love be so alone? Unless she had a steady lover hidden in the background? She never brought a male companion to any of the functions. Michael studied her figure but caught no softness or satisfaction, just the usual low hum of energy she always exuded.

His thoughts flashed to their first date almost a year ago. Alexa begged him to meet Maggie, citing some strange female instinct that they'd be perfect together. The moment their gazes locked, Michael knew sexual chemistry would never be their problem. She seemed just as startled by their instant connection but played it off with an expert ease until he realized she was a contradictory bundle of emotions—a tigress caught without her roar. The stimulating, edgy conversation only heightened his desire for her, but he knew she'd never be a one-night stand, as badly as she wanted to pretend that was all they could have.

He'd briefly ached to be the man to challenge her limitations and offer more. But his close relationship with Alexa and the threat of a messy breakup kept him from extending the evening to another date. He sought a woman who would fit in with his close-knit family and not keep herself distant. Maggie was the opposite of everything he believed he needed in a mate. Boring, no. But a mass of contradictions, emotions, and work, yes. If they tore each other apart, Alexa and Nick would become the victims, and since he viewed them as family, he never put anyone he cared about at risk. Not because of his own selfish needs.

He'd practiced that move most of his life.

Still, he'd screwed up. Her almost shy offer of the possibility of another date incited a fear he'd never experienced from a woman.

The raw vulnerability on her face from his rejection startled him. But there would never be a second chance with Maggie Ryan. She'd never allow herself to be put in such a position again, and she loved to remind him of it constantly.

Alexa lifted the baby charm up. "Isn't it beautiful, Maggie?"

"Charming."

Michael smothered a laugh at Alexa's warning look. Like a sulky child, Maggie backed off. "I have to get going, babe," she said. "I have to leave for Milan soon and still have tons to do."

Alexa groaned. "God, what I'd do to go to Milan and get a new wardrobe." She looked down at her fashionable dress and wrinkled her face.

"Lily was worth a couple of pounds," Maggie said firmly. "I'll bring you back a pair of sexy heels that'll drive Nick mad." Her gaze veered directly to Michael's face as if to prove a point. "Not that it takes much the way you two go at it."

"Go at what?" Nick appeared and slipped his arms around his wife's hips.

"Never mind," Alexa said sharply.

"Sex," Maggie stated. "I'm going to Milan and bringing back Alexa some sexy shoes."

Nick looked intrigued. "How about one of those silky nightie things, too?"

"Nick!"

He ignored his wife's embarrassed hiss and grinned. "What? She's going to the fashion capital of the world and you don't want lingerie? Hell, I do. The way you look is just . . . delicious."

Maggie laughed. "Done. She'll look hot in red."

"I hate you both."

Nick pressed a kiss to his wife's neck. Michael turned his head for a moment and caught the look on Maggie's face.

Longing.

Emotion lodged at the back of his throat as he registered the wistfulness on her face while she gazed at her brother, then the shutter slammed down and the moment disappeared.

He straightened and decided to make his move. "Maggie? Before you leave, can I talk to you for a minute?"

She shrugged. "Sure. What's up?"

"In private, please."

Nick and Alexa shared a look. Maggie rolled her eyes at them. "Give me a break, guys. It's not like he's going to ask me to marry him or anything."

Michael winced. Nick shook his head at her antics but she only stuck out her tongue and led the way down the hall toward one of the back rooms. She jumped on the high platform bed and kicked her legs out in front of her. With her arms propped behind her back, her breasts pressed against the silvery top in a demand to be freed. God, was she wearing a bra?

Michael tried to be casual as he leaned against the wooden beam of the four-poster bed. His curiosity was rewarded when twin points poked against the soft fabric. He shifted in an attempt to get comfortable, annoyed she couldn't have picked the formal den to have this conversation. It was too easy to imagine her spread out on the champagne quilt as he dragged her top over her breasts with his teeth. He bet her nipples were ruby-colored and very sensitive. Seemed like the fabric alone caused them to respond. Michael fought a shudder and clawed for focus.

"I have a proposition for you."

She threw her head back and laughed. The smoky sound beckoned like a witch casting a spell. "Well, then, you've come to the right girl." She licked her lips with deliberate precision. The faint sheen of wetness gleamed in the light. "Proposition away."

He smothered a curse and decided to go for the blunt approach. "I need a pretend wife."

She blinked. "Huh?"

"*Si*." He despised the slight flush his ridiculous admission caused and forged on. "I am having some family difficulties and I'm required to marry. I need someone to go to Italy with me for a week, pretend to be my wife, spend some time with my family, then leave."

"Why do I suddenly feel like I dropped into the Lifetime movie of the week?"

"What is Lifetime?"

She waved his question off. "Never mind, a girl thing. Um, let me think about this for a moment. You need me to pretend to be married to you, hang with your *famiglia*, stay in their house, and then return like nothing ever happened?"

"Yes."

"No, thanks." She jumped gracefully off the bed and headed out. Michael cut in front of her and kicked the door closed. She arched a brow. "Sorry, not into the dominating thing."

"Maggie, please hear me out."

"Hell, no. I heard enough. First off, I'm going to Milan to work, not to be a mail-order bride. Second, we don't really care for each other, and your family would pick that up in a moment. Third, we're not even close friends, which negates me from owing you any favors. Surely, you have some lovely young thing just begging for the opportunity to shine in this role?"

Michael held back a groan. Did he really think this would be easy? "Actually, that's why you'll be perfect for the job. I need someone who won't get any strange ideas. Anyway, I'm not seeing anyone at the moment."

"What if I am?"

"Are you?"

She pulled back. The temptation to lie glimmered in those eyes, then cleared. "No. But I'm still not doing it."

"I'll pay you."

She smirked. "I don't need your money, Count. I make enough on my own, thank you."

"There must be something we can bargain with. Something you want."

"Sorry, I'm a pretty happy girl. But thanks for the offer." She reached past him for the doorknob.

She was his only candidate, and he didn't think America had a store to buy fake brides. The final option flashed before him. It would never work, of course, and Nick wouldn't approve. But if Maggie thought it was a possibility, she may drop right into his hands. He pushed past his conscience and played his trump card. "Fine, I guess I'll need to ask Alexa."

Maggie stopped. Her hair flew, then slid into place as she whipped her head up to eyeball him like a prizefighter. "What did you say?"

He sighed with mock regret. "I didn't want to ask her to leave Lily so early, but I'm sure she will help me."

Pure temper oozed from her pores. She clenched her jaw and spoke between gritted teeth. "Don't even think about it, Count. Just leave her and Nick alone. Solve your own damn problems."

"As I am trying to do."

She lifted herself up on tiptoes and got in his face. Her breath rushed over his lips, a heady combination of coffee and cognac and arousal. "I swear to God, if you even present such a crazy idea to them I'll—"

"What? Once I explain the situation, Nick will understand. Alexa has always wanted to travel to Italy, and it will only be for a few days. This is a family emergency."

"You're not family!" The words breezed past his ears with a *whoosh* and he caught the edge of resentment in her tone. "Stop interfering in their life and get one of your own."

He clucked his tongue. "So angry, *la mia tigrotta*. Are you jealous?"

Her hands reached out and clenched around his upper arms. The bite of her nails dug into his muscles and only upped the swirling sensual tension between them. "No, I'm pissed you're still hanging around Alexa like a lost puppy dog, and now my own brother doesn't even see it. I wish there was a way to get rid of you. I wish I could—"

Her mouth snapped shut. Very slowly, she removed her nails from his arms and took a step back. His body mourned the loss of her female heat. Michael watched with trepidation as the gleam in her eyes brightened. Somehow, he didn't think her next words would be good. Somehow, she looked a bit dangerous.

"If I agree to this insane plan, you'll give me anything I want?"

Her sudden turn of direction made his stomach lurch. "Yes."

Her lips curved into a smile, stained red and perfectly formed. He stared helplessly at that sensual mouth, made for carnal delights beyond his fantasies. *Dios,* his body throbbed with a painful pressure and distracted him from rational conversation. He thought of the nuns in the Catholic church he grew up with and some of the pulsing blood calmed.

"Okay. I'll do it."

He didn't celebrate. Just stared at her with suspicion. "What do you want?"

The triumph on her face superseded her words. "I want you to stay away from Alexa."

Michael flinched. Somehow, his clever ammunition misfired. He mentally cursed for leaving himself wide open for her sneak attack. Her continued insistence he was secretly in love with Alexa usually amused him, but now he faced something more vital. He decided to pretend to misunderstand. "Of course," he agreed. "I'll keep my distance if you'd like."

Her gaze narrowed. "Don't think you understand the agreement, Count. When she invites you over for Sunday dinners, you will be busy. No more visiting Lily. No more attending family functions. You can deal with Nick in a business capacity, but from now on, you will no longer consider yourself a close *friend* of Alexa. *Capisce*?"

Oh yeah. He understood. His irritation grew at her inability to state his first name. The elegant title became mocking uttered from her lips, and a dominant need to force her to use his birth name shook through him. Preferably while she was on her back, thighs parted, crazed with lust for him. He retreated behind a cool facade and prayed she wouldn't notice the bulge in his pants. "Why are you so threatened, *cara*? What are you afraid will happen between Alexa and me?"

Her chin lifted. "I've seen how easy it is to ruin something good," she said with a tinge of bitterness. "Alexa and Nick are happy. She doesn't need a man sniffing around the sidelines. They may trust your intentions, but I don't." Maggie paused. Her final words came out in a harsh whisper. "I see the way you look at her."

Michael fought for air as her blunt words attacked him like wasp stings. She really thought so little of him. To imagine he'd try to break up a marriage and betray a trust sliced deep. Still, within his own anger and pain at her beliefs, he admired her gutsy move. Once she devoted herself to another person, she'd be loyal for life. Perhaps that's why she avoided long-term entanglements.

Her body vibrated with tension and raw emotion. "I'm sick of everyone saying I'm crazy. Just this once, admit to me you love her. Tell me the truth, give me your promise to stay away, and I'll pretend to be your bride."

He studied her in brooding silence. Arguing was fruitless. Alexa reminded him of his sisters whom he'd left behind in Italy, and she soothed a need for comfort in a sometimes lonely world. She owned the impulsiveness of Venezia, the responsibility of Julietta, and the sweetness of Carina. Obviously, the warmth that radiated in his face when he looked at her had been misconstrued by her best friend.

Perhaps this was for the best.

Maggie's delicious body and sharp mind already attracted him. He didn't need any scenarios where they ended up in bed together and things got . . . awkward. Not while around his family pretending to be married. If she kept her belief he was in love with her best friend, there would be an extra barrier of defense between them. Of course, his own sacrifice was greater than he'd imagined. He'd lose a close friend who meant the world to him, and he may even hurt Alexa in the process.

His choice lay before him. He thought of not being able to hold Lily or to have her call him Uncle. And then he thought of Venezia and her hysterics and grief, her desire to start her own life. His responsibility lay with taking care of his family at all costs. He'd learned that lesson young, and he never intended to forget it. No, in a way, there really was no other choice.

Michael forced himself to utter the lie Maggie needed to hear. "I love Alexa as a friend. But I will agree to your terms if you will do this for me."

She flinched, but her gaze remained steady as she nodded her acceptance. A strange flash of anguish lit her eyes, then vanished. His instincts told him her trust had been betrayed in an irreversible way no man had ever been able to fix. An old lover? An ex-fiancé? Fascinated, he longed to dig deeper, but she was back to her controlled self. "Fine. Give me your vow you'll stay away from her when we return. No exceptions."

"How do you suggest I neatly disappear without hurting her feelings?"

She shrugged. "We'll be in Italy for the week, and then you'll be busy. Pretend you're dating someone new and caught up with her. After a while, Alexa will stop asking questions."

He disagreed, but figured Maggie would help take care of that part. A sliver of grief pierced through him before he said the words aloud. "I accept your conditions." Then he took a step forward. "Now, I will tell you mine."

He enjoyed the slight widening of her eyes as he loomed over her. Awareness jumped between them. She refused to cower, though, and held her ground. "Wait. How do I know you won't break your promise?"

He reached out and gripped her chin. Her question attacked the core of who he was, and an icy chill threaded through his tone. "Because I do not break my promises. *Capisce*?"

She nodded. "Yes."

He released her chin, but not before sneaking a casual touch by running his finger down her cheek. Soft, silky skin tempted him to continue the caress. He cleared his throat and got back to the topic. "The rules are simple. I'll call my mother tonight to break the news, but it will seem suspicious unless I'm prepared. I'll need to agree to get married in Italy."

"What? Hell, no. I'm not going to really marry you!"

He waved off her shocked protest. "Of course, we're

not really going to marry. But we need to pretend. Mama is quite sharp and will remain suspicious if we don't seem willing to recite our marriage vows in front of her and a priest. I'll tell her we legally married in the States, but will apply for a license in Italy so she can take part in a second wedding."

"What happens when the priest shows up ready to marry us?"

Michael's lips quirked at her sudden panic. "It takes a long time for a priest to agree to marry a couple when he does not know the bride, especially if she isn't Catholic. It will never happen within our short visit. I'll tell Mama we're staying for two weeks, but we'll leave after one and cite an emergency."

She relaxed, back to her confident, sarcastic self. "You didn't tell me why you suddenly need a wife. Can't find your true Juliet, Romeo?"

Michael gave her a brief rundown on his family's background and his sister's desire to marry. He prepared himself for her ridicule of such an old-fashioned culture, but she nodded as if she completely understood—and managed to keep him off balance.

"I admire your mother," she finally said. "It's hard to keep your beliefs when others mock you. At least your family believes in something. Tradition. Promises kept. Responsibility." Fascinated by her words, Michael watched the emotion flicker across her face before she shook off the memories. "I just hope your plan works the way you want it to."

"What do you mean?"

Her elegant shoulders lifted. "Your family may not like me. I photograph underwear models for a living. And I'm not pretending to defer to you, either, so don't get your hopes up."

He grinned. "Didn't I tell you wives obey in every way? Part of the bargain revolves around you treating me like royalty. You'll cook my supper, serve my needs, and defer to my wishes. Don't worry—it's only for a week."

Her sheer horror ruined his ruse. He chuckled, and her fist fell back to her side. He had a feeling he'd just missed a black eye. Did she bring all that fiery emotion to the bedroom? And if so, was there anything left of her men in the morning other than a brainless smile and a desire for more?

Her lips quirked. "Funny. Nice to see you have a sense of humor, Count. It'll make the week go faster."

"Glad you approve. I'll make the arrangements and we'll leave tomorrow evening. I'll give you the rundown on my family during the trip, and you can tell me the important things about yours."

She nodded and eased her way to the door. Her obvious discomfort at their close proximity soothed him. At least he wasn't the only one experiencing sexual chemistry. She seemed dedicated to *not* being attracted to him, which made it easier to ignore the physical connection and get through the week.

Maggie Ryan may be an explosive woman, but he could handle seven days.

No *problema*.

Chapter Three

Maggie glanced at her fake husband and tried hard not to panic.

The familiar shortening of breath and hammering heart alerted her to trouble. She swallowed, hid her face behind Italian *Vogue,* and prayed she'd keep it together. She hated the idea of anyone knowing about such a weakness, especially Michael. The whole crazy plan hit her full force as soon as his private plane shot into the air. Her finger itched with the snug band of platinum gold, and the two-carat round diamond sparkled like icicles catching the glint of the sun. The ruse seemed doable in Alexa's house. A day later, though, with a ring, fake husband, and family to con, she realized she was a complete idiot.

What the hell had she agreed to?

And what was it about the Ryan family that necessitated fake marriages? She'd laughed her ass off when Nick told her he needed to marry in order to inherit their uncle's company, Dreamscape Enterprises. Thank God, setting him up with Alexa proved to be the best decision, especially when they fell in love and made it real.

Of course, the only reason Alexa agreed to a marriage of convenience with her brother was to save her family. Maggie had no lofty reason to save a business or childhood home. *But you have the opportunity to protect family,* her inner voice whispered. Alexa and Nick had something real. Michael remained a constant threat: his sensual smile, lilting voice, and come-hither bedroom eyes wrapped her best friend in a false state of protection. Finally, her suspicions confirmed truth.

He admitted he loved her best friend.

When the words fell from his lips, a strange flare of grief pierced her heart. Ridiculous, of course, and she quickly buried the embarrassing emotion. Of course, he wrapped it up in the term friendship, but it was only his way to throw her off base. A powerful man like the count would not be content to wait on the sidelines for long—not if he believed he'd have a shot with the woman he loved. Maggie couldn't live with herself if she didn't use the available weapon to keep Michael away from her family.

But at what price? Meeting his sisters and mother.

Sleeping in his bedroom. Pretending to be someone she wasn't?

Her fingers tightened around the glossy pages, and she breathed in through her nose, and out through her mouth. The shrink she'd forced herself to visit prescribed yoga and stress-reducing exercises. She absolutely refused to be medicated and controlled by anxiety. Starting from one hundred and going backward, she forced away the crazed need to gulp for air and reigned herself in. Visualizing her heartbeat slowing, she breathed.

Ninety-eight.

Ninety-seven.

Ninety-six.

Ninety-five.

"Studying for your shoot?"

She waited a few beats until she was under control, then looked up. He leaned back in the seat, one ankle crossed over his knee, a relaxed smile on his face. Funny, she'd always had a thing for long hair on a man, enjoying the modern-day pirate image. His powerful frame was wrapped in a black sports jacket, jeans, and low black boots. His eyes filled with humor as he motioned to her fashion magazine.

A quick lash of irritation caused her to cock her head and adopt a southern drawl. "Sorry, darlin', pictures are all I can handle. Too many words on a page makes me all aflutter."

She'd always hated the easy assumption she couldn't handle literature more challenging than a fashion magazine. Of course, she did nothing to convince anyone otherwise. She boasted no college education and made her own way in the photography world. She liked the control it gave her in a relationship to keep things hidden. Especially her addiction to crossword puzzles and Civil War literature. If only her dates knew she DVR'd the History Channel more than *Project Runway*.

He reached over to the minibar and poured himself a Scotch with ice. "Nothing wrong with *Vogue*. It was my sister's bible."

"I read, too. The articles in *Playgirl* are entertaining."

He laughed, the sound coating her skin like the slow slide of creamy caramel. "Why don't you tell me a little about your work? How did you end up being a photographer?"

The true answer skittered across her mind but she refused to say it aloud. Because the world was better viewed through a lens? Because photography gave her control to watch others—almost like legal voyeurism? She sipped at her glass of Chianti. "One Christmas I got a Nikon with all the trappings and was told to show up at photography camp for a week. The nanny had a vacation coming and they had no one to watch me, so off I went. The instructor was top rate and taught me a lot. I got hooked."

His probing stare burned through barriers and demanded the truth. Fortunately, the mess of emotions had been steeped in deep freeze for so many years there was nothing left to show. "Sounds like you received money but no emotional support. The fashion industry is quite competitive, especially in Milan. You must be extremely talented and dedicated to be so much in demand."

She shrugged. "I've always had an eye for fashion." She gave a fake leer. "Especially ones including muscled, half-naked men."

Maggie expected a laugh, but he kept quiet and studied her. "Have you ever tried to expand your focus?"

She stretched her legs out and settled back in the comfy seat. "Sure. I've done shoots for the Gap and Victoria's Secret during a dry spell."

"You don't like to talk about yourself much, do you, *cara*?"

The intimate rumble ruffled her nerve endings and made her want things. Bad things. Like his tongue deep inside her mouth and those hands all over her naked body. Oh, this man was good. All charm and humor and sensuality wrapped up in a power package deadly to women. His sinful eyes practically forced confessions from a woman's lips. "On the contrary. Ask me anything you want. Boxers or briefs? Mets or Yankees? Disco or hip-hop? Hit me with your best shot."

"Tell me about your parents."

She refused to hesitate. "My father is on his fourth

wife. He loves money, hates work, and only sees me to rack up brownie points with his new wife. Seems she likes family closeness, and he's trying to make her happy. For now. He's handsome, charming, and completely empty. My mother envisions herself a celebrity and despises the fact she's aging and has two grown children. She's currently shacked up with an actor and begging for two-bit parts as an extra on various sets."

"And your relationships?" His aura burned with a curiosity that made her uneasy. "What about them, *la mia tigrotta*? Have you given up on commitment because of your parents?"

Her breath caught at his directness, but she forged on. "I have many healthy relationships on my own terms." She uttered the lie without a shred of guilt. "Do I believe finding real love in this lifetime is almost impossible? Hell, yes. It's proven over and over again. Why bother? Why dive into obvious pain and heartache unless you find someone you'd die for? And personally, I don't think he's out there. But I have a damn good time finding Mr. Right Now."

The low hum of the plane's engine was the only sound between them. "I'm sorry."

His softly spoken words made her lips tighten. "Why?" she challenged. "I wasn't beaten, starved, or abused. I grew up in a mansion with nannies, cooks, and any toy I asked for. I do what I want, when I want, and don't answer to anyone. Why on earth would you be sorry for me? I got more than most." He nodded, but she sensed he didn't believe her. "I feel sorrier for you."

Michael jerked back. "Me?"

"Sure. After all, I already know your secrets."

The taunt hit the bull's-eye. He stiffened and deliberately took a sip of his Scotch. "Ah, but I feel the same way. I am what you Americans call an open book." The matching wedding band flashed as he waved his hand in the air.

She practically purred with the delight of taking the focus off her. "You had a close family with plenty of support. Money and success on your own terms. And you couldn't find one woman to pretend she loves you for a lousy week. No wonder your mother is insistent on keeping to tradition. Has there been even one serious relationship in your past?"

Anger flashed in his coal-black eyes.

"I date," he responded coldly. "Just because I haven't found The One yet doesn't mean I'm closed off."

"Nice recovery. So what are you looking for, Count? What type of woman gets you all hot and bothered to settle down?"

He muttered something under his breath, and she settled back to enjoy the show. "I'd love to settle down and give my mother what she wants," he finally stated. "But not at my expense. You see, *cara,* I believe in the love you say is impossible. I just believe it's hard to find, and I refuse to compromise."

"So all these women you take to your bed, do you seduce them for the challenge, the pleasure, or because you hope she's The One?"

His eyes glittered as she threw down the gauntlet. Again, he impressed her with his dual ability to switch from smooth charmer to a man who refused to play games. "I hope. I take them to bed, concentrate on their pleasure, and hope in the morning I want more."

Her breath strangled in her throat. Her surroundings tilted as his words echoed her own empty search for someone to slay the demons in the evening and be enough under the harsh morning light. Her heart galloped but this time it wasn't panic that caused the blood rush.

It was Michael Conte.

Her fingers clenched around the delicate stem of her glass. The leashed sensuality radiating around his figure pulled her in and kept her caught in his web as he stared at her in sudden realization. "You experience it, too, don't you?"

His harsh question made her flinch.

"Do you take them to bed to escape the loneliness, hoping it will end up to be more? Do you wake up in the morning with a sick feeling in your stomach, knowing you lied to yourself again? Do you wonder if you're meant to be alone? Wonder if something deep down is holding you back?"

God, yes.

Sudden tears threatened. The horror of such messy emotion made her fight back for her control. She'd never admit such weakness and want to this man. He'd use it against her, to climb under her skin and probe for secrets. She knew what drove her, knew the empty hole inside of her started at sixteen when a boy she trusted took everything hopeful and good and bright and crushed it beneath his heel. But she'd gotten strong and chosen revenge in her own way. She'd never let anyone take away the choice of her sexuality or her control.

If Michael stripped her bare, she'd have nothing left.

So she smiled and lifted her glass in a salute. "Sorry, Count. I take them to bed because they look good. But thanks for sharing."

The insult did what she hoped. The openness closed up as if a thundercloud passed over the sun and choked off the light. Her stomach flipped as the gleam of disappointment flashed in his eyes along with a tinge of regret. For one moment, she'd felt more connected with a man than ever before. Even in bed.

"I see. We shall play by the rules then, yes?"

She didn't answer. With deliberate motions she picked up her magazine and tuned him out. Michael took the hint and they passed the next few hours in silence. Finally, the intercom lit up and the pilot's voice came over the speaker.

"Sir, we are due to touch down at Orio al Serio within fifteen minutes. Please fasten your seat belts."

Michael pressed the button. "Thank you, Richard."

They clipped their buckles. Maggie drained her wine and ignored the empty ache in her gut.

· · ·

Michael glanced at the poised woman by his side as he wound his way through the curvy hills toward his home. The top was down, and her gold-red hair blew in the wind in a tangled mass, but she didn't seem concerned. Her pursed lips told him she was thinking hard, probably getting into character to meet his family. During the last twenty-four hours, he'd learned a lot about Maggie Ryan.

Unfortunately, the tiny glimpse only made him crave more.

The vivid green of trees and brown earth flashed by and welcomed him in a way that soothed his soul. His family owned land from generations back, which had all been passed to him. But he'd always known from his first visit to New York City that he longed to make his mark there. Papa took him to visit his uncle, and the bustle of Manhattan fascinated his sense of challenge. Unfortunately, the crowds and chaos did not call to his need for privacy and land. When he decided to expand La Dolce Famiglia in the States, he sought the excitement of Manhattan in a location that offered a more laid-back atmosphere. As he traveled upstate, a hidden jewel revealed herself in the majestic mountains of the Hudson Valley, and he knew he'd found the place he could finally call home.

Though he was happy in New York, his birthplace always gave him a certain strength. A reminder of the man he was and where he came from. On his own land, there was no bullshit or pretending. In the spinning world of technology and money and competitive business, he needed to remind himself of the things that were important.

The walled city of Bergamo reminded him of a treasure surrounded by a fortress. Snugly situated at the foothills of the Alps and separated into upper and lower towns, the combination of Old and New World mingled into sheer perfection. He enjoyed the sleek feel of the sports car as he moved from the Città Bassa to the Città Alta and the bustling city fell away to a quiet, country hush. A sense of peace and satisfaction coursed through him as he neared home.

He caught the musky scent of sandalwood in the air and shifted in his seat. Everything about Maggie was a sexual contrast. The hunter in him longed to dive underneath her surface and find what made her tick.

Her stunned look when he confessed his secret punched through his chest. He'd never told of his empty search for a woman to complete him. After all, most men would laugh, and women may take up the challenge to storm the barriers of his heart. She'd gotten him so pissed, the words burst out of his mouth. But her obvious recognition revealed her own deepest longing.

He reached the top of the hill, pulled up to the sprawling terra-cotta villa, and cut the engine. "We shall have a minute before they come running out."

"It's beautiful, but not the billionaire mansion I expected."

He took in the simple lines of his family home through her eyes and sighed. "Mama refuses to leave. I planned to build her a castle worthy of what she accomplished, but she laughed at me. Said she refused to leave her family land and the home where Papa lived."

"I like her already."

"She even refused help. No maids or cooks for Mama. I have a woman who sneaks in to do deep cleaning when she's in church." He shook his head. "Ah, well. Are you ready?"

Her face was impassive and cool. Yet those jade-green eyes mirrored a tiny flare of uncertainty. He caught her hand within his and entwined their fingers. Her small gasp sang in his ears and stretched his pants more than a notch. God, she was so responsive to his touch. The low hum between them beckoned, promising a deep physical satisfaction he ached to experience but never would. Her hot-pink nails dug into his palm, and his thumb pressed the sensitive pulse point at her wrist to confirm her response. Yes. He turned her on. She refused to buckle, though, and tossed her head with a devil-may-care attitude.

"Let's rock and roll," she said.

She climbed out of the car the same moment the door flung open and his sisters came running down the stone pathway.

In perfect unison, they flung themselves into his arms. Joy exploded through him as he hugged them back, their excited chatter a familiar noise to his ears. He pressed kisses to the tops of their heads and studied their appearances.

"You are all more beautiful than I remembered." A dual vision of thick black hair, strong features, and dark eyes stood before him. Venezia's generous curves had caused him to interrogate many of her dates regarding their intentions, and Julietta's independent streak gave him sleepless nights. These two sisters were bullheaded and full of sass, but they always bowed to his final orders as the family rules dictated. Carina at twenty-three was a late bloomer. He recognized instantly the awkward stooped posture as she tried to hide her height and curves under baggy clothes. Regret coursed through him at not being able to keep an eye on her at this tender age.

She giggled at his statement, but the older two only rolled their eyes.

"Is this how you wooed your bride?" Venezia demanded. "Corny compliments and sweet smiles in an effort to placate us? Though you don't come to visit for months, and then spring a new wife on Mama without any buildup."

Carina glanced back and forth between her sisters and Maggie, chewing on her lip with sudden unease.

"Watch your temper, Venezia," he commanded. "Perhaps my wife understands better than you that I do what is best for the family."

Maggie stalked away from the car, her hips swinging in the ancient rhythm of Eve. Her sleek hair swung past her shoulders, and she stopped beside him as if in full support. "I'm Maggie, by the way, your brother's new wife. And no, he didn't woo me with compliments. He did it the old-fashioned way." She paused for dramatic effect and twisted those full lips in a mocking smile. "With great sex."

The chirp of birds was the only sound that broke the deafening silence. Michael half closed his eyes in sheer horror. He was going to kill her. His older sisters stared at her with open mouths. Carina gasped.

Why did he think he'd be able to control her?

Venezia choked on a laugh. Julietta looked at her with a touch of admiration, and now Carina seemed as if she had met her new heroine.

Well versed in damage control, his mind spun with an appropriate response to make it all go away.

"Nothing wrong with sex to enslave a man." A familiar voice echoed from the doorway, and a slight figure made her way down the path. "It's what you do with him afterward that counts. At least you married him and made him honest."

"Mama?"

Everyone swung around to watch the progression of the short woman with the carved wooden cane. With each step, the cane banged with an authoritative air that sent shivers down his spine. Her long, gray hair was held back in its usual bun, and her olive skin was heavily wrinkled from the sun and old-fashioned laugh lines. She bore four children who all towered over her and boasted their father's genes, but the whiplash of her voice terrified anyone who got in her way or disappointed her. She wore comfortable slacks, sandals, and a simple white blouse with a cardigan wrapped around her shoulders.

She stopped in front of them. Her lips quirked, but her face showed no humor as she studied Maggie with sharp eyes. Long moments passed as they waited for her response.

Finally, Maggie broke the silence. "*Signora* Conte, I am honored to finally meet you." Her tone held the highest respect as she met his mother's gaze head-on. "Your son is an idiot for not telling you about our engagement sooner. I apologize for him."

His mother nodded. "I accept your apology. Welcome to my family." His mother kissed Maggie on each cheek, then frowned. "You are too thin. Always too thin these young girls. We shall fix that immediately." Her head came around sharply. "Girls? Did you not greet your new sister?"

The tension dissolved as his sisters hugged and kissed Maggie. The breath he'd held whooshed out of his mouth and he hugged his mother. The delicacy of her frame contradicted her steely stare. "Hello, Mama."

"Michael. I am angry with you but will make you pay later."

He chuckled and ran a finger down her wrinkled cheek. "*Mi dispiace*. I promise to make it up to you."

"*Si*. Come inside and get settled."

His senses swam with the familiar sights and scents of his home. He took in the sloping terra-cotta roof, wrought-iron balconies, and the elaborate stone pillars flanking the front door. Bright yellow and red surfaces competed with masses of wildflowers in vivid colors. Set atop the peak of a hill, the three-tier home sprawled like a queen over her subjects, boasting more than five acres of grassy fields. The carved-stone pathways led to a private terrace and pool area surrounded by lush gardens and walkways. The Alps shimmered in the distance, their massive white-peaked tips visible from the balcony.

While his sisters buzzed over Maggie's ring, he made his way through the doors and was assaulted with the smell of garlic, lemon, and basil. Ceramic tile gleamed clean and bright and set off the pine cabinets and heavy table. Massive counters surrounded the space that was covered with fresh herbs, tomatoes, and an array of pots and pans. This was his mother's domain and heaven on earth when they were first introduced to the sweet lure of pastries and luscious fillings. She'd passed her talent down to each of her children, but none had her expert skill, and they relied mostly on the famous chefs chosen to run their bakery empire. Funny, they all seemed to favor their father's genes for business, but Mama had never forced them to be someone they weren't.

The memory of his own dreams teased the fringes of his memory, but he refused to linger on regrets. Not then. Not now.

Not ever.

He glanced over at Maggie. She chatted with his sisters and seemed smugly at ease after her shocking entrance. Obviously, she assumed he'd meekly accept her outrageous actions in gratitude for her agreement to the whole farce.

"Maggie, I need to speak with you for a moment."

As if she sensed his irritation, she shot him a look and hiked up her brow. He smothered a chuckle.

"Bring your luggage up to your room," his mama ordered. "I've gotten it ready for you. After you settle, we shall meet in the garden for some coffee and snacks."

"*Si*."

He retrieved the luggage from the car, walked back in the house, and motioned for Maggie to follow. She broke away from his sisters and they ascended the stairs toward their bedroom. He dropped the luggage, kicked the door closed with his heel, and faced her.

"A very amusing opening to our week, *la mia tigrotta*. But I think it's time you realize who makes the rules here." He took a step closer and towered over her. "Now."

Chapter Four

More than six feet of irritated man loomed before her. Though he didn't touch her, her body stilled as if restrained. His usual relaxed charm disappeared and a dangerous aura crackled in the air. She'd seriously pissed him off. Unfortunately, instead of fear, excitement tingled along her nerve endings. Damn, what would he be like in bed? Naked and muscled and . . . demanding.

Usually, she stayed far away from men who had any dominance or control tendencies, but Michael didn't scare her. At least, not in a bad way. Her lips parted in an unconscious invitation for him to take it a step further. Onyx eyes sharpened on her mouth and darkened. She ached to know how he tasted. Craved to experience his tongue claiming her mouth, his hips slamming against hers, without forcing her to make the choice.

A beat passed. Another.

The words slipped out of her mouth before she caught them. "What's the matter, Count? Cat got your tongue?"

He turned away and a stream of colorful curses shot in the air. Her body relaxed from his retreat, but his threat caused a shiver to work down her spine. She ignored the flare of disappointment from a missed opportunity.

"Be careful, *cara*. Toying with me may be fun, but eventually I will tire and force your hand."

Maggie snorted. "You sound like those erotic romances I love. But I'm no sub, baby, and you're not my dom. My gamble paid off. I figured I'd challenge your family from the start so I don't have to play a role I'm not comfortable with. Eventually they'd realize I'm not a great pleaser or traditional Italian wife." She grinned. "Your mom's a pisser."

"She's ill, so please be careful."

"Oh, no, Michael. What's wrong with her?"

He gave a deep sigh and rubbed his hands over his face. "Besides an arthritic knee, her heart is delicate. She needs to watch her stress and activity, so I intend to humor her this visit." His brows lowered. "And I hope you will, too."

"I can play nice for a week."

"I'll believe it when I see it," he murmured. "Be sure

you don't try to deck me when I kiss you." He looked thoughtful, and Maggie almost gulped with unease. "In fact, perhaps I should kiss you right here. Right now. For practice, of course."

She hissed like a ticked-off snake. "I can manage not to jump when a man touches me."

"I'm not convinced." He stalked over and invaded her personal space. The heat of his skin pulled her in. "One slipup and this charade ends. I can't afford it. Especially when a simple kiss beforehand may make the difference."

"I'm real good at faking it." She tossed him a mocking smile. The delicious scents of musk and man beckoned her to steal a sample. Her heart tripped at the thought of him calling her bluff, which only made her more obnoxious. "No one will ever know I'm not interested in kissing you. No need to put ourselves through a practice run."

He studied her in silence and she began to relax. "Let's test the theory, shall we?"

He grasped her shoulders and yanked her forward. She collided with a rock of carved muscle, and her arms came up in automatic protest to push against his chest. When she hit resistance, her fingers gripped the soft material of his T-shirt. His feet straddled hers and kept her off balance. His lips stopped inches from her own.

"Take your hands off of me." Sweat beaded her brow. Oh, God, what if she melted and looked like an idiot?

What if she moaned when those full lips slid over hers? She could not respond. She could not respond. She could not—

"What are you so nervous about?" Humor danced in his eyes. "You've done this a million times, remember?"

"I don't like to be manhandled," she shot back.

His lip quirked. He lowered his voice to a husky purr that promised her pure bodily pleasure. "Maybe you haven't had the right man handling you."

"Give me a break. Do women really fall for that line? Because if they do, they must come from the land of the stupid. Take your hands—"

His lips covered hers.

His warm, soft mouth stopped the angry flow of words and distracted her from any other thought she'd ever had except how this man kissed.

Her senses short-circuited. She liked kissing and had experienced her fair share, but with Michael everything seemed different. His body heat reminded her of a were-wolf in those *Twilight* films she secretly loved. His tongue probed the seam of her lips, then dove in without apology. She could have fought him if he got greedy; instead, the slide of his tongue seduced and asked for her to come and play. His stubble rubbed the sensitive curve of her jaw. His hips slanted against hers as his arms came down and cupped her rear, bringing her up to meet the hard bulge between his thighs.

She moaned. He caught it and pressed a bit deeper, and Maggie opened her mouth and gave in.

He plundered and commanded in complete thrusts, reminding her of how he'd claim her body if she gave him a chance. She tried to surface and gain control of the kiss, but her mind crumbled and her body sang. He murmured her name, and her legs got shaky as she held on to him for dear life and kissed him back.

How long had passed? Minutes? An hour? He finally pulled away, slowly, as if he regretted ever breaking the contact. She hated herself in that moment. Instead of slapping him away, or coming up with a smart-aleck comment, she just stared helplessly. Her tongue ran over her swollen lower lip.

He groaned. Uneven breaths lifted his chest. "You're right," he said softly. "You fake it really well."

She jerked back and prayed her cheeks didn't look flushed. She forced out the words. "Told you."

He turned and stacked the luggage in the corner of the room and opened the closet door. "There's plenty of space for both of us. This will be our room for the week."

Reality crashed over her. Rich details made the room comfortable yet masculine, from the royal-blue throw rugs, cherrywood furniture, and lack of frilly clutter. A deep red quilt finished off the polished look of the bed that took up the center of the room. Maggie stared at the bed, a bit smaller than what she expected, and realized there was no sofa or cushy rug. The knowledge they'd be squished together rattled her nerves. Dear God, she'd just melted from a lousy kiss. What if she rolled over in her sleep? What if her fingers accidentally hit one of those sleek pec muscles and she made a fool out of herself?

Irritation bit at her from the ridiculous situation so she did what she learned best. Go on the attack first. "Nice bed."

He cleared his throat. "Is this acceptable? If not, I can always put a blanket on the floor."

She rolled her eyes. "I'm a big girl, Count, just stay on your side. I'll take the left."

"As you wish."

"You don't snore, do you?"

A twinkle of amusement glinted in his eyes. "I've never had anyone complain before."

"Well, I'll let you know for future reference if they're lying."

He gestured toward the bathroom and glass doors that led to a balcony. "Why don't you take some time to freshen up and come downstairs when you're ready? I'll show you the property and the rest of the house then. When is your Milan shoot?"

"Tomorrow. I'll be there most of the day."

"Very well. I'll meet you there in the afternoon so we can file our Atto Notorio and Nulla Osta at the consulate's office. I've already arranged for witnesses. Don't forget to bring all your papers—I had to pull some strings so Mama wouldn't suspect we wish any delay."

Maggie swallowed a gulp. "I thought you said it was impossible to get a priest to marry us?"

"It is quite difficult to get a priest to perform a ceremony last minute, and Mama will only accept this type of wedding. There's no way they can be approved in a week."

"Okay."

They stared at each other for a few moments in silence. He shifted his weight, and the fabric of his jeans strained against the bulge dead center. His black T-shirt did nothing to hide the breadth of his shoulders and chest. Or the corded, sinewy length of his arms covered with dark hair. Her traitorous body responded to his confidence as heat burned between her thighs and her nipples tightened to achy points.

When was the last time she'd been so turned on by a man? Maybe it was the chase. Women always craved men who were off-limits. Especially if they obviously had it bad for another woman.

Right?

"Maggie? Are you okay?"

She shook off the reaction and blamed it on jet lag. "Sure. I'm going to shower. I'll meet you downstairs."

He nodded and shut the door behind him.

Maggie groaned and quickly rummaged through her suitcase for a change of clothes. All she had to do was get through seven days without making an ass of herself, and she'd be free of Michael Conte for good. She wouldn't have to worry about bumping into him at Alexa's home, and she'd have her family all to herself.

The bitterness of the image mocked her satisfaction and screamed she was a liar. She'd gotten used to him over the past year. Too much so. And every time she gazed into those wicked dark eyes, the thought of her humiliation flashed in her mind and made her squirm.

The bathroom was small but boasted a deep marble tub and a shower stall. She decided to keep it quick and have a long soak later. She stepped under the stinging jets and let the heat relax her knotted muscles. Accustomed to forced blind dates from many colleagues, Maggie hadn't thought twice when Alexa swore she'd found the perfect man for her. She remembered entering the expensive, intimate Italian restaurant and expecting a certain sort of man. A little cocky. A little too smooth. A little too attractive.

She'd been wrong.

Except for the attractive part.

Maggie scrubbed her skin and tried to whisk the memory away. But the images flickered before her eyes. The instant connection when their hands touched, like lightning bottled up tight and released from the cap to scorch. She'd almost jerked back. Almost. The walls she'd built held firm, but his conversation pulled her in and wrapped her like a warm hug. Yes, he was smooth, and charming, and funny, but there was a sense of realness in his core that spoke to her.

When dessert came, for the first time in as long as she could remember, she didn't want the evening to end. And she sensed that he didn't, either.

She learned her one motto from experience. Control the date, control the result. For some strange reason, she opened up and gave him a peek of her inner soul. The sensual pull twisted between them, and a lightness spread through her body. Maybe she was finally ready for something more. Maybe Alexa had been right all along. Maybe she'd discover a rainbow or a waterfall on that hidden path, or something that could finally surprise her and fill the aching void inside.

"I enjoyed this," she said softly. "Maybe we can do it again." When the impulsive invitation stumbled out over the rich tiramisu, she almost bit her tongue in horror, but it was too late.

He studied her in silence. "I don't think that's a good idea, Maggie."

Her name drifted to her ears in a caress, but his words bit like the family dog gone mean. Rejection had never been considered.

"I'm sorry, *cara*. You're a beautiful woman, and I'm extremely attracted to you. But I think this could end up a mess."

The lightness shriveled and turned dim. Yes, she understood it was a sticky situation, but for the first time she had been willing to take a chance. She must have misjudged the situation. Or their connection. She almost laughed it off, but a strange fear glinted in those eyes and made her pause. He smiled, but she noted his discomfort by the way he shifted in his seat and grabbed his wineglass. Almost as if something held him back from taking her home. Almost as if . . .

The realization shook through her. The pieces of the puzzle slid and locked into place. Pain sliced deep into her core, and she barely managed to get the words out. "It's Alexa, isn't it?" she whispered. "You have feelings for her."

"No! Alexa is my friend, nothing else."

His denial screamed untruth as he looked away. Her skin flushed, and humiliation made her want to gag and run from the room. No wonder he didn't want to date her. Her mind wandered over the conversation and found all the remarks he'd dropped along the way regarding Alexa. How wonderful she was. How caring. How smart. He'd even asked how they met, intrigued by her telling of their first encounter on the school bus when they'd gotten into a fight, then became best friends. He'd never been interested in her. This date revolved around gathering information on another woman.

He was in love with Alexa.

She choked back her shame and swore to get out with

her pride. "I understand," she said. Her words were laced with an icy distance. Her fingers didn't shake as she pushed back her plate and slid out of her chair.

"Maggie, let's talk about this. Please don't go with the wrong impression."

Her chuckle came out a bit brittle. "Don't be ridiculous, Count. I'm a big girl—I can handle a little rejection. As long as you realize I'll be keeping an eye on you. Especially around Alexa."

He gasped, but Maggie saw right through him. "I told you—"

"Bullshit." She grabbed her Coach purse and slung it over her shoulder. Her eyes narrowed. "See ya, Count."

He called her name again but she ignored him and left the restaurant.

Maggie turned off the water and grabbed a towel. Even now his rejection hurt, as ridiculous as it sounded. He dragged her to the recurring nightmare of her youth.

Never good enough.

Angry with her thoughts and bad memories, she changed into a pair of jeans, green tank top, and leather sandals. No use going into the past. She controlled her relationships, her sexuality, and her own choices. And she sure as hell would never be sloppy seconds.

Especially not for Michael Conte.

She ran a brush through her damp hair and slicked on a coat of gloss. Then, pushing her disturbing thoughts to the back of her mind, she made her way downstairs to meet her new family.

Maggie stepped out in the back and found everyone gathered around the wrought-iron tables and matching bistro chairs. The alcove was surrounded by a walled garden of vivid blooms—a twist of yellows, bloodreds, and purples all screaming for attention. The sweet scent drifted on the warm breeze and tickled her nostrils. An elaborate fountain with a carved angel trickled water into a pond covered with floating moss. The sun washed over the rough terra-cotta cobblestones. Immediately, Maggie relaxed in the peaceful space. Her fingers itched for her camera in an effort to capture the almost mystical quality of quiet, even when invaded by the loud Italian family chattering at the table.

"Margherita, come join us." She almost flinched at the sound of the full name, but Michael's mother made it sound like magic, so she let it go. Rule number one: never criticize the matriarch of the family you just married into.

"*Grazie.*"

Michael poured her a glass of red wine, then intermingled his fingers with hers and smiled. Her heart hitched, but she smiled back with warmth. His sisters all looked eager to hear all the gory details. Maggie made an executive decision. The faster she spilled the story, the faster they'd move on to Venezia's wedding.

She sipped her wine. "Would you like to know how we met?"

Michael's brow shot up with surprise. A clamor of female voices rose in agreement. Maggie hid a smile. This one would be easy.

"My close friend Alexa set us up on a blind date. You see, my best friend is happily married to my brother. When she met Michael at a business dinner, she thought we'd be a perfect match." Maggie threw a cloying smile at him and caught a warning gleam in his eyes. "The moment we met, he told me I was The One. Usually, I never believe men on the first date, but he courted me and won me over."

Carina sighed and rested her plump chin in her hands. "That's so romantic. Almost like Fate."

"Yes, just like Fate." Maggie squeezed Michael's fingers. "We were going to set a wedding date, but when we heard Venezia was also engaged, we decided to elope. I hope you're not too upset we skipped a full-fledged wedding, but I despise being the center of attention, so we thought this would be best."

Michael brought her palm up to his mouth and placed a kiss in the center. Her skin tingled. "*Si,* Maggie is a very private person."

Michael's mother's sharp stare contradicted her frail body. Unease tickled her belly. Anyone who raised four children and led a family business had brilliant instincts, and Maggie made a note to be careful when they were alone together. Knowing there weren't many things to count on in life, she'd made sure her word was ironclad and never broken. Therefore, the stakes were high for her, too.

"What do you do, Maggie?" Julietta asked. Her long fingers held her wineglass with a delicacy that also belied her serious stare. Maggie remembered she was the head of the business end of La Dolce Famiglia. Polished and refined, Julietta was definitely the rational, down-to-earth sister.

"I'm a photographer. I have a shoot tomorrow in Milan so I'll be gone most of the day."

"How wonderful. What do you photograph?" Julietta asked.

"Men. In their underwear." A silence fell over the table and Maggie shrugged. "It's designer underwear, of course. I'm shooting Roberto Cavalli tomorrow."

Venezia burst out laughing. "I love it! Can you get me a discount? Dominick would love a new pair of Cavallis."

Carina giggled. Mama Conte gave a long-suffering sigh. "Venezia, we do not need to know what Dominick wears under his clothes." She glowered. "And you should not know, either, until you are married. *Capisce*?"

"Maggie is a very gifted photographer," Michael said. "I'm certain she will be broadening her experience, especially with so much to see in Italy."

Maggie frowned. His almost apologetic statement to his family stung, but she swallowed her outburst with a gulp of Chianti. Just because she didn't photograph cute puppies and babies did not make her choices less valuable. It was as if he knew that in her gut, she ached for more. Annoyed at her thoughts, she refocused on the conversation.

Venezia chattered as her hands confirmed each statement with dramatic gestures. Maggie pegged her as the emotional drama queen of the family. Still, her chocolate eyes burned bright with fire and enthusiasm, and her lithe body clad in expensive jeans, floral halter top, and Jimmy Choos told her she adored fashion. Michael seemed to disapprove of Venezia's choice not to work in the family bakery, but her career as an assistant to a well-known stylist seemed to satisfy her creative flair. Maggie couldn't picture her frosting cupcakes, buying advertising, or doing the bookkeeping.

"We'd like to hold the wedding here on the grounds," Venezia continued. Her face softened. "Of course, we'll have it catered with cake from our bakery. September is such a beautiful month."

Julietta gasped. "That's three months away!"

Her sister tossed a glare. "I don't want to wait another minute to start my life with Dominick. Now that Michael is married, we can move ahead with our plans. We've already decided on the fifteenth. That's okay with your schedule, right, Maggie? And of course you'll be one of my bridesmaids."

Maggie gulped as the guilt of their lie suddenly hit. She

swallowed past it with another sip of wine. "Of course, I'll clear my schedule."

Venezia squealed with delight and clasped her hands together. "Wonderful. Oh, and why don't we shop for our dresses this week?"

Julietta rolled her eyes. "I detest dress shopping."

"Well, get over it. You're my maid of honor and if you ruin it by whining I'll never talk to you again."

"I could only wish."

Maggie twisted her diamond ring around her finger as it suddenly burned. She fought the slight panic of the reality of her situation. "Um, I'll be busy with work, and I know Michael wanted to show me some of the sights while we're here." She smiled, but sensed it came out more like a grimace. "Maybe you and your sisters can go this week. If you find something, I'll give you my size and you can order it. I'm sure I'll see the dresses when Michael and I come back to visit."

"Absolutely not." Venezia's eyes gleamed with hard resolve. "You are also my sister now, and you must come. Besides, I refuse to put you in something that doesn't look good. It would ruin my reputation as a stylist."

Julietta snickered.

"Maggie and I are on our honeymoon, and we need some alone time. Traipsing around dress shopping is not my idea of romance." He smiled gently at her, and Maggie fought the melty sensation in her tummy.

Carina shot a pleading glance at Maggie. "Oh, please join us," she said. "We're a family now, and we missed out on all the excitement of your wedding. It's only one afternoon."

The pulsating walls closed in. How could she put on a bridesmaid dress and pretend she'd be in the wedding? Michael opened his mouth and Maggie caught a glimpse of his mother's face.

Suspicion.

A tiny frown marred her brow. Her discomfort was obvious, and the elderly woman sensed something was up. Which it was. But Maggie made a promise, so she needed to fake it.

She placed her fingers over Michael's lips to shush him. The soft curves made her ache to feel his mouth once more on hers, plunging deep and demanding everything. "No, Michael, your sisters are right." She tried to look happy. "I would love to spend an afternoon dress shopping. It'll be fun."

His mother leaned back, nodded, and crossed her arms in front of her chest in satisfaction. More chatter buzzed in Maggie's ears. She made a mental calculation of the hours left before she could collapse into slumber. A quiet dinner, an early night pleading exhaustion, and one day would be down. Tomorrow she'd work all day at the shoot, go file their papers at the consulate, and—what did Julietta say?

"Party?" Maggie asked. The word flashed in neon like a warning sign in her brain. Michael also looked surprised.

Mama Conte rose and settled her cane on the rough stones. "*Si.* The party tonight, Michael. You did not believe I would miss holding a celebration in my son and new wife's honor? We must get started on dinner."

"Is Max coming?" Carina asked in a breathless tone.

"*Si,* of course he is coming. And your cousins."

Michael winced, then shot her a reassuring nod. Holy crap, she was drowning, and her fake husband threw her a life preserver with a leak in it. Bridesmaid dresses and now a marriage party. "Mama, we are really not up for a party tonight. We had a long flight, and Maggie has to work in the morning."

She cut off his protests with a wave of her hand. "Nonsense. It is only a few people to extend their congratulations. It is nothing. Why don't you pull some wine from our cellar and visit the home bakery site? Bring tiramisu and cannolis, black and white. Julietta will go with you for the ride."

Maggie gulped. "Um, maybe I should—"

Mama Conte wrapped her hand around Maggie's arm. Her frailty seemed nonexistent. Sheer strength pulsed from those delicate muscles and squeezed like a death trap. "*Niente.* You stay with me, Margherita, and help me with dinner."

Michael shook his head. "Mama, Maggie does not cook. In the States, most women work and many do not know how to prepare food."

That caught Maggie's attention. Her head whipped around and she glared. "Screw you, Count, I can cook." She gave a fake simper. "I just pretended not to know how so you'd take me to dinner more often."

Mama Conte gave a proud cackle and led her inside, leaving an astonished count in their wake.

With every step toward the giant, shiny kitchen, a new bead of sweat appeared. Maggie seethed as one thought danced in her brain.

If she got out of this alive, she'd kill him.

. . .

Maggie wanted to give in to the urge to run from the house screaming. She hated kitchens. When she was younger, most of the cooks would turn mean when she'd enter their sacred space, until just the sight of that shiny equipment wrung a shudder. Still, she kept her head up and her attitude positive. She was a capable woman and could follow a recipe. Maybe dinner would be something easy and she could show Michael her unbelievable culinary talents and finally shut him up.

Michael's mama already had a variety of bowls and measuring cups stacked on the long, wide counter. Various containers of powdered things were neatly lined up. Definitely not like that crazy show *Iron Chef* with all the chaos and running around to prepare a meal.

Maggie always believed cooking was done for survival—not pleasure. Since she earned lots of money, she spent most of it on take-out. She frowned and tried to feign enthusiasm for the task ahead. God, she wanted more wine. If she got drunk enough, she'd be more relaxed for the upcoming torture.

"What are we making?" she asked with fake cheer.

"Pasta. We shall eat a quick dinner before the rest of the family arrives, then put out pastries and coffee. You know how to cook pasta, Margherita?"

Relief relaxed her tight muscles. Thank God. Mama Conte picked the one meal she excelled at. She often cooked pasta late at night and knew how to get it to the perfect consistency of al dente. Maggie nodded. "Of course."

Satisfaction flickered over the older woman's face. "Good. We need a few batches. I've already gotten the ingredients."

The massive countertop held flour, giant eggs, oil, rolling pins, and a variety of other equipment. She glanced around for the box of ziti and a pot to boil the water in as Mama Conte handed her an apron. Maggie wrinkled her nose at the odd choice of clothing just to stick something in water, but what the hell. When in Italy . . .

"I am sure you cook pasta differently in America, so you may watch me first, then prepare your batch."

Confusion fogged her brain for a moment, and Maggie refused to give in to panic. Where was the blue box? What was she talking about? In growing horror, she watched as wrinkled hands moved like lightning cracking eggs, straining yolks, and mixing everything in a bowl. The flour was dumped in the middle of a large board, and slowly, Mama Conte poured the wet stuff in the middle and began some kind of ritual that blended it all together. Like magic, dough suddenly appeared, and she kneaded, stretched, and danced over the blob for endless minutes. Completely fascinated by the hypnotic ritual, Maggie couldn't believe this stuff would end up looking like anything you could actually eat. Never breaking the rhythm, Mama Conte glanced toward her. "You may begin when you are ready."

Oh. Shit.

Reality hit her as she stared at the mass of stuff piled in front of her. Homemade pasta! She had to make the actual dough? There was no heavenly box to open, or a jar of sauce to heat up. The stakes were much higher than she thought, and Maggie felt the beginnings of an attack nibble on her sanity. She breathed deep. She could do this. No way would she be broken by a lump of dough and an Italian mother just waiting to pounce. She'd show them all.

Maggie pulled the bowl close. The flour part was easy, but the eggs scared the hell out of her. Hm, one good crack in the middle, pull apart the shell, and the inside should slide out easily. With fake confidence, she slammed the egg against the edge of the bowl.

The slimy stuff slipped into her hands and white shell scattered. One quick glance at Mama Conte confirmed she wasn't looking over, and she trusted Maggie to get her batch done. Humming some Italian song under her breath, she kept kneading.

Maggie scooped out as much of the shell as possible and left the rest in. A few more and she had some kind of wet ingredient that looked acceptable. Kind of. Screw it, she needed to move fast before his mother looked over. She poured a mass of flour in the center, then dumped the stuff in the bowl in the middle.

Liquid ran over the edges of the board in a runny mess. Trying not to pant, she wiped her brow with her elbow and scooped up the mess with the apron. The damn fork didn't help stir it at all, so Maggie took a deep breath and stuck both hands into the junk.

Oh, gross.

Flour caught under her nails. She squeezed over and over and prayed for some sort of miracle that resembled dough. Powder flew around her in a dust cloud. The more she panicked, the faster she rolled. Maybe more flour or another egg? The rest was a blur until a pair of firm hands stilled her movements. Maggie closed her eyes in pure defeat. Then slowly opened them.

Mama Conte stared at the mess that was supposed to be pasta. White shells scattered within the lumps of gooey junk that slid over the counter and dripped on the floor. Tiny puff clouds rose and drifted around them. Her apron was filled with sticky clumps, and the so-called dough covered her bare arms up to her elbows.

Maggie knew it was over. Michael would never marry a woman who couldn't cook homemade pasta. Mama Conte would never approve of such a match, or even believe in the possibility. With the last shred of pride she held, Maggie lifted her chin and met the woman's gaze head-on.

"I lied." Mama Conte lifted a brow in question, and Maggie rushed on. "I have no idea how to cook. I use the dried pasta and dump it in water. I heat up sauce in the microwave. I eat take-out almost every night."

There. It was done. She prepared herself for the ridicule and accusation. Instead, Michael's mother grinned.

"I know."

Maggie jerked back. "What?"

"I wanted to see how far you would go. I am impressed, Margherita. You never show your fear. Once you commit, you see it through, even if you think you will fail. That is exactly what my son needs."

With quick actions, Mama Conte dumped the oozing mess into the garbage, redusted with the flour, and turned to her. "We begin again. Watch me."

Maggie watched as she was showed each step with careful precision. As the fear of discovery slid away, she relaxed into the lesson, her hands steeped in dough as she worked the mound with a strength that quickly tired her. The hand weights at the gym had nothing on cooking, and the muscles in Mama Conte's arms and wrists never seemed to tire as she sought the perfect blend. Maggie caught up the lilting melody Michael's mother hummed, and a sense of peace settled over her. She'd never cooked with a woman before, never been allowed in such a warm, domestic space. As the rolling pin worked the dough and was stretched delicately, Mama Conte handed her a portion.

"The earthiness of pasta dough is the true element in a good, simple meal. We must stretch it to a delicate thinness without breaking. Work the edge."

Maggie bit her lip. "Mama Conte, maybe you should do this one?"

"No. You will serve your husband dinner tonight, Margherita, by your own hand. And this is not because you are beneath him, or he believes you are less. It is because you are more. So much more. *Capisce*?"

The beauty of her statement shimmered around her with sudden truth. She reached up, wiped her brow, and smeared batter over her forehead. And smiled. "Okay."

They worked without speaking, humming Italian songs, listening to the soothing motions of the rolling pin and the chirping of birds in the distance. Maggie broke noodle over noodle, but dug in, until one perfect large strand draped over her hand. Uneven, but transparently thin without a break.

Mama Conte reached over and draped it on the drying stand, inspecting it carefully. Her cackle echoed through the kitchen. "*Perfecto*."

Maggie grinned and wondered why she felt as if she just emerged from a Mount Everest climb in the middle of winter.

. . .

Hours later, she sat at the large table with bowls of steaming pasta and fresh tomato sauce. The scents of sweet basil and savory garlic hung in the air. Three bottles of wine took up the corners, and plates squeezed between the platters of food like secondary characters in a book. She glanced over nervously at Michael. Would he laugh? Would he tease her about her inability to cook and her pathetic efforts at an expert table?

Laughter and yelling and loud discussion swarmed around her in confusion. She was so used to dinners eaten at her breakfast counter while she watched television or at structured restaurants with low, murmured conversation. Growing up, she ate alone, or with her brother in silence. But Michael was different.

He teased his sisters and relaxed under the warmth of his family, and Maggie realized his ease was brought into every situation because he knew exactly who he was. She respected that in a man and found it rare. He enjoyed life and liked a sense of humor, and she wondered what it would be like to eat with him every night. Sip wine, talk about their day, cook together, and eat together. A real-life couple.

Michael picked up his fork, twirled the noodles, and popped them in his mouth.

She held her breath.

He made a moaning sound. "Ah, Mama, it is delicious."

Mama Conte smirked and slid herself onto the seat. "You may thank your wife, Michael. Each noodle on your plate was made by her hand."

He drew back in surprise. A tiny frown marred his brow as he looked down at the meal, then swung his gaze to meet hers. An odd combination of emotion swirled in those eyes. A lick of heat. A flare of pride. And a flicker of gratitude.

He bowed his head and a smile bloomed over his face. Lightness filled her, and she smiled back, the busyness of the table fading away under his attention. "*Grazie, cara*. I am honored to eat something you made for me. It is *delicioso*."

She nodded, accepting his thanks. Venezia spoke about bridesmaid dresses and weddings. Carina spoke about art. Julietta spoke about the new ad campaign they were launching at the bakery. Michael kept eating, obvious pride in his fake wife's food.

And for a little while, she was happier than she'd ever been.

Chapter Five

They were in trouble.

Michael flanked the door and greeted a long line of relatives he hadn't seen in months. He'd suspected the intimate dinner party that was no big deal would end up in a disaster. Well, not as much for him as for poor Maggie. His *famiglia* flocked around her with a noisy affection they only reserved for blood. Cousins brought spouses, girlfriends, boyfriends, and all the *bambinos*. Close neighbors and some women who'd hunted him for years showed up to check out their winning rival. For him, it was a typical evening at his mama's house.

For Maggie, it must be hell.

He shook his head and tried hard not to laugh. She stood trapped in a corner with some of his female cousins, her cinnamon-colored hair a bright beacon in a room filled mostly with olive skin and brunettes. Her dress was short and flirty, the skirt flouncing above the knee and showing off a pair of endless legs that begged to be wrapped around a man's waist. Bright red and yellow splashed over the delicate material and made her easy to spot in the thronged mass. Her height had always been impressive, but she matched most of his cousins with her three-inch red sandals. Something about her shoes turned him on like no other woman's shoes had. Almost as if her lust for sexy, come-get-me heels confirmed her inner hellcat.

He refilled his wineglass and chatted with old friends as he kept an eye on her. He expected a chilled politeness that would put off his affectionate family, but each time his gaze snagged her, she was laughing or listening intently to the many stories regaling her ears. Fascinated, Michael inched toward her.

Sure, he knew she was socially professional and relaxed in work settings. He just didn't expect her to be so open in her ruse. Her childhood bespoke a cold familiarity, and she radiated a distance that was part of her core. Hell, she wore it like a cloak, which he spotted the moment she walked into the restaurant to meet him for their blind date. But something felt different tonight.

He studied her as his uncle Tony talked shop with him—problems with suppliers and increased rent and the possibility of owning properties. He nodded, listened with half an ear, and eavesdropped on his fake wife.

"How did you do it?" his cousin Brianna whispered to Maggie. She reminded him of when people dropped their voices automatically to say such words as "cancer." The question still sounded as harsh as a gunshot. "Michael has avoided marriage forever. He has a reputation, you know."

Maggie's lip twitched. "Really? What type of reputation?"

Brianna looked around and leaned in. Michael hid behind the breadth of Uncle Tony's back. "He loves the chase. Seems he likes to seduce a woman—the bigger the challenge the more skilled he becomes in gaining her affection. Then, as soon as she gives in, *wham*."

Maggie drew back. "Wham? What wham?"

That whisper again. "He leaves her flat. Heartbroken, seduced, and abandoned."

Anger cut through him at his cousin's impression. *Dios,* did he ever get a break? He never led a woman on, yet his reputation preceded him all the way to America. Nick had informed him many times of the murmurs of his prowess among women and how he'd once been concerned Alexa would fall vulnerable to his charms. Michael took another casual step in and listened for her answer.

Maggie clucked her tongue. "How horrible! Maybe that's why he married me, then. How strange."

Brianna widened her eyes. "What's strange? Tell me. We're family now—your secrets are safe with me."

Maggie took a deep breath and looked around as if worried who'd overhear. Her whisper was as soft as his cousin's. "I refused to sleep with him until he married me, of course."

Michael choked on a piece of bruschetta. When he recovered, he looked up to find Maggie's mischievous grin, followed by a wink. She touched Brianna's arm, then turned on those sexy heels, and her skirt flipped, showing off a perfectly curved backside. He clenched his jaw as the sudden want clawed at him. He imagined sinking his teeth into her firm flesh and taking a succulent bite. The echo of her cry as he held her down and pleasured her misted his vision. When he resurfaced, Uncle Tony still droned on, and Maggie had moved to the other side of the room.

What the hell was he going to do about her?

More important, what was he going to do about his sudden need to claim the woman who pretended to be his wife?

• • •

Something was wrong with her.

Maggie nibbled on salty prosciutto from the antipasto, drank her wine, and mingled. In only twenty-four hours, she'd experienced every event she always avoided and despised.

Long, chatty conversations focused on weddings and girly talk. *Check*.

Cooking and chopping and ruining her perfect manicure. *Check*.

Dealing with mother-in-law and sister-in-law and cousins all prying into her personal life and making judgments. *Check*.

So why wasn't she running from the room in terror, like one of those idiots in *Scream* who saw an obscene white mask?

Maybe because she knew it was all fake?

Had to be. There was no other rational explanation. Other than with her brother and Alexa, she didn't do family functions. She cooked on her terms, when she thought it'd be a fun distraction. And she never had to deal with a flock of females who giggled and asked a billion questions. She was used to silence—had lived with it most of her life—and had little experience with such open affection.

Yet, they all welcomed her into the fold wholeheartedly. All of his sisters were so different, yet Maggie actually liked them. They were real. His mother never laughed or criticized as she taught her to make her first homemade pot of gravy. A tiny part of her flamed to life, a part she was ashamed to admit she owned. What would it feel like to have so many people love you no matter how many mistakes you made?

Her gaze caught on Venezia wrapped up in her fiancé's arms, laughing at something he said. Their connection burned from across the room, and the adoring expression on Dominick's face smashed straight through the gut with one pure emotion.

Longing.

Maggie swallowed past the lump in her throat. As horrific as their ruse was, somehow it felt so right once she saw the couple together. Nothing should stand in their way—especially an ancient custom. What would that feel like? To have a man look at her with such possession and love? To belong to a person who actually gave a damn?

She pushed the question from her mind and made her way back to Michael. Time to get her head back in the game. He stood next to a very attractive man with burning blue eyes and scruffy facial hair. Thick, jet-black waves of hair spilled over his forehead. Crap, the man was sex on a stick, and she briefly wondered if he was a model. Carina stood with them, her head tilted up as she gazed at the stranger as if he were the sun and the only element that stood between her and a cold, frozen death.

Curious, Maggie eased her way into the inner circle to stand by Michael.

"Maggie, there you are," Michael said. "Meet my friend Max Gray. He's been like a part of our family for years, so I consider him my brother. He works for La Dolce Famiglia as my right-hand man."

Max the sex god turned his piercing eyes on her and smiled. Laugh lines carved the edges of his mouth. She blinked at the sensual aura coming at her like jet propulsions. Oddly, she didn't feel the burn of connection she experienced with Michael, but more of an aesthetic pleasure from such a visually stunning creature. She offered her hand and he shook it with a firm grip.

Nope. No sparks at all. Thank God. Maggie pitied the woman who fell in love with this man, doomed to walk in his shadow forever.

Then she realized Michael's little sister had the bug.

Bad.

Carina had not yet reached the age where she hid her emotions. Still caught halfway to a full-grown woman, her face reflected a longing that broke Maggie's heart and filled her with fear. Her past rocketed toward her with the dim memories of the girl she'd once been. Before her innocence and belief in happily ever after was ripped from her.

Poor Carina. If she had a thing for Max, she was doomed to experience a broken heart.

"Where have you been hiding her, Michael?" He glanced between them with a hint of curiosity and something more. Suspicion? "Here I am thinking of you as my best friend, yet I didn't have a clue you two were involved. When Page Six doesn't break the news about a hot single billionaire in New York getting hitched, something's up."

Oh yeah. Max definitely believed her to be a fortune hunter.

Michael snorted. "Seems the magazines are more interested in you than me, my friend. And I thought the last time we compared notes, you beat me by almost a million."

"Two."

"Ah, but you are not a count."

"That Swiss blood took me out of the running, I guess. But I still own more land."

Maggie rolled her eyes. "Why don't you both whip it out and I'll tell you who's bigger?"

Michael shot her a look. Carina clamped her hand over her mouth.

"If my sources are correct, you're keeping your own secrets," Michael said. "What's this in the gossip columns about you dating royalty? Italian descent not good enough? You need a blue blood to satisfy you?"

Max shook his head. "Serena accompanied her father on a business trip and is keeping me company. She's an heiress to a fortune, and not really royalty. Her papa would rip me apart—I'm not worthy enough to marry into that family."

Carina blazed with fury. "That's ridiculous! Anyone who marries for money instead of love deserves unhappiness! You're worth more than that."

Max put his hands to his chest. "Ah, *cara,* will you marry me? You are a woman after my own heart."

Carina turned beet red. Her lips trembled as she searched for words. What a mess. In love with her brother's best friend who was years older, and trapped in a girl-woman's body as she lusted after someone she couldn't have. At least, not yet.

Maggie opened her mouth to divert attention, but Michael dived in for a belly flop. He chucked his sister under the chin, his indulgent smile like that of an adult to a toddler. "Carina has many years before she can be serious about a man. She will be stepping into her rightful position in the bakery and will finish her business degree. Besides, she's a good girl, and you, my friend, only date the bad ones."

The men laughed, neither realizing the expense of their joke.

The color drained from Carina's face, and she lowered her head. When she stuck her chin back up, she blinked back tears of rage. "I'm not a child, Michael," she hissed. "Why can't you both see that?"

She turned and ran from the room.

"What did I say?" Michael asked. "I was only teasing her."

Max looked just as lost.

Maggie let out an irritated sigh and gulped the rest of her wine. "You two boneheads really did it this time."

"Did what? Her behavior is irrational and rude to our guests. I meant no harm."

Max shifted uneasily. "Should I go talk to her?"

"No, it's my responsibility. I will talk to her."

Maggie shoved her empty glass into Michael's hands. "Ah, hell, stay out of it. You've done enough. I'll talk to her."

Michael's face reflected skepticism. "Darling, you don't have much experience with young women. Sometimes she needs a firm hand to see reason. Maybe it will be better if I get Julietta."

Maggie somehow doubted his business-minded sister understood Carina at the moment, either. Once again, his tone pissed her off, basically telling her she was incapable of handling another situation. In the past twenty-four hours, the man had insulted her career, her cooking, and now her social methods. She forced a sweet smile that almost gave her a cavity. "Don't worry, *darling.*" She mocked the endearment in a private manner he understood immediately. "I'm going to give her some good news to make her feel better."

"What news?"

She stared up at the twin gorgeous men before her and gave a wicked smirk. "I'll fix her up on a blind date. With someone hot."

Michael's face darkened. "Absolutely not. My baby sister is not experienced with dating."

"That's exactly why this will be perfect for her. See ya." She added to the insult by raising herself on tiptoes and placing a kiss on his lips. The tiny zing between them distracted her for an instant but she ignored it. "Let's not argue on our honeymoon, love, when we can concentrate on other fun activities." She gave Max a wink, then strolled away, making sure to swing her hips as she felt his gaze on her rear.

Maggie held back a laugh. Damn, some of this was fun. Challenging his wit and bullheaded ways gave her some benefit. She made her way upstairs and searched for Carina's room. Let Michael stew with that disturbing idea for a bit. She'd confess later she didn't even know a suitable boy to set Carina up with. Unfortunately, her mouth got her in trouble again and she still needed to try to speak with Carina. She certainly had no experience with female advice. What could she possibly say to make her feel better?

Maggie sighed as she stopped behind a closed door and heard muffled sobs. Her palms were sweaty so she rubbed them on her skirt. Ridiculous. If Carina didn't want to talk to her, she'd just hang here upstairs for a bit so Michael would believe they'd shared a conversation. She raised her hand and tapped on the door.

"Carina? It's Maggie. Do you want to talk for a bit, or do you want me to go away?" Yep, she was a coward. A good advisor would demand she open the door for a talk. A few beats of silence passed. Relief caved through her so she turned to go. "Okay, I understand, I'll just—"

The door swung open.

Ah, crap.

"Why doesn't anyone understand I'm a grown-up?" the girl burst out.

Maggie paused in the doorway, tempted to run, but Carina stepped back and made room for her so she walked in.

"Because your older brother will never accept it," Maggie said easily. She took in the pink walls, fluffy stuffed animals, and lots of lace. Yuck. Something told her Carina kept the room like this to please others and not herself. The canopy bed looked soft and inviting, but held a quilt of various butterflies that made it seem childish.

Definitely a young twenty-three. Maggie doubted she'd ever dated, especially with Michael in charge. She stopped at the back of the room where a few stairs led down to a separate space that looked as if it could have been a play-room at one time. This area had a different feel to it, with blank canvases, paint, and an array of artists' tools. Various watercolors in vivid colors drew her attention, and clay models of embracing lovers lined the shelves. Hm, inter-esting. This seemed more of a fit for Carina than the main area.

"I hate my life." Misery etched every feature of her face. She flopped on her bed as more tears leaked from her eyes. "No one understands or lets me make my own decisions. I'm not a baby anymore, but my life is already mapped out for me."

Maggie mentally berated herself for getting into this mess with a girl she barely knew and a situation she couldn't fix. "Um, how so?"

Carina gulped. "I'm only allowed to date boys my family approves of. Not that any boys have ever asked me out. I'm ugly and fat."

Maggie let out an exasperated sigh. "That's stupid. Your body is naturally curvy. You have breasts. Have you seen your sisters? They may be rail thin, but their boobs are flat as pancakes."

The girl's eyes widened in shock, and then an actual laugh escaped her lips. "Maybe. But boys like thin. And my hair looks like I stuck a finger in a socket. My lips look puffy and swollen and stupid." More tears and another gulp. "And Michael says I have to help Julietta at La Dolce Famiglia, but he never asked me what I want! I wanted to go away to college but he made me study at the university. Now I have to get my MBA and then do a long internship. Why can't I go to America and work for him? Nothing's fair!"

Maggie shook her head. Geez, the dramatics in this family were off the charts. She sat gingerly on the bed and let Carina cry it out. She searched desperately for all the right things a mom or Alexa or Michael would say. Ah, the hell with it. At this point, Maggie figured she couldn't make it much worse.

"Okay, babe, sit up."

The girl swiped at her cheeks and obeyed. Those lips she hated pursed, and Maggie bet one day Max would be seeing a whole new persona of Michael's baby sister. But not now. Not yet. Carina needed some time to find herself and be comfortable in her own skin.

"I'm sure you've heard this before, but life sucks."

Another faint smile. At least she humored the girl.

"Look, I know we don't know each other well, but let me tell you what I see. Max is smoking hot and you're crazy about him."

Carina's mouth fell open. Her skin flushed bright red. "N-n-no, I don't—"

Maggie waved her hand in the air in dismissal. "I don't blame you. The problem is you recently passed legal drinking age. You're practically jailbait to a thirty-year-old man."

"What's that?"

"Hm, never mind. I mean, you're too young for him to see you as a woman yet. That may change, but instead of spending the next few years not living and waiting for him to notice you, you need to get out and live a little. Find out who you are. Then everyone will see you as your own person."

She looked so bleak and hopeless, Maggie's heart tore. God, she remembered how it felt, how confusing life was. But Carina had people to guide her, people who loved her, and Maggie hoped it made the difference. "How do I do that? Look at me. I'm a mess."

"Do you like studying business in college?"

"I don't mind. I'm very good with numbers—one of the few things I can do well." Her chin tilted up stubbornly. "But it would be nice if someone asked my opinion."

Maggie laughed. The girl had spirit. She'd need it. "Business and accounting aren't bad degrees to get. You can do lots of stuff with it and meet new and interesting people." She pointed to the art room at the back. "Is that your painting?"

Carina nodded. "Yeah, I like to paint, but I don't think I'm good."

Maggie took in the stark images of faces in different emotional turmoil. With a critical eye, she noticed the sweeping lines of the brush, the vivid expressions pulling the viewer in, and the beginnings of real talent. "No, you're good," she said slowly. "Don't ever give up on the art. Take some classes on the side to nurture your talent, and don't let anyone tell you that you can't. Get it?"

Carina nodded, seemingly fascinated by her new sister-in-law.

"Michael has your best interests at heart, but as an older brother, he's always going to suck at this. You're going to need more of a backbone to let him know what is and is not acceptable."

Her eyes widened. "But whatever Michael says is law," she whispered. "He's head of the family."

"I'm not telling you to disrespect him. Just be clear with communication. Try."

"Okay."

"As for Max, maybe one day things will change. Until then, you need to concentrate on other boys."

"I told you, boys don't like me."

Maggie shook her head. "You're not presenting yourself to your full potential." The invitation hovered at the edge of her lips, but before she could swallow the words Maggie sealed her fate. "Why don't you come with me to my shoot this week?"

The girl studied her with suspicion. "Why?"

Maggie laughed. "I'll give you a makeover. Show you the world of photography and introduce you to some of the models. It won't fix your problems, but maybe you can see how other people view you. You're beautiful, Carina. Inside and out. You just need to believe it."

As she said the words, Maggie suddenly fought back tears. What she would have given for someone to say those words to her. Would it have made a difference? At least she had an opportunity to tell another young girl, whether or not it made an impression. Disgusted with her burgeoning emotions in the past twenty-four hours, she tamped down her silliness and stiffened her spine.

"You would do that?"

"Sure. It'll be fun."

Carina threw her arms around her in an all-consuming hug.

A beat passed before Maggie hugged back, then pulled away awkwardly.

"Thanks, Maggie. You're the best sister-in-law in the world!"

"I'm your only sister-in-law, babe." Guilt pricked her conscience. It was one thing to pretend to be Michael's wife, but another to actually form an attachment to his family. She regretted the invitation immediately but it was too late to change her mind. Maggie rose from the bed and walked toward the door.

"*Grazie!*"

"*Prego.*"

She shut the door behind her. Oh, boy. Michael was going to be pissed.

Chapter Six

D^{*ios,*} he was going to kill her.

Michael watched his fake bride calmly gather her belongings for the upcoming shoot and move about the room like she was alone. Unfortunately, she was not. He was getting more and more irritated at her fake ignorance of the chemistry that burned through the room.

This was getting complicated. She was supposed to stay out of his business, remain distant, and depart with not even a ripple. Instead, she caused a tsunami the first day here. Everyone seemed to like her mouthy attitude. Now his baby sister was going to a shoot to see half-naked men, and Maggie thought this was a good thing.

"You did not even ask permission before you invited

her," he stated coldly. "Do not disrespect me with matters of my own family, Maggie."

She didn't bother to glance at him as she packed her day bag. She wore black satin pajamas that rippled over her like water, emphasizing every sweet curve of her body. Her silky hair brushed back and forth past her shoulders and put him in a meditative trance. "Hm, I don't think the word 'obey' was in our vows, Michael. Anyway, I told you I was kidding about the blind date thing. At least you don't have to worry about that."

"This is not funny."

She snorted. "Listen, I had no choice. She was hysterical, and I needed to calm her down. If you hadn't treated her like a five-year-old, maybe I wouldn't have had to do it."

"Carina is an innocent and I intend to keep her that way."

She snorted again and his temper reared. "Wake up and smell the coffee, Count. She's on the edge of exploring her sexuality. She's gonna do it anyway, and we might as well be her guides."

"Not under my roof. I have a duty to protect her and I will. She needs to finish college and start her career. Boys are not in the picture."

"She's hot for Max."

"*What?*" His roar boomed off the walls. "Did he do something to lead her on? I'll kill him."

"Geez, calm down. He didn't do anything. He sees her as a child, too. I'm just trying to tell you to cut her some slack. It's not easy crushing on your brother's best friend."

He jumped up from his relaxed position on the bed and paced the room. In minutes, she'd elicited arousal, anger, and frustration. At this rate, he'd be dead by the end of the week. "Max is family and Carina would never view him like that." A horrible thought occurred to him. "Why? Are you attracted to him? Did you put these ideas in her head?"

That made her whirl around. He almost stepped back from the blast of ice vibrating from her body. Green eyes narrowed dangerously. "Contrary to your opinion of me, Count, I don't come on to every man I see. And Carina is capable of making up her own mind. You just have to get your head out of your ass and actually listen to her."

She turned her attention back to packing.

He closed the distance, grabbed her upper arm, and spun her to face him. "You are on dangerous ground, *la mia tigrotta*," he growled. "I will not have any interference from you this week with my family. You are not taking Carina to this shoot, and I will handle this problem with her myself. *Capisce*?"

Another woman would cower. This one stood on tiptoes and got right back in his face. The sensual scent of amber and sandalwood swarmed him and wrecked his concentration. "I have no interest in messing with your

family. Go ahead and play dictator if it makes you happy.
I'm trying to tell you your sister needs a listening ear, not
a lecture."

"And you are the convenient listening ear?"

She gave a cheeky grin. "Guess so. Lucky I'm here,
huh?"

Her dismissal of his authority burned and tilted his
temper toward something else. Something more dangerous.

The slippery fabric of her pajamas slid through his fingers and he imagined an endless expanse of smooth golden
skin beneath. He craved to hold her head and plunder her
lips and see how sweetly he could turn anger to surrender.
He grew hard at the thought, challenged on every level
to claim and possess and conquer. When had a woman
wreaked such havoc? Dimly, he wondered: If he allowed
himself to take her to bed, would the need disappear by
morning? It always did. Maybe he needed to satisfy his
craving in order to rid himself of the itch to push between
those thighs and make her forget anything and everyone
but him.

"You put bad ideas in a young girl's head. I take care
of my own," he warned. "One lousy day and you've already made a mess of things. You don't know what my sister needs. You don't know what anyone needs. Hell, you
don't even know what *you* need."

He regretted the words the moment they left his lips.

She stiffened in his arms, and raw pain flashed within those eyes. The memory of something in her past reared its ugly head, and he watched as she battled the monster and slammed it back into the closet.

An aching need to hold her and make it all better squeezed through him. What was this crazy combination of lust and tenderness? What was happening to him?

Her smile was distant and forced. "You're right of course," she mocked. "I'll stay out of things from now on. But I'm not telling her she can't go."

She tried to back away, but he slid his arms around her back and tugged her toward his chest. "I'm sorry, *cara*," he said softly. "I didn't mean to say such a nasty thing. You bring out the beast in me sometimes."

Surprise flickered over her face, but she remained unyielding against him. "Accepted. Now let me go."

Instinct made him draw her closer. She arched upward as if to get away, then hit against his rock-hard erection. She gasped, then immediately stilled. "Seems like the beast side is pretty happy to see me. Insulting me turns you on?"

He laughed. Her razor-sharp wit never bored him, but lately he learned to push past her comedy routine and glimpse a hidden vulnerability that intrigued him. After all this time, was he finally spotting the real Maggie? He remembered the American expression "all bark and no bite" and wondered if he'd get to test his new theory. "No, *cara, you* seem to turn me on. As you are well aware. What I need from you now is just to hold you."

Her body froze and her voice lashed at him in the need to draw blood. "Trust me, Count, I've heard much worse and was never bothered. I don't need you to hold me."

"No, I need you to hold me," he whispered. "You deserved more than that cheap shot and I need to feel better."

She fought as if terrified of a little comfort.

"Shhh, just for a moment, I promise it won't hurt much."

Michael lifted her up, wrapped his arms tight, and tucked her head against his chest. Her breath came out choppy and uneven, as if she was almost on the verge of panic, but he kept his patience and slowly, she relaxed against him. Her body molded perfectly to his. The taut thrust of her nipples told him of her own arousal, and he bet if he slid his fingers to the pulse by the base of her neck, her heartbeat would thunder like a racing thoroughbred. Still, he made no move to deepen the embrace. He breathed in the exotic scent of coconut from her hair and savored the moment. For a little while, he ached to hold her and remove the pain he caused by his thoughtless remark.

He didn't know when the moment slid from warmth to fire. He swore to push her away before anything sexual occurred. His gut told him Maggie rarely experienced the tenderness of an embrace without ties or the culmination of sex. Sadness leaked through him at the thought, and he cursed her parents for raising her in an icebox with a goal to avoid emotions. He wanted to prove he was trustworthy. But once again, she broke his self-control, and in a mad rush of heat, she practically shimmered with sexual electricity.

He held his breath. Slowly, he slid her back down his body so her toes reached the ground. The hard nub of her nipples dragged across his chest, and his palm settled perfectly on the full curve of her ass.

Ah, *merda.*

His penis ignored his prayers and stiffened to an almost painful length. Michael gritted his teeth and held on.

Then she looked up.

Stormy emerald eyes filled with fire. Passion. And stark demand. She shook in his arms as she fought her reaction, but Michael was past politeness and damned himself to hell. At least the road was paved in gold.

He lowered his head and captured her mouth.

Her little catchy moan urged him on. He swallowed the sound and plunged his tongue through the seam of her lips. She opened immediately, meeting him thrust for thrust as she hung on to his shoulders and dug her nails in hard. The tiny bite of pain made him nip at her lower lip, the plump, ripe flesh reminding him of a sweet, juicy peach, and then he was lost.

Somehow, he backed her against the wall and lifted her up. Wrapped her legs high around his waist. Fit his throbbing erection into the notch between her thighs. Then dove back in.

He slipped one hand under her pajama top. His fingers closed around her breast, the silky skin a delicious contrast to her stiff nipple. She moaned again and arched upward for more. Crazed for the taste of her, he ripped open her buttons and lowered his head.

He sucked and bit until one of the tips was ruby red and glistening. She panted, but managed to move her hands to grip into the length of his hair, yanking his head up. Through misty shimmers of want, he stared at her, waiting for her to tell him to stop.

"More," she demanded. "Give me more."

He bent his head again and gave the same treatment to her other breast, teasing her on the fine line between pleasure and pain. She twisted and moaned in his arms, her open response like a drug injected in his veins. Her musky scent rose to his nostrils and taunted him, and with one quick movement, his hand dove beneath the waistband of her pants. The damp curls tickled the tips of his fingers. She sucked in a breath and he moved his hand downward, ready to plunge in deep and—

"Michael!" The pounding on the door slammed through his brain. His hand paused in its travels, trying to fight the fog. A giggle. "Are you guys doing anything naughty in there?" Venezia called out. "If so, save it for later. I need you downstairs for a minute." Another pause. "Michael, Maggie? Are you there?"

He fought for breath. Fought for normalcy. And wondered if he'd ever be normal again.

"I'm here. I'll be down in a minute."

"*Grazie.*"

Footsteps echoed. The heat turned lukewarm between them and kept dropping. By the time he'd removed his hand and Maggie had rebuttoned her pajama top, he felt as if he were in Antarctica instead of Italy.

Michael realized he'd lost some of the fragile trust between them. If he'd stepped away without being intimate, she might have respected him.

"Next time you want to cop a feel, just be honest. I'm not one of these women who needs to wrap sex up in a warm, fluffy cocoon of emotions."

"Maggie—"

"Don't!" She ducked her head, but not before he caught the sheer vulnerability in her face. Her hand shook slightly as she pulled back the covers. "Please. Not tonight. Go talk to your sister."

He stood beside the bed, torn between his need to tell her the truth and his need to save his family. Dear God, what had happened? He had to convince her he wasn't in love with Alexa; this was getting way too sticky. But what if it was too late and she didn't believe him? And if she did, would she walk away, pissed off he'd deceived her?

No, his blood must have rushed to his other head. He needed to keep it together, get through six more days, and get back to New York. He'd keep his bargain and stay out of Alexa's life and never see Maggie again. Everything would go back to normal. In six days.

He remained silent and walked out the door, leaving her in bed, alone, in the darkness.

"So who are we meeting again?"

Michael led her toward the Piazza Vecchia as the sun sank and bathed the square in golden light. She caught her stiletto heel on the broken pavement and he gripped her around the waist. Firmly ignoring the blast of electricity between them, he lingered over the warmth of her skin under rose silk before releasing her. He figured she'd put up a fuss about the long walk and business dinner, but her enthusiasm to accompany him caught him off guard.

Of course, she'd just gotten back from bridesmaid dress shopping with his sisters, so maybe she was desperate.

"Signore Ballini. He owns many restaurants and may be open to partnering with La Dolce Famiglia." He paused and tried to roll his tongue over the word without a stumble. "He has heard about my marriage and insists on meeting my wife."

She snickered and stopped by a stand to linger over the taleggio, which was a soft, fragrant cheese, and an array of salty cold meats. Her quick conversation with the vendor in rapid Italian surprised him, but then again, Maggie Ryan seemed full of surprises lately. Every time he seemed to figure her out, she threw him a slider. Or whatever that American expression was.

"Need me to help close the deal, Count?" She batted her eyelashes in mock admiration. "Want me to sing your praises and play the doting wife?"

He held his patience. He'd been tempted to make an excuse to the older man, but the opportunity was too great. Still, he prayed Maggie played her part. "I'll pass. Signore Ballini is a bit conservative, and I'm looking to make an impression. Perhaps you can play the part of the doting, silent wife?"

"Dare to dream."

The hem of her dress flirted with her knees as she strolled leisurely through the square, seemingly enjoying the character of the ancient city he called home. The elaborate water fountain rose from the center of the square and set off the majestic columns and breezy, open spaces, accentuating the classic architecture.

As if sensing his thoughts, Maggie spoke. "Nick would go crazy here. The balance of nature with man-made objects always calls to him. Bergamo has such deep character. I can see how happy you were here growing up."

He smiled. "*Si.* I adore living in America but must admit I'd never give up my childhood. Alexa would love it here, too. We host a very famous poetry event each year called Bergamo Poesia. Perhaps we can arrange a trip for them one day?"

Maggie stiffened and he cursed his mention of Alexa. Did she honestly think he lusted after her married friend? "Hm, convenient. Get her on your home turf with the lure of poetry. Just remember our deal, Count."

He had no time to answer. They reached the Taverna del Colleoni & Dell'Angelo and after a brief chat with the waiter were led inside. The medieval-looking decor with the high vaulted ceilings elicited a murmur of approval from Maggie, and then they were seated in a cozy corner while Michael made the introductions.

Signore Ballini emitted the old-fashioned demeanor of an Italian gentleman. He enjoyed culture, travel, good food and wine, and beautiful women. He'd aged well, with a stylish salt-and-pepper cut, and he couldn't resist flirting a bit with Maggie, who seemed to not only accept his compliments but genuinely enjoy them.

Michael's breath loosened a bit as he straightened the knot on his royal-blue tie. Perhaps the evening would play out smoothly after all. They chatted about nonsensical items as the waiter discreetly served platters of food with an explosive array of textures and tastes. Grilled radicchio with earthy Gorgonzola, firm noodles flavored with porcini and blueberries, and shrimp sitting on a bed of polenta with saffron. The Valcalepio Rosso was a local wine rich and blunt on the tongue, and two bottles were quickly consumed over conversation.

"Signora, since you are from America, I am sure you have a career. Tell me what you do besides make Michael a happy man?"

The square-cut bodice of the rose dress slipped an inch and showed off just a hint of firm, high breasts. Her hair glimmered red under the play of light as the silky strands brushed her shoulders. "I'm a photographer," she answered. "I've loved being behind the camera since I was young."

The older man nodded with approval. "Do you shoot landscapes? Babies? Weddings?"

"Underwear for Calvin Klein, Cavalli, and many other well-known stylists. I fly to Milan often on business, so it was a wonderful opportunity to combine both business and pleasure on this trip."

Michael held his breath, but Signore Ballini laughed in delight. "How refreshing. It is good to make your husband a bit jealous, no?"

She laughed with him and redirected the conversation back to business as she lustily groaned over the food. Neatly led into the dessert menu, she mentioned La Dolce Famiglia and its raging success, and like she planned it that way, Michael was able to go smoothly into his pitch.

Before long, espresso steamed hot and rich from tiny cups and he'd secured another meeting, in Milan. He was about to end the evening on a strong note when the careful building blocks shook in their foundation.

"I am trying to arrange a skiing trip in Aspen and having a terrible time with a villa," Signore Ballini commented. "That awful American actress who owns a home there won't return my calls. I read she will rent out her home to only the best. I guess an Italian is not good enough for her."

Maggie razored in on the conversation. "Are you talking about Shelly Rikers?" she asked.

Surprise flitted across the older man's features. "Yes. I refuse to watch any more of her movies. She is quite rude."

"Actually, I know Shelly and she's very personable."

Michael clenched his wineglass as an awkward silence descended. Signore Ballini stiffened his spine and a new chill crept into his voice. "I would not know this, signora, since obviously she only deigns to speak with Americans."

Michael opened his mouth to cut the dinner short, haul Maggie out the door, and hope to God the man didn't cancel their meeting. "Maybe we should—"

"Don't be silly, *signore*. Let me fix this for you." She whipped out her flashy leopard cell, punched in numbers, and spoke briefly to someone on the other line. With a stunning efficiency, Michael watched while she spoke with three more people, firing orders and chatting nonstop. She paused and slid the phone away from her ear. "*Signore,* is the first week in September acceptable?"

The older man beamed. "*Perfecto.*"

"Yes, that is fine. Give Shelly my love and tell her I'll call her when I arrive home. Thank you."

She slid the phone back in her bag and smiled. "You are all set. I will make sure to give the information to Michael so you can set things up. I think it was all a misunderstanding. She is looking forward to seeing you."

"*Grazie.* Not only beautiful, but efficient."

Half in shock, Michael followed them out of the restaurant and said his good-byes. With a casual grace, his fake wife hooked her arm through his in an effort not to trip on the cobblestones and took a deep breath of the mild evening air. They walked in silence for a moment as he tried to wrap his brain around the reality of the situation.

"I thought you were going to screw that up for me," he admitted.

Her tinkling laugh stroked his ears and other places. Places that hardened instantly and ached to be buried inside her. "I know. I thought I'd make you sweat first. It was fun watching your face while you tried to keep the conversation neutral. Did you really think I couldn't handle myself in business situations, Count?"

The raw truth hit him full force. Yes. Because the alternate reality scared the crap out of him. If she wasn't what she appeared, she was much more. A woman with soul and grit and passion. A woman of such charm and intellect she'd never bore a man. A woman worth more than one night.

A woman worth everything.

His heart hammered and her scent swarmed around him. She led him toward a gelato stand and ordered two chocolates, quickly paying and handing him the cup before he could protest. The center of the square fluttered with activity and couples hand in hand, and he let his worried thoughts slide away as he sank into the moment.

"See that fountain over there?" he asked.

"Yeah."

"My friend Max and I came into the square one night and dared each other to go skinny-dipping."

She quirked one brow. "No way. Did you do it?"

"Max did. I bribed him to first. Bare-ass naked he stepped into the fountain and one of our neighbors was out with his dog and caught us. He chased us out of the square, but Max had to leave his clothes behind."

"What was the whole point of this male escapade?"

"To see who had bigger balls, of course."

She laughed out loud, the sound spilling into the night, and he gazed down at her. A spot of chocolate rested at the corner of her mouth. Her face was open and soft in a way he'd never caught before. And without thinking, he lowered his head and kissed her.

Michael didn't linger. Just captured her lips with his for one brief moment. Tasted rich chocolate, red wine, and warm female. She kissed him back and relaxed, giving herself to him on borrowed time. When they broke away, something had changed between them, but neither was ready to explore. She tossed her cup of gelato in the trash and they walked home the rest of the way in silence.

But Michael wondered if it was already too late to deny what was between them. Too late to believe this was still a no-strings, no-emotion *fake* marriage.

Chapter Seven

"Okay, Decklan. Drop 'em."

His pants hit the floor. The harsh light accented the carved muscles under his oiled skin. The briefs hugged the critical parts and left the rest of his flesh proud and bare. Already Maggie's mind clicked relentlessly about the best way to get the shot she needed, picking and discarding as she warmed up. These were a crop of new male models she worked with by invitation from the Italian designer, and they were a bit green around the edges.

Comfortable in her role, she let the pull of the camera take over. For a while, all thoughts shut off and she was captivated by the moment. She'd always been happier behind the lens than in front of it, as if the voyeur inside of her burst free and got permission to invade another person's privacy while remaining safely distant. She liked to push barriers and comfort zones in order to get the perfect shot, and she never quit until she hit pay dirt.

Sweating under the hot lights, she called for a break and guzzled a bottle of water. Her makeup artist had whisked Carina away to transform her. Maggie still laughed at the expression on the young girl's face when she got a glimpse of the half-naked men onstage—like a female set loose on a designer clearance sale. Hopefully, she'd gain a bit of confidence, have some fun, and Maggie could safely return her to Michael in a better mood.

The image of Michael pushing her against the wall, ripping open her top, and sucking on her breasts shuddered through her. Heat rushed and settled between her legs. What was going on with her? She'd never had such a strong reaction to a man. Attraction, yes. Raw, naked, crazy lust to jump his bones? No.

She'd been stupid, though. Hadn't seen that move coming. The man distracted her with his comforting embrace. Men believed she hated cuddling, which she normally did, but when had a man even tried to hold her without sex getting in the picture?

The kiss last night was worse. Sweet, tender, and full of promise.

Maybe if she slept with him, this wanting would go away. It always did. Maybe one hot, sweaty night would flush him out of her system, and she could go on with the rest of the week without teenage hormones.

She finished her water and studied the lineup of three models. All bodily perfect. Oiled up. Ready to go. What was she missing?

The underwear was edgy and screamed *designer*. But if she didn't do her job, it would look just like Calvin Klein and the rest of them and wouldn't stand out. Damned if she'd have her work rated second class. Frustrated, she nibbled at her lower lip.

The expression on all three men's faces suddenly changed. Maggie paused, then peeked behind her shoulder.

Wowza.

Carina stood before her. The makeup artist preened and Maggie took in the vision of a girl turned into a young woman. Her skin glowed as if lit from beneath, with light foundation and a hint of peach in her cheeks, and she had a touch of a smoky eye. Her pouty lips held a glossy sheen, both virginal and tempting. Her once frizzy hair now lay in neat, shiny ringlets surrounding her face, giving her a pop that forced people to pay attention. She still wore her jeans, but had traded her plain T-shirt for a red camisole over a gauzy shirt that emphasized the ripe swell of her breasts but still kept her modesty.

Sheer pleasure rushed through her as Carina walked over with confidence. And by the reaction of all three men on the stage, well, she'd hit her mark perfectly.

"You look gorgeous," Maggie said. She touched the girl's springy black curls. "Do you like it?"

Carina nodded furiously. "I can't believe I look like this."

Maggie smiled. "I do. And I think my men agree."

Carina blushed and shifted her feet, then snuck a glance at the models. The men looked suddenly enchanted with the girl who had practically been ignored before her transformation. Maggie suspected the look of lusty innocence was a rare combination, and her confidence being ratcheted up was like a siren call to men. Nothing more attractive than a woman who liked herself. But something else in their current expression pulled at her, an emotion she rarely caught on a male's face, and—

Lightbulb.

Maggie ignored her galloping heart as a rush of adrenaline took hold. The perfect shot. Right there in front of her. "Come with me." She grabbed Carina's hand and dragged her up to the set. With quick movements, she rearranged the set, moved her camera, and adjusted the lighting. "Decklan, Roberto, Paolo, this is Carina. She's now in the shoot with you."

"What?" Carina squeaked.

She positioned Carina to the edge of the stage and cast her in shadow. "Cross your arms like this." Maggie adjusted Carina's pose to lean against the wall in a casual stance. "Now, look out the window as if you're dreaming of something. Something that makes you happy. Don't worry, your features will be blurred and your figure in shadow. Okay?"

"But I can't—"

"Please?"

Carina shook a bit, then slowly nodded. Her features tense, she tried to give Maggie what she wanted. Maggie whirled back to the models and lined them up in a jagged line. The slight bulges in their underwear didn't embarrass her—in fact, it was exactly what had been missing in the shot. "Listen up. Your target is her." She pointed to Carina, who looked stiff and uncomfortable. "Imagine what it would be like to approach her, to give her her first kiss, to make her feel like a woman. That's what I want. Now."

She grabbed her camera and pressed the shutter release. Calling out instructions, she moved like a madwoman to capture the element of the elusive . . . of innocence . . . wanting . . . temptation. It was more than a shot about pretty-looking underwear. This was about buying an emotion.

As the time ticked, her surroundings faded away. Finally, something flickered across Carina's face. A small smile rested on her face. The men shifted, studied her, and then—

Click.

Got it.

Satisfaction surged and her body loosened with relief. "We're done. That's a wrap."

A combined shout of approval rose from the models and staff. Maggie grinned with pleasure, turned on her heel, and came face-to-face with her husband.

Uh-oh.

He stood before her in a black Armani suit, a crisp royal-blue shirt, and bright red tie. His perfectly controlled posture contradicted the seething emotions in those dark eyes. His gaze deliberately raked over her, then swept back to the stage. Carina's chuckle drifted in the air and Maggie didn't have to turn to know she was probably talking and flirting with Decklan. A supermodel in tiny briefs.

She was so screwed.

Fear rushed through her and caused her back to straighten in pure rebellion of the messy emotion. "I can explain."

His voice came out whisper-soft and rattled her nerve endings. "I'm sure you can."

Why did he seem rough around the edges? As if he called for a woman to dive beneath the polish and discover all that primitive maleness beneath? He grew up with money, a good family, and relatively few problems. She didn't resent it, but most men she met with staid backgrounds left her cold and a bit flat. Not Michael. It would take ages to discover all his layers, and she'd bet he'd still keep surprising her. Fortunately, she had no intention of getting to know anything about his Italian temper.

Her mouth worked to spit the words out. "Well, I decided to treat Carina to a makeover while I worked so she wouldn't have to see the models in their underwear, because I knew you wouldn't be too happy about that."

He snapped his voice like a whip. "And that is why I saw her on the stage with the same naked models. Because of your *protection*."

She winced. This wasn't coming out the way she'd planned. "You didn't let me finish. And they're not naked. So I was having a terrible time getting the shot I needed. Then Carina came out, and she was so happy about her appearance, and so much more confident . . . the men got this look on their faces, it was quite incredible, really—I've never seen anything so pure in this business, and I knew I had to capture the expression in order to get something fresh."

"Pure?" His brow hiked up and fury sparked from his eyes. "You put my baby sister in your shot to be gawked at by strange naked men in order to capture purity? Is this your defense, Maggie? Would you sacrifice anything just to sell a few ads?"

Whoa. Her fear melted away. How dare he? She sneered and threw her head back. "They. Are. Not. Naked. You're twisting my words, Count. As for sacrifice, it seems I'm willing to do a lot of that in the name of true love. Even have a fake marriage with you."

He pushed his face toward hers and hissed under his breath. "You didn't do it for true love, *cara*. Don't ever forget you got your pound of flesh for this bargain."

"Oh, yeah, so sorry I won't let you pant all over my sister-in-law and make moony eyes at her from across the room."

His mouth fell open. "You are crazy. I told you over and over I am not in love with Alexa. It is your delusions and need to control everything around you. And what does this have to do with Carina and your bit of exhibitionism?"

"I cast her in shadow; no one will really see her face. I would never expose her to anything inappropriate."

His body shook with hot male frustration. "You already did!"

"Michael?" Carina flew between them and gave her brother a big hug. The affection and worry in his gaze clearly showed Maggie he did not know how to deal with his youngest sister growing up. "Did you see me up there, Michael?" she squealed. "I was a real model."

"You were wonderful, *cara*." His hand gently touched her springy curls. "Who did this?"

"I got a makeover. You should have seen Maggie work, I've never been at a shoot before and it was ultracool. Now I may be in the real ad, and the models are supernice. Decklan invited me to dinner with some of the other models and—"

"Absolutely not." His brows came together in a fierce

frown. "I'm glad you had fun, but the shoot is now over. You will not be going out with some strange men you don't know. Besides, you're babysitting for Uncle Brian tonight."

Maggie opened her mouth to say something, then quickly shut it. Hell, no, she would not get involved. This wasn't her real sister-in-law. She was not in Michael's family. She was not really his wife.

Carina glared. "I babysit for Uncle Brian almost every Saturday night while other people date."

Michael rubbed a hand over his face. "I will not argue with you on this point. Now be a good girl and wash your face, get back to normal, and let's go. We have an appointment at the consulate soon."

Silence.

Maggie winced. Oh, this was bad. Very bad. Like an oncoming train wreck, she watched Carina's face fall at his comment. Carina pressed a trembling hand to her mouth in order to stop herself from crying, but her voice came out broken and wispy. "Why can't you see I'm not a baby and respect me? I wish you'd never come back to Italy!"

She walked out of the studio and a door slammed in the distance.

Maggie closed her eyes. *Ah, crap.*

Michael shook his head and let out a litany of creative phrases in Italian. He paced and muttered, and Maggie gave him wide berth, because she didn't know at the moment whether to hug him since he looked so frickin' lost, or slap him in the hope he gained some sense.

She decided to compromise.

She jumped in front of his quickly moving feet and he almost barreled into her. "Michael—"

"What did I do now? Huh? Is it so wrong to deny her to go off on a drunken fest with a bunch of naked male models to be lost forever? We are one of the richest families in Italy. She's too young! She could be kidnapped and ransomed. And why did she look so different? She always babysits for Brian and said she loved doing it. Suddenly, she wants to change her routine and prowl the town so someone can kidnap her? Absolutely not."

Maggie mashed her lips together. The absurdity of his comments struck her hard, and she tamped down on her instinct to burst out laughing. Her powerful count was really a crabby Papa Bear, not wanting to deal with the reality of his sister flying the coop. At twenty-one she'd been running her own life, and no one had cared whom she went out with and if she came home at night. She coughed into her hand and concentrated on trying to look serious. "Well, I agree, I wouldn't let her go on a drunken fest either."

He narrowed his eyes as if daring her to mock him.

She threw up her hands in defense. "Hey, it sounds like babysitting four rambunctious nephews would be a blast, but the girl got invited to dinner with a nice, handsome man and wants to go. You can't blame her for asking."

He practically gasped. "You would let her go?"

"I would let her go with provisions," she corrected. "I don't know the group well enough to let her go alone, either. But I do have a close friend who could join them. She has a daughter Carina's age, whom I think Carina would get along with. I usually visit Sierra when I'm in Milan, and she's someone I trust. I don't know if she's free today, but I can make the call. She can chaperone, and drive her home after dinner. If not, then I agree with you completely—she shouldn't go alone. But at least it looks as if you are trying to compromise."

He practically moaned. "How does Mama handle her temper? Carina is usually so calm and reserved. What's happening to her? Why won't she listen?"

Maggie gentled her voice. "Why are you trying so hard to keep her from growing up?"

He lifted his head. For a moment, she caught a glimpse of grief and fear in the blue-black depths of his eyes. She touched his hard cheek, needing the contact of skin on skin.

"I made a promise not to fail."

His words rose to her ears in a whisper of sound. Her heart squeezed but she pressed further, needing to delve deeper. "Who did you make a promise to, Michael?"

"My father. Before he died." The normal confidence he carried faltered. "I'm responsible for them all."

The realization of the weight he carried on those broad shoulders hit her full force. She'd never imagined someone could take the words so literally, but it seemed Michael believed every success and failure of his family rested on him. The sheer stress and pressure of making decisions for them all blew her mind.

God, she had only herself to rely on for so long she wouldn't know how to make hard choices for others. Any man she knew would've walked away and cleansed his hands of the mess. But not him. No, once a person belonged to Michael's world, he'd look out for them forever.

A burning need to be the woman he cared for so passionately rocked her mind, her body, and shook her soul. What would it feel like to be claimed so completely by him?

Maggie's throat tightened with emotion. His delicious spicy scent surrounded her, and his body heat burned through his clothes and reached out to entangle her. She craved to unbutton his shirt and smooth her palms over all that naked flesh, open her legs, and allow him to dive in and stop the endless ache inside of her. Instead, she dropped her hand from his and took a step back. She was tired of running sometimes, but it seemed the only thing she knew how to do well.

"If we don't let them make some mistakes, how will they ever know?" she asked softly. "Carina is crazy about you. She just needs a little breathing room." She paused.

"Your family is lucky to have you watching over them. Now, let me make a phone call to see if we can fix this."

She grabbed her smartphone and dialed.

• • •

Michael watched the closed door and waited for his sister to exit. *Dios,* he was trapped in female hell and saw no way out. Yes, Venezia had been difficult, but once she fell in love with Dominick she'd calmed, and he was able to relax. Of course, her decision to take a career outside the family business caused fireworks, and he was still disappointed, but that was mild in comparison with Carina's sweet innocence on the verge of decay.

Julietta had been a breeze, not interested in boys and driven to succeed in her career and prove her worth. She reminded him so much of Mama with her ability to focus and a sharp business sense that built La Dolce Famiglia. His papa may have turned the place into a successful chain, but without his mother's vision and drive, there would have been nothing.

Carina was different. She'd always been Papa's little girl and held a lightness of spirit no one else claimed in the family. She experienced emotions more deeply, saw things no one else did, and her ability to give without caution had worried Papa.

The scene at his father's deathbed flashed in his mind.

The promise to keep his family safe and protected. To always take care of the girls. And to lead the bakery into a successful chain. Failure was never an option.

Sweat pricked his brow as he gazed at the three men hanging around, waiting for Carina. They were definitely older. Was he nuts to even consider letting her go?

He marched toward the small refrigerator and grabbed a bottle of water, giving the cap a vicious twist. His fake wife had done it again. His innocent sister had been in a photo shoot for male underwear, had a makeover, and wanted to run around with models. Why did he bring Maggie here again?

Oh, yeah. Because she was his wife.

He brooded as he drank his water and watched her. He hated the tiny leap his heart gave when she first turned and met his gaze. He was becoming used to the fiery connection that zinged between them, the tiny flare of awareness that lit those cat-green eyes and tempted him to push boundaries. The physical temptation he could handle.

It was the other things that were starting to bug him.

Her ability to surprise him was the worst. He'd expected a certain intimacy on the set with Maggie and the models. He'd never been on a live shoot, and her sharp eye and easy manner fascinated him. At first, Carina distracted him on the stage, but soon Maggie pulled his gaze until everything else fell away. She took control of her scene in a way that never threatened, but in fact encouraged teamwork.

Oh, she flirted. It was part of the woman's core. But as he continued to study her, he spotted so much more beneath the rippling, cool surface, like discovering a vivid coral hidden beneath the muddy brambles of dull sea plants.

She always kept her distance.

Not physically. She touched, often, until even he squirmed when she had to actually adjust the bulge between the models' legs. She laughed and teased and gave naughty winks in good fun. But there was a cool detachment in her aura, surrounding her like a thicket of thornbushes bushes with nasty-looking spines. Look, but don't touch. Touch, but don't feel. Her emotions were locked up and controlled to a point of strangling. Yet, when she looked at him, she seemed tempted to give him more. And he wanted more.

But would she say no? Her pride battered from their first encounter—her false belief he was in love with her best friend—all of the factors conspired to form a big fat No Way.

Unless he took what he wanted.

Her lithe frame clad in sleek black pants, a matching sleeveless black tunic blouse, and ridiculously high black sandals emphasized every graceful motion and luscious curve. Her gorgeous cinnamon hair played a game of hide-and-seek, showing off the tender nape of her neck, her soft cheeks, and her long, refined nose that always looked down upon him. To be the prince to break down those cut-throat defenses pulled to his Italian core. When had another woman ever challenged him like this?

He wanted her.

The sound of his name snapped through his thoughts. Maggie pointed to her phone, then motioned him over. "Okay, Sierra's free. She can be here in a bit and drive her home tonight. You can trust her. But it's up to you."

His heartbeat sped up at the thought of sending his sister off with men and a strange woman he didn't know. But something in Maggie's words rang true. What if he didn't let Carina experiment a bit and then she exploded? He couldn't screw it up. Carina and his promise to Papa were too important.

"Maggie, can I trust my sister with this woman?"

Something flared to life in his fake wife's eyes. A memory of pain, then regret. "Yes. I would never put Carina in a vulnerable position where she could be hurt. I know Sierra well, and she will not let something happen to your sister."

He nodded. "Set it up. I'll talk to Carina."

"Talk to me about what?"

He turned and she stood beside him. Chin up in defiance. Eyes glittering. She'd left on the makeup, but even Michael admitted it was so much better than that goop she'd put on before. Now, she looked fresh. Herself, only better. "Maggie made arrangements to have her friend chaperone you," he said.

Carina gasped. "*Dios!* Are you kidding me? For real, I can go?"

Michael put up his hand. "There are rules. You text me and let me know where you are at all times. Sierra will be in charge and will take you home. And before you go, I have a talk with them." He stabbed his finger at the models, now donning T-shirts and jeans and combing their designer haircuts. "*Capisce*?"

Carina nodded frantically. "*Si, grazie,* Michael."

His heart bloomed at her happy, open expression.

"They have the photos ready," Maggie said.

They joined her at the small computer, which flashed a bunch of photos in a rapid stream. He listened as Maggie went through them, pointing out problems and deficiencies, what she liked and didn't. Her opinions were bold, bossy, and turned him on big-time. Nothing like a strong woman in business—he'd always craved that in his mate. Unfortunately, many of the women he dated loved the idea of him taking care of them, and though he may come from a traditional household, he yearned for something more in his wife. Someone with a little brass.

The screen clicked on an image and everyone stopped. Michael sucked in his breath.

"That's it," Maggie whispered. "I got it."

Michael stared at the photo. Carina leaned against a fake wall, staring out into space. Cast in half shadow, her figure was blurred, luminous. The features of her face were hidden by a wave of thick, curly hair, and her lips were pursed in longing for something . . . out there.

The three men were carefully positioned behind her to show off the product, but it didn't seem posed. As if they had spotted an angel, they seemed rooted to the floor, entranced by her, expressions of need flickering across their strong features. The physical aspect of the picture paled in relation to the unexpressed emotions in each body, compelling the onlooker to stop and look deeper.

A whoot sounded from the production guy and he high-fived Maggie. She tilted her head and looked at him. "Can I use it, Michael?"

Carina shook her head, still gazing as if in a trance. "How did you do that, Maggie?" She breathed in awe. "It's so beautiful."

Maggie chuckled. "Part of my job. You're the star, though. You're the one who's beautiful."

Michael watched his sister blush and squirm in delight. His body shook slightly, as if preparing for a lockdown. How was she able to see exactly what his sister needed? Yes, she was a woman, but she'd always touted herself as disconnected from the usual woman stuff. Cooking, gossipy chatter, kids, domestic scenes. Yet, she offered his sibling a compliment that simply came from her soul, with no thought to sugarcoat or be fake.

Michael leaned down and pressed a kiss to Carina's head. Then he looked into the eyes of a girl who was no longer a girl. "She's right, you know. You are beautiful. And yes, Maggie, you can use it."

The sudden emotion choked at his throat until he made himself turn abruptly and disappear down the hallway. Damned if he didn't need a moment to get himself together.

Chapter Eight

She was approved to be married in a civil ceremony right now. Today. This moment.

Maggie sank down in the luxurious bubbles and blew out a breath. A spray of foam shot up and sprinkled the air with tiny pockets that caught the last rays of light and shimmered. She wiggled her feet, propped up her legs on the sides, and soaked.

Their visit to the court office in Milan terrorized her. Talking about a fake marriage was one thing; actually filing papers was another. After obtaining the Atto Notorio with two witnesses, they obtained their Nulla Osta—the final declaration of their intent to marry—after stacks of paperwork were approved, notarized, and filed.

Maggie groaned. Because of Michael's high-ranking and

well-known contacts, his mother had eased the paperwork chain so they were able to take care of everything in one busy afternoon. Maggie lifted up her hand and looked again at the cheery sparkle of the diamond ring encircling her finger. Michael's plan seemed foolproof. He'd string his mother along for the next few months until Venezia was safely married, then advise them of a terrible fallout and their breakup.

Messy, but necessary. Maggie gave a deep sigh as the delicious scent of sandalwood calmed her senses. It was truly amazing the lengths Michael was going through just to help his sister, and his actions bespoke a respect for his mother that touched her. Instead of waving off her crazy demands that he marry and allowing his sister to take the brunt, he'd composed a plan to make everyone happy.

Except himself.

Her skin tingled and she rested a hand on the swell of her breast, stroking gently. What type of woman would make Michael happy? Someone sweet and undemanding? Or would he get terribly bored within the month? And why did she care so much?

Because she wanted him.

The truth slammed into her like a rear-end jolt. Yes, she'd always known they had sexual chemistry. But sleeping in the same bed, seeing him in his element, was doing terrible things to her. She craved to finally sate her appetite and be done with it. After all, if her track record was any indication, she'd be happily satisfied by morning and could move on. Nothing was worse than that empty, gnawing feeling in her stomach when she rolled over and realized the man next to her was not The One. Would never be The One. Surely, a good bout of healthy, satisfying sex would finally quiet her hormones.

But what about Alexa?

She nibbled on her lower lip at the thought. He may want to deny it, but he loved her best friend. Of course, after this trip, he'd finally stay far away from Alexa and her family, and Maggie wouldn't need to worry he'd muck things up.

It was just sex. They played at being married anyway, so it might give their ruse a bit of punch. Nobody would ever need to know. They were adults and could handle a strictly physical relationship.

She wanted to have sex with Michael Conte. Excitement slithered down her spine. Her nipples pebbled under the slap of water. She wouldn't be settling for second best because, once again, the bargain was on her terms. Her rules.

Oh, yeah.

Her fantasy exploded in front of her when the door opened.

A girlish yelp escaped her lips. She slithered farther down underneath the bubbles and hastily pulled back her leg from the edge. Michael strode in, a glass of white wine in one hand, a plate with a luscious crème puff in the other, and a full, wicked grin curving his lips.

"*Buon giorno, cara.* Are you enjoying your bath?"

She spluttered and tried hard not to blush like a school-girl. "Are you kidding me? What are you doing here? As most married women would state, I have a headache."

He had the audacity to chuckle. "Ah, I have heard that expression before. We just uncorked one of our best bottles of pinot grigio, and I thought you'd enjoy a sip while you soak."

She frowned. "Well, okay. Thanks." Maggie grabbed the half-filled glass and breathed in the scent of lemony citrus and tangy oak. "You can put the plate over there."

He set it on the small ledge at the end of the tub and stared at her. Refusing to squirm under his open, hot stare, she glared right back, sticking her lip out to blow some stray wet strands of hair out of her eyes. "You can go now."

He sat down on the small lip a few inches away. He'd changed out of his suit and looked crisp and casual in worn jeans and a white button-down shirt. His feet were bare and his hair fell loose to his shoulders, which some-how made him even sexier. His presence squeezed out all the breath in the room and left none for her. Already that familiar zing tried to stab her like some sort of Sex Superhero. What was with that?

She waited him out but since she was the naked one, he didn't seem to feel the need to make conversation. "What are you still doing here?"

"I thought we'd chat."

"Fine. Strip off your clothes and let's talk."

He didn't move, but his features shifted and suddenly, he was all hot male predator. "Sure about that request?"

Damn, her usual snarky comments were having the wrong effect. Why wasn't he walking away? A light of challenge gleamed within his eyes, and in horror, her body lit to life. The water swished between her open thighs. Her nipples hardened beneath the bubbles. She caught her breath as his gaze deliberately dropped and caressed her hidden, naked form. What the hell was going on?

She changed tactics. "What do you want to talk about?"

"Our deal."

Maggie shrugged. "Thought we were on course. Papers are filed so your mom knows we're legit. Did you see how she asked a zillion questions to make sure everything was in order? She's a crafty one."

"Always was."

"My shoot is over. Dress shopping is behind me."

"Good."

"Another family dinner is Friday night, oh, and Julietta wants me to visit the bakery with you tomorrow."

"Fine."

She frowned. "Why are you still here?"

"Because I want something."

"What?"

"You, *cara.*"

Her tummy plummeted. She worked her jaw up and

down but nothing came out, just weird squeaks because she had no air left in her lungs. Michael never moved, just remained poised on the edge of the tub. His easy posture contradicted the heat and demand in his eyes as he stared at her like a hungry cat ready to pounce on his evening meal. Oh, and just the thought of him biting her somewhere made her limbs go loose and liquid. What had he said?

"What did you say?"

His lip quirked. "You heard me. Here, try a bite of this."

"I don't want a frickin'—"

He reached out and pushed the crème puff slowly between her lips. She opened on reflex, then bit down. The flaky, buttery taste of the pastry exploded in her mouth. Rich crème coated her tongue in sheer pleasure. He watched her chew, and his thumb ran across her lower lip to catch the last bit of crème lingering. With deliberate motions, he put his finger in his mouth and sucked.

Her thighs tensed. Wetness seeped from between her legs and she knew it had nothing to do with the water. Her eyes widened as he tipped the glass to her lips. One precious drop fell on her tongue, and the icy sting of liquid slid down her throat and seduced a moan. He set the wine on the ledge and leaned in.

"Good?" he murmured.

Maggie blinked.

His gaze held her spellbound. Rough stubble covered

his jaw and matched the image of a civilized man gone bad. The intoxicating scent of musk and soap filled her nostrils.

"Uh. Yeah."

His hands skimmed her shoulders, teasing a line through the bubbles and leaving a trail of peppered goose-flesh. "What scent is this?"

"Huh?" Oh, dear God, she'd become a mute. She struggled to surface from the physical torture of his touch right above her breasts. "Sandalwood."

"It's been driving me crazy. When I finally taste you, will you remind me of earthy musk, sweet against my tongue?"

She realized then he was the master. He'd pretended she was in charge the whole time. No wonder she amused him! Her limbs hung limply, her center ached, and her skin burned even underwater. The man had bided his time and got her when she was the most vulnerable. Why did he suddenly want to change the rules of the game? Maggie forced her brain to work through the sensual haze.

"Why are you doing this now?" She hung fiercely to the thread of irritation, knowing if she lost it she'd throw herself at him and beg him to take her. "Are you playing some sick game with me?"

His face tightened with determination. "You're the one playing games, *la mia tigrotta,*" he growled. "I've wanted you from day one, and I never denied it. I'm tired of fighting with you when we can be doing other things. More pleasurable things . . . for both of us."

The fact he'd come to the exact realization she had pissed her off. *She* was supposed to proposition *him*. Michael was mad if he thought she'd meekly sit by and let him seduce her and stay in charge. It was her idea to finally have sex and get him out of her system. Damned if she'd allow him to win this round.

"I need time to think."

He rose from the tub and nodded politely.

"Please hand me a towel."

He glanced back at her. The struggle on his face, whether or not to push, finally settled. Maggie realized a layer of trust had begun to build, and knowing that as angry as he would get, he'd always remain in control softened a fear deep inside that had been buried for way too long. He grabbed the pink fluffy bath towel off the hook and handed it to her, then discreetly turned around.

Maggie grinned in triumph. Slowly, she rose from the bath, wringing out the dripping ends of her hair and wiping down most of the bubbles. Then she dropped the towel on the floor.

"Okay, I'm ready now."

• • •

Michael turned.

She was naked.

Gloriously, vibrantly, bare-ass stark naked.

He dimly remembered the first time he'd seen a pair of naked breasts. As a young man on the brink of sexuality, he'd thought nothing could ever beat that moment for him.

This one did.

She stood at full towering height, head thrown back, with the towel pooled around her feet. An endless expanse of golden smooth skin lay before him, damp from the bath, glistening with the remains of the bubbles. Her breasts were high, full, and crowned with red nipples. His mouth watered to taste and suck on the ripe fruit. Her legs went on forever, lean and muscled. And a perfect triangle of cinnamon-colored hair hid her most intimate secrets. Barely. He scented her arousal and her body beckoned him.

Yet, he stood stock-still in the middle of the ceramic tiled floor, completely unable to move.

She'd tortured him all afternoon. The brush of her hair on her shoulders, her sarcastic wit, her vibrancy that shimmered even when she stood still. He remembered those few precious inches the other night. If his hand had dipped just a tiny bit lower, he would have been able to touch liquid fire.

The woman was under his skin and there was only one way to remove her. Sleep with her. Wring her out of his system, and in the morning, maybe they'd both be normal. Hell, they weren't right for each other. They wanted different things—craved different lifestyles. He wanted a big family and a settled home with minimum drama. He wanted someone sweet, fairly pliable, but with enough spunk to keep him from getting bored.

Sex could fix everything. He was sure of it.

Maggie's rejection had stung, but he refused to force her. The deep disappointment in her inability to be honest with him only proved his point that they weren't evenly matched. He touted honesty as one of the most important factors in a relationship, and whatever secrets she hid, he bet those would never be shared. With him. With anyone.

But, again, she'd surprised him. On her own damn terms.

She had the gall to shrug and look down her nose at him like she was dressed in a royal gown. "I agree with your proposition to sleep together. But since you can't even speak, I'll go get dressed and we'll revisit the topic later. When you're more"—her gaze drifted downward to his rapidly rising erection and she smirked—"functional."

She headed toward the door.

Two steps and he closed the distance. Locked the knob. And slowly turned her around.

Her eyes widened. With deliberate motions, he backed her up against the door. Tilted her chin. And pushed his knee between her thighs to spread her wide open. She caught her breath as he lowered his mouth to hers.

"I'm ready, *cara*," he whispered. "Are you?"

His mouth took hers.

He loved to seduce women. Loved the slow slide of tongue, the catch of breath, the easy climb of desire as each step led toward completion. He considered himself a master in the art of pacing, but one thrust between her lips wrecked any type of control he'd ever had.

Her body slipped against his, as wet as the heat between her thighs and as blistering as flame. This was no easy, gentle, let's-get-it-on kiss. This was a no-holds-barred war with no survivors. And Michael loved every inch of his total surrender.

He dove deep into her taste. She moaned and pushed her hips up, her fingers digging into his hair as she held him against her and demanded more. His hands slid over her body and reveled in every glorious inch, palming her breasts and tweaking the tips with his thumbs as he swallowed her moans. He nudged her legs farther apart while she panted, then hooked one of her thighs around his waist to secure her. He ripped his lips from hers and stared into mossy-green eyes dazed with lust.

His hand moved from one of her breasts and traveled downward, stopping at the top of her belly. "I've been dying to sink my fingers into you," he murmured. "Are you ready for me?"

Her breath was a sexy whisper of sound. "You talk too much, Count."

He smiled and slid his fingers into the swollen folds.

She cried out and threw her head back against the door. Her silky, pulsing channel closed around him and squeezed. He muttered a curse at her response, her need for him evident in the rush of liquid that soaked his fingers. *Dios*, she was the most beautiful woman he'd ever seen, so open to every sensation. He stroked her deep, curling his fingers, and hit the sweet spot as she pumped her hips and reached closer to the edge.

His erection grew painful, but her face was a creation of erotic beauty he didn't want to miss. Her teeth sank into the swollen flesh of her lower lip, and her eyes half closed as she fought off the growing need for release. Her body bloomed beneath him, but her hands clenched into fists and pushed against his chest. Her endless need to control the result of every encounter taunted him to make her completely surrender. To him. To this.

He swiped the tight, pulsing bud once. Twice. Then lowered his mouth and sucked on her nipple.

"Michael—"

"You talk too much yourself, *cara*." His teeth scraped over the swollen tip while his fingers teased mercilessly. Her thigh muscles trembled, and her heartbeat rumbled in his ear. Her glorious musky scent rose to his nostrils and he knew she was about to explode. For the first time, she belonged in the present, surrendering to her body, and open to everything he gave her. His erection throbbed, and the blood roared in his veins.

"Michael! Don't, I'm going to—"

"I want you to come. Now. Come, Maggie."

He bit her nipple as his fingers plunged one last time.

She cried out and squeezed him mercilessly. Her scream ripped through the air as she shuddered and arched against him, and he held her as he prolonged her orgasm, keeping her body against his.

She grew limp. He muttered soothing words and pressed a kiss to her temple, slowly removing his fingers. He'd been right about the chemistry between them, but nothing prepared him for the surge of emotion and connection that suddenly squeezed his gut. He wanted to lay her out on the bed and claim her completely. Spend hours in a tangle of sheets until she couldn't think of another smart remark and only knew how to murmur his name. Where had such tenderness come from?

She lay still in his arms, her breathing returning to normal. He nuzzled her cheek and decided to carry her into the bedroom so they could talk and make love and—

"Well, thank goodness. I needed that." Her cool, no-nonsense tone contradicted her slight shaking, but before he could soothe her, she gave him a push and scooped the towel off the floor, wrapping it around herself. She tossed her head and let out a long, relieved sigh. "Thanks. Do you want me to take care of you?"

Her flippancy cut deep. He took a step back, wondering if he'd been an idiot. Why was she so determined to act carefree when a minute ago she was crying out his name and clinging to him with a fierceness he'd never experienced from a woman? His gaze picked and shredded, but she remained perfectly at ease. And distant.

"Do you want to take care of me?" he asked coldly.

She shrugged. "If you want. Tit for tat. No time for a long marathon—I promised your mom I'd help her with dinner, so I have to get dressed. Well?" She raised a brow and waited. A sinking sensation told him he was in trouble. For a few moments, she belonged to him completely. Yet she was incapable of maintaining any sort of closeness. Why was he so bothered by her inability to connect? Why did he care?

"Why are you doing this, *cara*?" he asked gently.

Maggie jerked back as if smacked. She practically snarled. "Sorry if I don't want to talk about touchy-feely things after an orgasm, Count. I thought we were past that."

The silence simmered with unspoken emotion and words. Finally, he nodded, then shut down the blossom of tenderness like a delicate flower ripped from the stem. "You're right, Maggie. I thought we were past this, too."

He snatched the knob and opened up the door. "After

dinner we're babysitting. Since you were the one to convince Carina to break her promise to Brian, we will take over the responsibility."

Her mouth dropped open. "Brian has four boys! I'm exhausted. No way am I babysitting tonight."

He leaned forward with a menacing air and snapped his voice in command. "You will be babysitting tonight. We'll go after dinner. Get dressed and meet me downstairs."

He closed the door on her loud protest and stalked off with a hard-on and a boiling temper.

· · ·

She'd screwed up.

Maggie peered at her fake husband from under lowered lashes as he fought with his bawling nephew who refused to go into the crib. Michael had rolled up the sleeves of his crisp white shirt, and his strong forearms flexed as the baby kicked and spit with growing fury. If she weren't so miserable, she'd get a chuckle out of the scene. His normally cool appearance now showed a disheveled, tired man who looked as if he craved the couch and a remote.

And it was only 8:30 p.m.

The room looked as if it had thrown up. The cheerful yellow and blue paint with vivid sea animals sketched on the walls now seemed like a scuba diving mission gone horribly wrong. Crayon marked up the walls, books were flung everywhere, and stuffing poked out from a blue teddy bear that had been ripped apart in some sort of weird experiment.

"Is he still hungry?" she asked, taking a step forward and crunching on some sort of cereal.

"No. Lizzie said one bottle is all he needs to get to sleep." The baby squirmed in his crib, wet drool pooling out of his mouth and ruining the third bib of the night. The playful ducks on his onesie mocked their inability to make him happy as he renewed his screaming. "Do you think he needs to be burped more?" he asked with a frown.

She blinked. "I don't know. When Lily cries for too long, I just hand her back to Alexa."

Michael gave a sigh. "Where are Luke and Robert?"

She shifted her feet. Somehow, she had a bad feeling about his next reaction. "Playing."

"I thought you put them down to bed."

"I did. But they didn't want to go to sleep so I told them they could play."

He muttered something under his breath and wiped more drool from baby Thomas's mouth. "Of course they don't want to go to bed, Maggie. But we're the adults. Just tell them no."

"I did. Three times. But Robert started crying because he wanted his mother, and then Luke joined in, so I told them five more minutes." No way would she admit those crocodile tears broke her heart and she'd give them anything they asked for.

He huffed out a breath. "They played you big-time. Fine, keep it to books. Nothing messy."

Maggie wondered why she was suddenly afraid to tell him about the Play-Doh. Wasn't that kid-friendly stuff? That's what the commercials always advertised. Robert told her his mother always let them play with the stuff when they couldn't sleep.

Suddenly, she realized Michael was right. She'd been played. Big-time. No wonder they'd both been so excited when she took it out from the top shelf of the closet! She nibbled her bottom lip and decided to sneak back in and take it away before Michael found out. His directives began pummeling her faster than angry bees. "How about Ryan? Is he asleep?"

She blinked. "He kept popping up because he was thirsty. I gave him some water in that sippy thing."

He placed a pacifier into the baby's mouth and lifted his eyes up to God. "Don't tell me this, Maggie. He wets the bed and he's not supposed to have liquids after seven."

She cut him a glare. "You didn't tell me that. He grabbed his stomach and said it hurt because he was so thirsty. You've been in here over an hour while you left me with the sons of Satan. Let's switch. I'll put the baby to bed, and you handle the *Outsiders* gang."

"Outsiders what?"

"Oh, never mind. Here." She snatched Thomas from the crib, slanted him in a football stance so he hung loosely from one arm, and stuck her finger in his mouth. The cries stopped and he sucked on her knuckle like she was surf and turf. His eyes half closed in ecstasy. "See, he's teething."

Michael looked in disbelief at the happy baby. A blessed silence soothed their ears, until they heard a weird half yell from down the hall. "Stay here. I need to get Ryan and make him go potty again."

Maggie watched the baby suck furiously. She always knew she'd make a terrible mother, and now the fact was proven. How did Lizzie handle so many requests all at once? This whole evening was becoming an even bigger disaster since she'd had an orgasm. How the mighty have fallen.

She paced and brooded. What was wrong with her? Maybe she needed therapy. A man gave her intense pleasure, tenderness, and emotional warmth. What did she do? Blast him away from her faster than a Buzz Lightyear laser gun and pretend not to care?

Because it wasn't just the orgasm.

It was how she felt wrapped up in his arms.

For the first time in her life, she felt out of control. Way past her comfort zone. And she honestly didn't know how to handle it. Her entire life revolved around controlling her relationships while she hoped to find the man who could feed her heart and soul. She figured she'd be able to break down the wall once she found her mate, but instead, Maggie began to realize she was way past the point of turning back.

She didn't know what it was like to have a normal, real relationship. To give up a part of herself and offer it to another. Maybe it was too late for her. Because just a taste of what Michael Conte could offer rocked her world and the very ground she'd rebuilt herself on. So instead, she acted like a total bitch and deliberately hurt him. Her gut wrenched from the memory of the look on his face. The total disappointment as he stared at her dead-on and challenged the basic soul of who she was.

She had to get out of here. Cut the trip short. Do anything possible to stop the oncoming train wreck she saw hurtling toward her. But what if she woke up and discovered he was The One?

The one man she could possibly love. The one man who loved her best friend and could only offer her second best.

"Maggie!"

Her name ripped through the room and she winced. The Play-Doh? Or something worse? Her head hurt with all the instructions and fear she'd do something wrong. "What?"

"Did you give Luke one of those juice box things?"

Damn, which one was Luke again? All of them had gorgeous curly brown hair, dark eyes, and mischievous grins. Like the Three Stooges gone horribly wrong. "Yes!"

she screamed back. "He saw Ryan get a drink and cried, so I gave him one of those."

"Can you come in here?"

The yelling back and forth was getting ridiculous. She hitched Thomas higher on her hip as he madly sucked and picked her way around the toys down the hallway. "Talk to me like a human being, please," she said, wondering why she suddenly sounded like a parent. She skidded to a halt and stared at the once clean kitchen. Five juice boxes lay discarded on the floor. Juice splattered the counters, refrigerator, and walls in a crazy homicide pattern. Luke shifted his feet and looked guilty. "Oh, my God, what happened?"

Michael crossed his arms and glared at his nephew. "Luke. Why don't you tell Aunt Maggie what occurred here?"

Luke cocked his head in a way he thought was cute. Maggie refused to admit he was right. "Played rocket blaster," he declared. "See?"

"No!" they both yelled in unison.

Too late. Luke stomped down on the last juice box. The liquid exploded in a spray and drenched everything in sight. Including them.

Michael grabbed him and hauled him up in his arms. "You are in big trouble," Michael warned. "Wait till your mother gets home and I tell her what you did."

Maggie smothered a mad giggle at the whole ridiculousness of the situation. Her fake husband stared at her in astonishment. "You think this is funny?"

She bit her lip. "Well, kind of. I mean, it's so bad I feel like I'm on *Punk'd*."

"Can you clean this up while I give Luke a bath?"

She glanced at the mess. "But I have the baby. He's quiet, and I'm not removing my finger until it prunes and falls off."

He seemed caught between the two scenarios, unsure which was worse. "*Dios*, fine. Come help with the bath then."

She trudged after him, and he peeked in on the other two. "You guys stay right here and play until Luke is out of the bath. Then bedtime for everyone. *Capisce*?"

"Yes, Uncle Michael," Robert stated solemnly.

Maggie glanced at him with suspicion. Somehow those chocolate-brown eyes seemed funny, as if he had some other master plan in mind. She ignored the crazy gut instinct and sat on the toilet seat while Michael plopped Luke in the bath. "So you're telling me your cousins do this for fun every night?"

He poured in bubbles and shook his head. "Something tells me they are more organized than us. But yes, I am sure this is what most of their evenings are like."

She rocked Thomas and tried not to sound curious. "What about you? Is this what you want, too?"

He seemed to think about the question. Then nodded. "*Si.*"

"Really? All this glamour?" She lifted a brow. "Do you realize there won't be any sophisticated dinners, or work-

ing late to close a deal, or jetting off to some tropical is-
land on a moment's notice? You'd willingly give up your
freedom?"

For a brief moment, a melting tenderness passed over
his features as he gazed at the naked boy in the tub. He
ruffled his nephew's hair and looked straight into her eyes.

"Yes."

His answer rocked through her and made her want.
Imagine a man who wanted to come home to this type
of chaos? Who willingly chose to be part of the mess and
enjoy every crazy part?

"Hi, Uncle Michael!"

They both turned toward the sound. A four-year-old
ghost boy stood in the doorway grinning. Maggie blinked
and stared harder. The only features still visible were his
eyes, a touch of golden-brown hair, and a flash of red lips.
The toddler looked like a demented child Joker. And why
was he naked?

She braced herself for an explosion but Michael remained calm. "What did you do, Robert?"

"I found this bottle in Aunt Maggie's purse!" he declared with pride. "Lotion!"

Maggie closed her eyes.

Michael pinned her with his own assessing gaze. "Hm.
I thought I told you to put your purse on top of the refrigerator so it wouldn't be a temptation."

She huffed out a breath. "I hid it behind the couch because

I had no time! As soon as I got through the door Lizzie and Brian shot out like their asses were on fire. Now I know why. Why would someone ever want another one after Robert?"

The giggling mad Joker cackled. "Ass! Aunt Maggie said 'ass'! Ass means butt. Ass, ass, butt, butt." The song went on and Maggie shuddered.

"Use that word again and I will wash your mouth out with soap," Michael said. "Now, get into the bath."

"Um, Michael?"

"What?"

"You're going to have some trouble. The lotion is waterproof. Won't come off for hours."

Michael plucked his second nephew off his feet and placed him in the tub. He rested his hands on his hips as if anticipating a huge business deal. Damn, why did he look so adorable mussed, wet, and smelling of apple juice? "We can do this." He rubbed his hands together, knelt beside the tub, and grabbed the washcloth. "Can you check on Ryan for me?"

Maggie shifted the baby to her other hip. Her finger released with a wet pop. Thomas stared back with wide eyes and a drooly grin, and her heart shifted. The trusting innocence in his gaze made her want to be worthy. What was happening to her?

She walked into the boy's bedroom. "Ryan, where are you?"

"Here!" He crawled out of the closet with his Thomas

the Tank Engine T-shirt hiked up over his belly and stuck his hands in the air with sheer pride. "I do dough!"

Yep. He did dough all right. Maggie took in the red and green clay that plastered his body and face. Thomas shrieked in pleasure and stuck both hands into her hair. The laughter bubbled up inside and threatened, but she wasn't sure if it was the giggles of a person turning insane like the Joker, or a way to cope with madness. "You did great, buddy. Follow me; it's bathtime."

"Bath!"

He darted out the room and into the bathroom and she followed. With a decisive click, she closed the door behind her and trapped everyone into the tiny bathroom. Steam billowed and fogged the mirrors.

"You gave them the Play-Doh, huh?"

Maggie nodded. "Yep. In my defense, I thought it was child-friendly. Live and learn. Figured if we're all in here together, nothing else can happen." She shot him a worried look. "Right?"

"Let's pray." With efficient motions, he stripped Ryan and placed him in the tub with his brothers. "I think I need help here. I'm on the second washcloth and the lotion is only half off. Can you scrub Ryan?"

"What about the baby?" Thomas cackled and reached up and shoved a handful of her hair in his mouth. He emitted sucking sounds of ecstasy. "Ah, gross," she moaned, trying to disengage herself. "Can I put him down on the ground?"

"Yeah. Make sure there isn't anything he can reach first."

She gave a good scout to make sure there was nothing but a messy floor covered with bubbles from the splashing. She yanked two towels from the rack and spread them down, then placed Thomas in the middle. His fists clenched in her hair again and he howled, refusing to let go.

"Ouch, ouch. Michael, help me." Firm hands carefully disentangled the baby's fists from her aching scalp. The lower lip quivered. A howl echoed through the small space and her nerves screeched in agony. No wonder they said a baby's cry could make a person crazy. She'd do anything to stop him. "Oh, God, he's crying again. Give me the rubber ducky there."

Quickly, Michael handed her the squishy toy and she stuck it in the baby's hands. He shoved it in his mouth and gummed the toy madly. "Smart move," Michael commented.

She grinned with pride, crawled over to the tub, and grabbed a washcloth. They worked in efficient silence until Maggie spotted the lovely olive skin beneath the clay and the water turned white. The boys chattered nonstop, alternating between Italian and English in a musical melody soothing to the ears.

"Uncle Michael, who is the bestest superhero? I think it's Superman."

Michael crinkled his brow as he pretended to think

hard. "Superman's pretty awesome because he can fly and bend steel. But I like Batman."

Luke gasped. "Me, too! Batman beats up bad guys."

"But he can't fly," Robert pointed out.

"Yes, he can," Michael said. "He uses his equipment to fly like a bat. And he has cool gadgets and the best car in the world."

Robert considered it while his brother practically oozed adoration. "I guess so. Aunt Maggie, who is your bestest?"

She slanted Michael a naughty look. "Thor."

"Why?"

"I like his long, blond hair and hammer."

Michael laughed and shook his head. "You're hopeless. Such a girl."

"Yeah, such a girl," Robert mimicked.

"I don't feel like a girl right now," she muttered. Her pretty white peasant blouse stuck to her skin with sweat and steam. She used her elbow to push back sticky strands of hair, and she already knew her makeup had long ago slid off her face. No wonder mothers never wanted sex. Who'd crave an orgasm when a good night's sleep was even better? "I'm a mess."

She was about to laugh off her girly comment when his gaze snagged hers.

Coal-black eyes delved into hers and stripped past all the barriers. Energy hummed between them, ridiculous in the domestic setting, but burning real and bright. Her nerve endings tingled with awareness as she stared back, helpless to break the connection.

"I think you look beautiful," he said softly.

Everything inside her shook hard and broke open.

Maggie surrendered. Lifted her hand to reach for his, to beg his forgiveness for her crappy behavior, to tell him every last secret and emotion locked up inside of her.

Suddenly, Robert reached down between his legs and grabbed his penis. Luke caught him and giggled, pointing at his own while his brother began hitting it back and forth, like a Ping-Pong game. "Pee-pee! Boys have pee-pees, and girls have Vaselines!"

Robert stopped and gave a long-suffering sigh. "Vaginas, Luke. Vaginas."

The magic of the moment between Michael and Maggie blurred and disappeared. They both looked at the two boys, and Maggie fought back a blush. Maybe it was Fate stepping in. Or Earth Mother. Whoever it was, she grabbed on to the distraction.

"Yes, well, let's not touch our private parts. Here're the towels to dry off."

She refused to be embarrassed by a couple of toddlers. For God's sake, she handled grown-up male equipment on the set all the time without a stumble.

They ignored her. "Why don't girls have pee-pees, Aunt Maggie?" asked Luke.

She looked to Michael for help but a bad-ass grin curved his lips. She refused to back off from the obvious challenge. She could talk honestly with children. No problem. "God made them different. And you're right, Robert, girls have what we call vaginas." She shot Michael a satisfied smirk. Take that.

"But without a pee-pee, girls have nothing to touch! What do you do?"

Silence descended. Michael mashed his fist against his mouth in an effort to still his mirth.

Ah, hell. She gave up and waved the frickin' white flag. "Ask your uncle."

With her last ounce of dignity, she grabbed the baby and stalked out.

Jerk.

• • •

Hours later, she sank to the floor next to the boys' bunk bed and lay her head against the side. The soft sounds of little boys snoring drifted in the quiet air. They refused to go to sleep unless someone lay beside them, so Michael hurriedly took his exit and she was more than happy to delay any alone time between them. Her fingers still held Robert's—the tiny hand relaxed and warm in hers. Maggie sat on the carpet and stared into the distance, remembering.

She'd had nightmares when she was little. The monster with blood in his teeth and wild eyes who sprang from her closet and wanted to eat her. Once, she'd run from the room to find her parents, but they weren't in the bed. Nick wasn't big enough to protect her and kill it, so she drifted downstairs and stopped in the middle of the stairway.

Her father was with another woman on the couch. The woman giggled and made low moans, and Maggie saw clothes on the floor. She tried to be quiet, but she was so scared she called out to her dad.

She remembered the look he gave her. Distant. Annoyed. Completely unconcerned. "Back to bed, Maggie."

She gulped in terror. "But Daddy, there's a monster in my closet and he's gonna get me."

The strange woman laughed, and her father looked even more disgusted. "I'm busy and you're acting like a baby. Get upstairs now or I'll spank you."

"But—"

"Now!"

She scurried back upstairs to her huge room filled with toys and stuffed animals and emptiness. She crawled under the bed with her stuffed puppy and waited for the monster to get her. All night, as her sobs muffled into the plush carpet, she wondered why no one loved her. Wondered if anyone could ever love her.

Maggie squeezed the small hand. A bone-deep exhaus-

tion and grief overtook her. She leaned her head against
the mattress and breathed in Robert's sweet scent, closing
her eyes just for a moment. One moment.

• • •

Where was she?

Michael waited, but silence filled the house. He figured
she'd be back in a few minutes, but it was way past that,
and no voices sounded. He smothered a groan and got up
from the couch. *Porca vacca,* what if the boys had done
something horrible, like set a booby trap and she was stuck
in there, unable to cry out? He was reminded of the Peter
Pan story with the Lost Boys and held back a chuckle at
the ridiculousness of the evening.

Maggie confirmed his belief she would not be the
typical mother. He figured he'd be relieved. After all, she
handled most of the scenes with unease and slight terror,
though his nephews had been known to drive most baby-
sitters out of town after an hour.

His temper reared from her constant quick quips, yet
she managed to charm four boys who usually preferred
strangers to remain outside their circle. Odd, they'd
flocked to her almost as if they recognized a gentleness in
her soul, completely hidden by her demeanor. Even the
baby sucked madly at her knuckle and cried when Michael
tried to pull him away.

But Maggie Ryan was completely unsuitable for his lifestyle and his heart. She rejected any type of intimacy between them. He needed to get past this tangled mess of emotions and let her go.

He stopped in the doorway and stared.

She was asleep. Her head rested near Robert's, their breathing deep and even, their hands clasped together on top of the blanket. A peaceful silence settled over the room, and for the first time, Michael greedily devoured his fake wife's features, vulnerable in the slight shadow the night-light cast over her.

What was she doing to his family?

What was she doing to him?

Strange sensations bubbled up and grabbed him in a ruthless hold. He didn't need this. Only forty-eight hours in her company and everything seemed different. He never craved to dig deep to learn about a woman before; usually they were only too happy to fall to their knees, thrilled about his money and looks and easy nature. Not that he was arrogant, but he always knew things came a bit too easily for him. Especially in the female department.

Until Maggie.

A smile touched his lips when she snored softly. The poor woman was exhausted. There'd been little sleep and too much running around. He glanced at his watch and noted his cousins would arrive home within the hour. Not much time left, but he didn't want to leave her there on the floor with her legs curled up like a pretzel.

He disengaged her hand from his nephew's and scooped her up with ease. She murmured in protest, then snuggled into his embrace. Michael smothered a curse, then swore he'd keep his hands to himself. He settled with her back down on the couch and stretched his legs out on the coffee table, propping himself up on a cushion.

Maggie grunted, then mushed her face into the crook of his neck.

He stiffened.

She took a deep, relaxed breath, as if she liked his scent, then opened her mouth and ran her tongue down the side of his jaw as if dying for a quick taste.

He cursed and bore down on his need to claim her lips and delve deep. Her hands ran up his shoulders, sank into his hair, and urged him forward toward her lips.

Hell, no.

"Maggie."

She dreamily opened her eyes. Her gaze still reminded him of a cat's. Piercing. Mysterious. And full of attitude.

"Wake up, *cara*. You fell asleep."

"So tired."

"I know, baby. Why don't you close your eyes and sleep a bit before my cousins get home?"

He waited for her to slip back into slumber but she never blinked, just stared at him with a heartbreaking sadness that cut through to his heart. Unfortunately, another realization struck him like the weight of Thor's hammer.

She had so much to give, but no one to give it to. She buried all those messy, writhing emotions deep in a hidden secret place and pretended she was okay.

As if she sensed his desire for more, the words hesitated on her tongue. "I'm so tired of being alone. Tired of not being wanted by anyone."

Her words rocked through him like an explosion. Was she half-awake and had no idea what she'd uttered? And if so, would she despise herself in the cold light of day for revealing her secrets?

Hell, he no longer cared. He needed more—and his opportunities were few. He stroked her hair gently and she softened beneath the caress. "Why do you say that, *cara*?"

Silence fell. Her face shifted and he knew she was completely awake. He prepared for her icy retreat and excuses.

"Because it's true. My parents didn't want me. I tried very hard, but they didn't love me. Then one day I thought I was in love. He told me I was special." Stark pain ravaged her face, then smoothed. "But he lied. So I promised myself I'd never get hurt again. I promised I'd never be rejected again." She paused in the shattering silence, then dropped her voice to a whisper. "And I haven't been. I'm just alone."

Michael tightened his hold. Her body sprawled out across

his chest. Her lower lip trembled, then steadied with the truth that came from her lips. And in that moment, a wall crumbled between them—an inner glimpse of what made her choose such a path suddenly crystallized in his mind.

The need to drive away her pain took precedence as he cupped her face between his hands and lowered his mouth to hers. "You're not alone now," he murmured. "You're with me."

He kissed her. So different from the raw, carnal passion in their last encounter, the kiss shattered his soul to the very core. Her taste was pure sweetness as her lips opened under his, and her tongue met his with a humble giving that shook his body like a storm. He groaned and deepened the kiss, drowning in the silk of rose petals hidden beneath the thorns. She arched upward and let him in. He devoured her, claiming every slick, hidden recess of her mouth, then moved down her neck to nibble and bite, wringing shudders from her as she clung to him.

Michael readjusted his position and pushed her beneath him, deep into the pillows. Hip to hip, leg to leg, his erection pressed between her thighs, and she yanked the material of his T-shirt from his jeans and pushed her hands underneath the fabric. He uttered a half prayer, half curse at the feel of her warm palms tracing the muscles in his chest, the tiny bite of her nails in his back, the way she raised her legs to cradle him more intimately against her. Mad with the urge to strip her clothes off and take her on his cousin's couch, he breathed deeply in an effort to calm his nerves. "We have to slow down, *cara,* or I'm going to take you here."

He prepared himself for the chill once she came to her senses, but all she did was grip the back of his head and force his lips back to hers. Between deep, hungry kisses, her whisper raked across his ears. "I want you, Michael."

The sound of his name squeezed him like a hot vise and he grew harder. He slid his hands underneath the full curve of her buttocks and lifted her up. She gasped as he rocked against her with teasing motions, but while he was busy, the loud snap of his jeans ricocheted in the air. "Baby, I think we need to—*Dios!*"

Warm fingers dove under his waistband and grasped his erection. Fireworks exploded in his vision, and he'd never been so damn happy in all his life that he didn't like to wear underwear. She squeezed gently, then began pulling down his jeans to get more exposure and—

The door opened.

The sound of laughter cut through the scene like a bad sitcom. They both moved like naughty teenagers, removing hands and fingers, and adjusting clothing as his cousins bounded through the door. One look at Lizzie's rosy cheeks and Michael bet they'd gotten reacquainted in the car. After all, if four boys was any indication of their lifestyle, he figured they skipped the token movie and went straight for the fooling around.

Michael sat up and pulled Maggie with him.

Brian's grin widened. "Well, well, what do we have here?" He crossed his arms and clucked his tongue. "My four innocent sons are sleeping down the hallway and you're conducting yourselves like an X-rated movie."

Michael called him a dirty word, which only made Brian laugh harder. One look at Maggie's face caused his cousin to frown. "I'm just kidding, Maggie."

Her lip caught between her teeth, his *tigrotta* had lost her growl. She stood and shifted foot to foot, looking embarrassed, uneasy, and vulnerable.

Michael grabbed her hand and pulled her against him, snagging his arm around her shoulders. "Sorry, Bri, we're both exhausted. The boys are fine. They trashed the house and I didn't clean it up."

"Asshole."

"Ditto." They said good-bye, Lizzie and Brian giving Maggie hugs and kisses, and Michael got her into the car.

She rested her head against the seat and stared out into the night, not speaking. For the first time in his life, he felt completely uneasy around a woman, unsure what her thoughts were, and only wanting to comfort. No, he was a liar. He wanted to make love to her, *then* comfort her.

"I'm sorry."

Michael shook his head and wondered if he'd misheard her softly spoken voice. "About what?"

She gave a sigh. "About before. In the bathroom at your mama's house. I was a bitch."

Great. A woman who admitted she was wrong. What was he going to do about her? Why couldn't she just stay in character and stop surprising him? "Accepted." He paused. "Mind telling me why?"

She stiffened but didn't avoid the question. "I'm screwed up."

He laughed. "Who isn't? I moved too fast. These past few days have been overwhelming, and I surprised you."

She let out a snort. "Oh, please. I had planned to seduce you, so you didn't overwhelm me. Don't think I'm some ditzy shrinking violet you can manipulate with your charm."

He grinned. This was the Maggie he was used to and enjoyed battling with. "If that's so, I hope you make up your mind fast. I don't think I can take another night with a hard-on."

That remark earned him a sneer. "Maybe if you'd stop driving like an old man, we'd get home before you lose it."

He didn't answer. Just stepped on the gas.

• • •

They snuck inside the house and locked the door. Maggie kicked off her shoes and motioned toward the bathroom. "You go first. I need to grab something from my suitcase."

Michael rushed through the minimum of necessity, deciding to remove his shirt but leave his jeans on. Barefoot, he walked out of the bathroom, his heart pounding like his first woman was waiting for him, and he didn't know if he'd be able to last.

When he finally spotted her, he realized he was doomed. She was heaven and hell in one, and he'd greet the devil with a smile on his face.

She stood under one of the antique lamps cast half in shadow. The dim light emphasized the high thrust of her breasts encased in delicate black lace. The fall of her silky hair as it brushed her shoulders. The full curve of her hip and the bare expanse of leg where the slip stopped above the knee.

As he moved forward, he realized it was more than her body that mesmerized him. For the second time tonight, a flash of vulnerability shone from her cat-green eyes. Her feet shifted just an inch as if she was still unsure, but he already decided he'd waited too long to claim her.

He grasped her shoulders as he closed the space between them. The tips of her nipples teased his bare chest, and she let out a tiny gasp. Satisfied, he gazed down at her in silence, taking in every inch of her body that was about to belong to him. His tigress scrambled for footing.

"Um, Michael, maybe we should—"

"No, *cara*." He smiled and tipped her chin up. "It's time."

. . .

Maggie wondered if all those BDSM romance novels weakened her mind. Instead of taking charge in her normal sexual capacity, she watched with trembling knees as the man before her told her exactly what was going to happen.

God, she loved every moment.

The heat of his body pulled and tantalized as he lowered his head. A catchy little gasp escaped from her throat, but she was past caring. She needed his mouth and his hands and body to drive away the demons of doubt and vulnerability that tore her apart. The same ghosts that waited in her closet late at night to taunt her about not belonging dissolved in smoke as Michael Conte finally kissed her.

No-holds-barred.

The time of seduction and slow kisses was long gone. Maggie was completely overtaken by the assault that pushed and prodded every crevice of her mouth until she opened further and dived in. The taste of coffee and mint and raw hunger swamped her senses, and she slid her arms around his shoulders and hung on. He bent her backward and devoured her, promising her heaven and hell, while excitement pounded her body in waves. Control long gone, the kiss was pure survival, and she reveled in every stroke of his tongue, each nip of his teeth, until his thrusts parried his erection as he rocked between her thighs.

He ripped his lips from hers and breathed hard. Savage lust gleamed from the coal-black of his eyes while his gaze roved over her half-naked body. A thrill shot through her at the need that shook his hands as he traced a line down the valley of her breasts and around the cups. Her nipples rose in demand. His thumb tweaked one, then the other, and her knees grew weak as a spear of hot need shot straight to her clit.

He took half a step back and studied every inch of her. Then with a wolfish grin, he pushed her back on the bed.

Maggie had no time to gather her thoughts as he divested himself of his jeans in record time. The sheer power and length of his erection stole her breath. She reached out to touch him, but he moved too fast. His fingers grasped the fragile straps of her slip and worked the fabric down over her breasts, her thighs, her calves, her feet. He threw the lace away, then slowly eased her legs apart.

Maggie moaned as she lay open to his demands. The helplessness under his hungry stare caused a ripple of panic to flutter low in her belly. She lifted her hands to push him away, but as if he sensed her sudden unease, he raised his head to look at her.

"You are so fucking beautiful," he murmured. His fingers gently parted her swollen folds and dipped into her wet channel, thrusting slowly. "*Dios,* if I don't taste you I'll die."

"Michael—"

"Yes, Maggie, show me your pleasure. Tell me how much I please you."

His mouth dived. His hot tongue circled around her swollen clit as one finger joined the other and plunged deep. She arched upward and cried out. The overwhelming sensation of his thrusts, combined with the teasing licks around her bud, pushed her slowly toward the edge. Her fingers grabbed at the blanket in an effort to ground herself but he never let up, swirling and sucking with a gentle, steady pressure that heated her blood and drove her faster and faster toward orgasm.

"I'm going to—oh, God, I can't—"

"Come for me, Maggie." With one final thrust, he nibbled ever so gently on her clit and she flew over the edge. She screamed and convulsed, her hips arching up for more. Thrusting over and over, he took her deep and lengthened her climax until every muscle shuddered in agony and ecstasy.

Michael pressed kisses to her inner thighs, then slid down and came back with a condom. He threw the packet to the side and covered her body with his. Maggie moaned at the feel of his hot skin over hers, each muscle pressed into her curves, his hard length throbbing.

She tasted the musky essence of her pleasure as he kissed her long and deep. Helpless from the intensity of her orgasm, she let him take what he wanted, bringing her back up the slow ladder of tension, as he played with her nipples. As he rolled them between his fingers, the sharp pleasure rocketed her to the top until she surrendered completely and gave him what he wanted.

"Take me, Michael," she begged. Her hips thrust up in demand, and she hooked one ankle around his leg and tried to urge him down. "Please."

He laughed low and wicked, his teeth raking across her nipple and causing shivers to wrack her body. "You ask so nicely, *cara*. I can't wait to bury myself inside you."

He grabbed the condom and sheathed himself, then paused at her entrance. Wetness leaked down her thighs and welcomed him further. He teased her a bit, pushing in an inch, then another, until her head thrashed back and forth on the bed and her nails dug punishingly into his back.

"More," she demanded. "Damn you, give me everything."

He held her head still, his dark eyes drilling into hers with a promise to take and plunder everything she had. Then he plunged deep.

Maggie gasped as he filled her to the hilt, his massive size overtaking not only her body, but her mind and her soul. Panic hit her full force—the invasion by a man who'd be able to strip her of every surface barrier and unearth the truth.

"No!" She panted, the wild beating of her heart strangling her very breath. "I can't, I can't."

"Shush, *mia amore*. Relax. Let me in."

Her body eased, and the feeling of fullness caused a sharp rush of heat. He groaned, obviously struggling for control, and Maggie panted, his body pinning her down into the mattress with no escape. Helplessness flooded through her.

Tears pricked her eyes. "I can't."

He pressed a kiss to her brow, every muscle locked. "Here, baby, I know what you need." With one quick movement, he rolled until she straddled him.

The freedom and sudden control whooshed through her. She relaxed and arched, ripping a groan from his lips.

"Better?"

The joyous smile curved her lips and broke over her face. "Yes."

He cursed, his hands cupping her breast. "I'm never going to last. Ride me, *cara*. Ride me hard."

She threw her head back and moved up and down his penis, reveling in his raw, naked response, in her ability to make this man weak with want for her. She sucked him in deep and the bruising pace quickly brought her right back to the edge. Her hair fell down her back, and his fingers worked her nipples as she reached for the pinnacle, feeling free and beautiful above him.

"Now, *mia amore*. Now."

With one final plunge, Maggie shattered. She screamed his name, and heard his hoarse shout right behind her. The world broke around her in jagged pieces, and she rode out the pleasure to the very end. When she collapsed on top of him, and his arms came around her, one word echoed over and over in her mind, her heart, her soul.

Home.

Then she closed her eyes and slept.

Chapter Nine

Maggie sipped the strong, steaming brew and stared at the magnificent view before her. The sunlight washed over the green hills, highlighting the vast expanse of mighty, snow-tipped mountains. Terra-cotta sloping roofs spotted the horizon. The scent of olive and lemon wafted in the warm breeze, and she breathed deep, trying desperately to calm her racing heart.

Last night, Michael made love to her.

Pieces of memory flashed before her. The delicious heat and explosion of her orgasm. The gentle curve of his lips as he smiled. The strokes of his hands against her flesh as if she were breakable and precious, not just a one-night stand.

But she was. Or at least, maybe a two-night stand.

Because at the end of the week, this whole charade would end, and he'd leave. Like they all did.

How had it happened? She'd confessed her secrets freely at his uncle's house and had no one to blame but herself. His gentleness encouraged her to open up easier than any hot demands ever had. One moment she swore she'd be on the next plane out. The next, she'd challenged him to a bout of lovemaking with the stupid idea she'd be able to wring him out of her system.

She nibbled at her lip and took another scalding sip. When she woke up he'd left her a note that he'd run into town for a few hours and would be back to bring her to the headquarters of La Dolce Famiglia. The disappointment of an empty bed rattled her foundation. She always fought the need to escape as fast as possible once dawn hit. For the first time, she craved a morning snuggle with the man she made love with. He consistently surprised her, challenged her, and made her long for more. He was dangerous. Not just to her body. But to her heart.

She had to get out of here.

Her heart pounded and the blood roared in her veins. The oncoming panic attack gathered speed and Maggie grabbed her camera, desperate to control her ridiculous physical defaults. Breathe deep and clear her mind. She began snapping shots of the landscape, sharpening her focus to the frame in front of her, looking to find something unique and incredible. Her mind clung to the noise of the shutter and the flash of the light of the lens as she moved around the back terrace. Anything but the dizzy pull of alarm taunting her to lose all control.

"Meow!"

The half shriek of the cat caused her to stumble back and almost fall on her ass. She caught a whirl of black fur as the thing launched through the air, and she scrambled away, desperate to avoid the sharp sting of claws.

"Crap!" she yelled, heading toward the safety of concrete and away from the bushes. "Get away from me."

The cat, or whatever the thing was, stalked her. Blazing green eyes dominated the black face as massive paws closed the distance between them. Maggie jumped behind a wrought-iron chair and glared at it. She did not like cats. Never did. Dogs were sufferable because they were generally affectionate and only lived for you to pet them. Cats were different—they were like high-strung divas who assumed your only job in life was to serve them. They scared the bejesus out of her—even more than children— and there was no way she was sticking around a moment longer. But this creature was three times the normal size, almost like a small dog. He'd do a wicked witch proud because he stared her down like he was about to cast a spell, and he freaked her out.

"Ah, I see you met Dante."

Maggie spun around. Michael grinned down at her, clean-shaven, with his long hair neatly tied back. He looked rested and refreshed, while she still felt completely out of sorts and scrambling for her composure. "What do you feed it? Small children?"

He chuckled and knelt down, trying to call the cat over. Dante swished his tail and hissed. Maggie jumped back another step. "You're not afraid of cats, are you, *cara*?"

She shuddered. "I just don't like them. They're demanding and spiteful."

His lip twitched. "Seems like you'd go perfect together."

"Funny. Is he yours?"

Michael shook his head. "Nope, he's a stray. Visits a regular route for food, but won't let anyone near him. Even Carina, whom we call the animal whisperer, hasn't gotten close. Dante has issues."

She stared at the cat. Pretty clean, definitely not starving, but he seemed to dislike people. The sudden humor struck her. "So Dante gets fed and catered to by the same people he openly despises. Interesting."

"Yes, I guess it is," he murmured. Suddenly, she was in his arms. His minty breath rushed across her lips and made her belly tumble. "Did you sleep well last night?"

"Yes."

"Liar." His dark eyes glittered with promise and a hint of danger. Shivers raced down her spine. "But if three times still gave you enough sleep, I'll need to do better tonight."

Oh. My.

She cleared her throat and reminded herself another night with him may be dangerous. She blinked and pulled back, needing the distance. His arms closed around her. "Michael—"

"I love hearing my name on your lips." His mouth lowered and took hers, kissing her deep and long and slow. She opened up and thrust against each silky stroke of his tongue, pressing close. He caught her low moan, then slid over her bottom lip to nip. The sharp pleasure-pain shot a rush of heat between her aching thighs. He tasted so good she wanted to devour every inch and discover all those hard muscles straining under his clothes. Drowning in sensation, she let herself slide headlong into a pit of seething heat and fire and—

"Owww!" He thrust her away and jumped on one leg.

She looked down in horror to see Dante's teeth stuck in Michael's pants. The tiny puncture holes through the thin fabric caused her to freeze, afraid she was his next meal. The cat's face turned upward in a sneer and he disengaged from Michael. He hissed low, then stalked toward her with intention.

"Dante!" Michael let out a rush of Italian and waved him away with a threatening gesture. The cat ignored him and reached her. She closed her eyes, unable to move and—

Dante rubbed his body against her calf. The low hum of a motor reached her ears. She opened her eyes and realized that noise was purring. He pushed his face hard into her leg, his long whiskers twitching with pleasure as he circled once, twice, then settled beside her.

Michael just stared at the cat, then back at her. "I don't believe this. He's never done that before," he murmured. "And he's never bitten."

"What? It's not my fault—I told you I don't like cats. I didn't tell him to bite you!"

"No. It's deeper than that. Perhaps he sees something we've all been missing."

Maggie watched with widened eyes. "And you feed this thing so he comes back?" she asked in amazement. "What is wrong with you? He came at you like he smelled a tuna dinner."

The electricity between them jumped and burned like a live fuse gone wild. Her pulse rocketed. His eyes darkened with purpose, and he reached for her.

"Margherita? Michael?"

They both jumped back. His mother stood framed in the doorway, an apron covering her dress, her hair twisted neatly into a chignon. The aristocratic lines of her face shimmered with a classical power that had launched a successful business and raised four children. "What is happening out here?"

"I was just introducing Maggie to Dante."

Mama Conte gasped. "Why is Dante near Margherita?"

"Yes, that seems to be the question of the day." Maggie

shifted uneasily and took a step back from the man-eating cat. Dante only stared with disgust at her cowardly retreat. "Mama, we'll be going to the office with Julietta in a bit. Do you need anything?"

"I will give you a list of ingredients I'm running low on. Margherita, I need help in the kitchen. Will you join me?"

She hesitated. As much as she liked Michael's mother, a deep-seated fear lodged in her gut. The woman was too sharp and asked too many questions. What if she slipped up and blew the whole cover story? Michael motioned for her to go, but she shook her head. "Um, I really don't like cooking. Maybe Michael can help you."

His mother crooked a finger. "Michael already knows how to cook—you do not. Come with me." She disappeared back into the house.

Maggie cursed under her breath, indignant at Michael's shaking shoulders as he smothered his laughter. "I hate cooking," she hissed. "Your mother scares me. What if she suspects?"

"She won't. Just be nice, *cara*. And don't blow up the kitchen."

She scooped up her camera, shot him a dirty look, and stomped off. A low meow sounded behind her but she refused to acknowledge the sound. The irony of her current situation blew her mind. She seemed to be confronted at every turn with all the items she refused to deal with back home. Already, she felt responsible for Carina and her current activities, she had to make sure she didn't kill four small children, she had to deal with psychotic cats, and now she needed to please his mother by not poisoning the food. Muttering under her breath, she put her camera down on the table.

Michael's mama already had a variety of bowls and measuring cups stacked on the long, wide counter. Shiny red apples that would do Snow White's evil queen proud gleamed in a row. An expensive blender thing with wheels took up the center. Various containers of powder—which she guessed as sugar, flour, and baking soda—were neatly lined up.

Maggie tried to feign enthusiasm for the task ahead. God, she wanted some wine. But it was only 9:00 a.m. Maybe she'd spike her coffee—Italians liked their liquor.

She smiled with false cheer. "So what are we making today?"

Mama Conte slid a well-worn piece of paper over to her and pointed. "That is our recipe."

"Oh, I figured you knew enough not to need a recipe."

His mama snorted. "I do, Margherita. But you need to learn how to follow instructions. This is one of our signature desserts at our bakery. We shall start simple. It's called *torta di mele,* an apple breakfast cake. It will go nicely with our coffee this afternoon."

Maggie scanned the long list and got lost on step three. She'd made chocolate cake from a mix once because she wanted to try it. It sucked because she hadn't realized you had to mix the batter for so long, so clumps of dry powder got stuck in the middle. Her then-boyfriend had laughed his ass off and she'd broken up with him that night.

"I will supervise. Here are your measuring cups. Begin."

When was the last time an older woman ordered her about? Never. Unless she counted Alexa's mother, and that was only because she'd spent time at her house when she was young. Slowly, she measured each dry ingredient and poured it into the huge bowl. Ah, well, if she was going to be tortured, she might as well be nosy. "So Michael says you taught him to cook at an early age. Did he always want to run La Dolce Famiglia?"

"Michael wanted nothing to do with the business for a very long time," the older woman answered. "He had his heart set on being a race-car driver."

Maggie's mouth fell open. "What?"

"*Si.* He was very good, though my heart stopped every time he went out on the track. No matter how many times his papa and I tried to discourage him, he found a way back on the track. By then, the bakery was taking off, and we had opened up another one in Milan. His papa got into many riffs with him about his responsibility to the family and the business."

"He never told me he raced cars," Maggie murmured. The words escaped before she caught them. Holy crap.

Why wouldn't she know her husband's past? "Um, I mean, he doesn't say much about his previous racing."

"I am not surprised. He rarely talks about that part of his life anymore. No, Margherita, you crack an egg like this." A clean break sliced the egg open and, one-handed, she expertly dropped it in the bowl.

Maggie tried to copy her and the shell exploded. She winced, but Michael's mother took a bunch of eggs and directed her to start cracking. Maggie tried to concentrate on the eggs, but an image of a young Michael Conte defying his parents and racing cars stuck in her head.

"What happened?"

His mother sighed. "Things were difficult. A friend of his was injured, which made us even more upset. At this point, we knew Venezia wanted nothing to do with the bakery, and our dream of a family business began to die. Of course, we had other choices we could make. My husband wanted to expand; I liked cooking and wanted to remain with the two bakeries. Who knows what we would have done? God stepped in and Michael made his choice."

Maggie hit the side of the bowl with an egg. The egg slid neatly inside with no shell, and an odd satisfaction ran through her. Seven must be her lucky number. "Michael decided to quit racing?"

Mama Conte shook her head, an expression of regret flickering across her face. "No. Michael walked out and decided to race cars for a living."

Maggie sucked in her breath. "I don't understand."

"He left and did the circuit for a year. He was young but talented, and his dream was to race in the Grand Prix. Then my husband had a heart attack."

The image hit her full force. She stared at his mother, as if on the verge of a terrible truth. Every muscle tensed with the urge to run and cover her ears. Her voice broke on the two words that broke from her lips. "Tell me."

Mama Conte nodded, then wiped her hands on her apron. "*Si,* you should know. When Michael's papa had the heart attack, Michael came right home. Stayed at the hospital day and night and refused to leave his side. I think we all believed he would be all right, but the second one struck hard and we lost him. When Michael came out of the room, he informed me he had quit racing and was taking over the business."

Maggie remained silent as the older woman pondered the event with the flicker of demons in her eyes.

"I lost something in my son that day, the same day I lost my husband. A piece of wildness, of freedom from restrictions that always burned bright. He became the perfect son, the perfect brother, the perfect businessman. Everything we needed from him. But he left something of himself behind."

Her throat clogged with emotion. Maggie gripped the spoon so tightly she was amazed it didn't shatter. No wonder he seemed so faultless. He gave up his own dreams and became everything his family needed. With no thought of himself and no whining. Not once had he even hinted this was not where he wanted to be.

His mother shook her head and refocused. "So that is the story. You may do with it what you wish, but as his wife, I wanted you to know."

Maggie tried to speak but only managed a nod. As they peeled apples the image of the man she imagined she knew exploded into tiny pieces. His easy, carefree existence hid a man strong enough to make decisions for others. For the people he loved.

"Tell me about your parents, Margherita." The sudden command cut through her aha moment. "Why did your mother not teach you to cook?"

She concentrated on skinning. "My mother is not the domestic sort. She worked in movies and believed her children would be better raised by nannies and cooks. That being said, I never wanted for anything, and enjoyed a wide variety of foods at meals."

Pleased with her cool, calm reaction, Michael's mother glanced up.

She carefully lay down the apple and squinted as if to study every hidden nuance of her expression. "Are you close with your parents now?"

Maggie tilted her chin up and let her stare. "No. My father is remarried and my mother prefers we do lunch only occasionally."

"Grandparents? Aunts or uncles? Cousins?"

"No one. Just me and my brother. It really wasn't a big deal; we had all our needs taken care of, and life was quite easy for us."

"Bullshit."

Maggie's mouth fell open. "What?"

"You heard me, Margherita. You did not have it easy. You had no one to guide you, teach you, care for you. A home is not only about things or needs being met. But this is not your fault. They are fools, your parents, for missing out on such a beautiful, special woman." She scoffed in disgust. "No matter. You learned strength and stand on your own two feet. This is why you are good for my son."

Maggie laughed. "Hardly. We're completely different." She choked at the blunt admission. Damn, she'd screwed up again. "Um, I mean, well, we thought it wouldn't work but then we fell in love."

"Hm, I see." Maggie fumbled and the batter flew up toward the ceiling. "When did you get married, Margherita?"

She dug deep and remembered all the times she needed to lie and be good at it. *Please, Devil, don't fail me now.* "Two weeks ago."

"The date?"

She stumbled but forged on. "Um, Tuesday. May twentieth."

The older woman remained silent and still. "A good day for a wedding, yes?"

"Yes."

"Do you love my son?"

She dropped the spoon and stared. "What?"

"Do you love my son?"

"Well, of course, of course, I love him. I wouldn't marry anyone I didn't love." She forced a laugh and prayed it didn't sound fake. Damn Michael Conte. Damn him, damn him, damn him. . . .

Suddenly, strong hands enclosed hers and squeezed. Maggie winced as his mother's gaze shredded past the surface and sought the truth. She held her breath. She so did not want to blow up their ruse when they only had a few more days left. A dozen responses flitted past her mind to try to convince his mother they were truly married, but as if a sudden thunderstorm had passed, his mother's face cleared and softened with a knowledge Maggie didn't understand.

"*Si,* you are perfect together. You give him back his freedom. Before this visit is over, you will believe it, too."

Before Maggie could respond, the large mixer was dragged over. Mama Conte pointed. "Now, I will show you how to use this. Pay attention or you can lose a finger."

Maggie gulped. The insistent demon that lived within her and always whispered she would never be good enough took hold. "Why are you doing this? I still don't like to cook. I won't be baking Michael yummy desserts and catering to his whims when we get back to the States." She almost wished his mother would say something cutting and cold. "I work late and order take-out and tell him to get his own beer. I'll never be the perfect wife."

A ghost of a smile settled on Mama Conte's lips. "He's tried many times to love a woman who would be a proper wife. Or, at least, what he thinks a proper wife is."

A deep longing took root and grew. Maggie swallowed past the urge and tried desperately to ignore the emotion. After all, she'd fought it back before, many times. Like Rocky, she kept going round after round, knowing if she fell she'd be hurt beyond measure.

As if his mother knew her thoughts, she touched her cheek with a gentle caress that reminded her of Michael. "And as for cooking, I am doing this for one reason. Every woman should know how to make one signature dessert. Not for anyone else but herself. Now, mix."

When dozens of apples were peeled and the cake was safely in the oven, Maggie grabbed her camera, relieved she still possessed all ten fingers, and turned to thank Mama Conte for the lesson. Her fingers flexed around her camera as the image before her swallowed her whole. Trembling, Maggie brought the lens up and pressed the shutter release. Again. And again.

Mama Conte gazed out the kitchen window, seeing something not really there. Her hands held the mixing bowl to her chest, wrapped almost in a hug. Head tilted slightly, a small smile on her lips, her gaze held the dreamy, rapt expression of one caught in the past.

Stray strands of hair lay against her milky cheek, the lines in her face emphasizing her strength and beauty as the sunlight trickled through the window and warmed her. It was a photo of such emotional depth, Maggie's heart expanded in her chest. It was a moment caught in time that defied the past, the present, and the future. It was purely human.

And for a little while, in Mama Conte's kitchen, Maggie felt like she finally belonged. A glimmer of what a real home might feel like taunted her, but she firmly pushed it back in the box and shoved the lid closed.

Maggie remained silent and left the kitchen. Left the woman to her memories. And wondered why she suddenly wanted to cry.

• • •

"Absolutely not!"

Michael smothered a groan and faced his two angry sisters from across the conference room. Irritation prickled his nerve endings but he reached for the usual control and authority he used when dealing with family drama. The two advertising executives glanced back and forth between them, as if trying to decide whom to side with.

With a smooth smile, he focused his attention on the ad team. "How fast can you get us a new campaign?"

The men shared a look. Their eyes glittered with the

mad lust for money. "Give us a week. It will blow you away and make waves."

"Very good. I will discuss this further with my sisters and call you back in."

"*Si. Grazie,* Signore Conte."

The door shut and Michael faced the twin firing squad. "Always remember to keep conflict within the family, Julietta."

Bitterness tinged Julietta's voice. "You didn't even hear me out. Again. Michael, I spent months helping with this campaign, and I think you're going in the wrong direction."

He waved his hand at the photos on the cherrywood conference table. "I've seen the reports, and consumers want edge. A homey, plain-style bakery ad is not going to cut it in New York, and we need to freshen up things at home. I want to launch a whole new look. Hire a sexy model, maybe one eating a pastry, and come up with a catchy line playing off the whole comparison of sex and food."

Julietta gasped. "Excuse me? Are you nuts? This is Mama's business and I refuse to see you exploit it for money!" She threw the thick portfolio onto the table with a crash. "I'm in charge here, and I like our new ads. Profit is steady, and there's no reason to throw something away that's working."

"I disagree." Michael stared at his sister, his voice stone-cold. "You may be the CEO, Julietta, but I still own the bulk of this company. I believe we need to take a risk with the new opening in New York. I'll need new print ads, a television spot, and billboards, and we *will* go in this new direction."

The weight of responsibility deadened his shoulders, but he straightened and took it like he always had. *Dios,* he wished he didn't always have to make the hard decisions. "I know you are angry with my choice, but I feel it is best for the family. For La Dolce Famiglia."

There was a total of twenty bakeries spread throughout the Milan and Bergamo area, all a tightly run operation boasting fresh and creative pastries for both the casual pedestrian and four-star party catering. The headquarters stood proudly in the middle of Milan and took up the whole upper floor, and they'd finally added their own factory so they could consistently ship fresh ingredients and have total quality control. Running a massive empire required making hard decisions, even if he needed to overstep Julietta's boundaries. Though his sister impressed him with her business decisions, if the new campaign failed it would be his fault. He opened his mouth to explain, but his sister interrupted.

"I cannot believe you would disrespect me like this." Julietta clenched her fists, her normally reserved features set with fury. Her voice shook. Dressed in an impeccable navy suit with matching pumps, her hair twisted in a neat chignon, she came across as the perfect businesswoman.

Unfortunately, tears shimmered in her eyes. "I'm not doing this anymore. Hire someone you trust, because obviously you don't trust me."

Michael jerked back in surprise at her sudden emotion. He softened his voice and took a step closer. "Ah, *cara,* I didn't mean—"

"No!" She jumped up from the table. "I'm sick of the way you treat me. I'm good enough to run La Dolce Famiglia when you're not here, but as soon as you step back onto my turf, you disrespect everything I've worked so hard to build: respect, mutual admiration, work ethic."

"You're being ridiculous. I'm only doing what's best for the company."

Julietta nodded. "I see. Well, then I don't think you need me anymore. I'm resigning as CEO. Effective immediately. Go find someone else to boss around."

Ah, merda.

Venezia jumped in front of Michael and wagged her finger madly through the air. "Why do you always have to order everyone around?" she demanded. "You're our brother, not Papa."

His jaw clenched and unclenched. "No, perhaps if I was Papa, I wouldn't have let you flounce off to dress a bunch of Barbie dolls and call it a career. Perhaps if I was Papa, I would've made you take your rightful place in this company and not put all the weight on Julietta."

Venezia practically snarled like Dante and teetered on

her three-inch red heels. "I knew it! I always knew you never respected my career. Fashion is a huge industry, Michael, and I've made a name for myself in a competitive business. But no, just because I chose to do what I loved, that's not good enough for you. You don't respect any of us."

"*Zitto!* Enough of your childish tantrums, both of you. I do what is best for this family, always."

Venezia sneered and grabbed her sister's hand. "Who do you think you are? You order us around like children, refuse to respect the decisions and choices we make, and pretend you actually care. We're making a life for ourselves here and have been doing fine without you."

Pain shot through his chest and he struggled for breath. "How could you say this to me? After everything I've done?"

Venezia tossed her hair and led Julietta toward the door. "We don't need you anymore, Michael. Maybe it's time you return to America, where you belong now."

They shut the door behind them.

Michael stood in the shattering silence as the pieces of his life exploded around him.

His head pounded as he paced the empty conference room, searching for answers. The careful control he'd built to protect his family slipped under the weight of raw emotions. Julietta had always been the rational one, yet the hurt in her eyes when he'd overruled her cut him to the bone. Had he been mistaken? Should he have stepped out of the way, even when he knew the campaign wasn't the best, and let her fail?

The door opened.

Maggie peeked her head in. "Okay, I'm bored and I want to go home. I visited the cafeteria twice, hung out with Julietta's secretary, and was sufficiently impressed with your organization. I've done my wifely duty so I'm heading out."

He forced a nod, but she blinked and nudged the door wider. "What's the matter?"

"Nothing." He waved her out. "I shall meet you at home."

The blasted woman ignored him and stepped into the room. "Did you have a fight with your sister?"

He should kick her out and keep business in the family. Yet, the words rushed out of his mouth. "Make that *sisters*. I disagreed with Julietta's advertising campaign and they—what do you Americans term it?—blew up."

"Ah, I see." She looked uneasy as she shot a look at the exit. He waited for her to go but she shifted from foot to foot, her hands cradling her camera, which Michael now thought of as another appendage. "Is that the ad campaign?" she asked. She walked over to the table, and her legs flashed in her short skirt and high heels. Memories of those limbs wrapped snug around his hips and open to every thrust shuddered through him.

"Yes. It's outdated. I told them we need a sexy commercial equating food and sex. Americans like shock. It sells."

"Hm." She flipped through the photo ad, then closed the folder. "Okay, I'll meet you at home."

Damn her. He almost choked on the words when he realized how much he respected her opinion. "What do you think?"

"Of the campaign?"

"Yes. Am I right?"

She turned on her heel and stared at him. Her bangs slid over one eye. The sexy peek only made him fight harder to concentrate on business and not the low moans she made last night. "I agree."

The breath rushed out of his lips. He straightened, glad he made the right decision. "I thought so."

"But I hate your idea, too."

He frowned. "*Scusi?*"

She threw one hand up in the air as if dismissing him and wrinkled her nose. "Some shock sells but not for a family bakery. Your mama would hate it."

Coldness rushed through him. "I see. Well, thanks for your opinion, but you really have nothing to do with this. I'll meet you at home."

Annoyance flitted across her face. She threw her purse on the table and took out her camera. In typical fashion, his *tigrotta* marched over to him, stood on tiptoe, and got in his face. "Is that what you do to your sisters when you don't agree with their opinion? No wonder they walked out. Oh, trust me, I can never forget my *place*. I don't want to be involved in this shit, but you keep messing up. For God's sake, Count, wake up. You treat your sisters with a patronizing air they can't stand. Julietta is perfectly capable of running the business without you, yet instead of respecting her place, you challenge all of her decisions."

"Enough." His brows lowered in a frown. "You have no clue how my sisters feel."

She laughed without humor. "Are you kidding? It's crystal clear. They adore you and believe you practically walk on water. They just want some kudos from their big brother. A little respect for what they've accomplished. Do you know Venezia believes you think she's a joke? She may dress celebrities and gain respect in her field, but it means nothing because you don't acknowledge her success. And Carina? She loves to paint, but you term it a cute little hobby, pat her on the head, and force her to attend business school. She's got tons of talent and she aches to pursue it, but wants your approval. You're not seeing her, and the woman she's becoming. And Julietta keeps fighting the idea she's an imposter and the business will never truly belong to her. You've made her doubt her instincts."

A muscle ticked in his face. "I respect them and love them more than you know. *Dios,* they are my life! I sacrificed everything so they can be happy."

Suddenly, her face softened. "I know," she whispered. "You've done everything a father would have done. You supported them with money, discipline, and good advice. You kept them safe. You made sure they did the right thing and wanted for nothing. But you forgot the most important part. They don't want a substitute father. They want an older brother who can joke with them, support them, and let them shine. On their own. They don't need you to take care of them anymore, Michael." She touched his cheek and tenderness slipped through the cracks and right into his heart. "They just want you to tell them you love them. Exactly the way they are."

Her words rocked through him and tore down his comfortable blinders.

She held up her camera. "This is what I see for the image of La Dolce Famiglia," she said. The screen showed the shot of his mother, bowl clasped in her embrace, a dreamy expression on her face in her homey kitchen. "It's not about sex and food. It's about this. Her dreams for her family, her determination to be the best, and the quality she strives for every day. That's what your motto and advertising campaign should be."

He stared silently at the screen. When he looked up, an array of emotions flickered across her features.

"You're so lucky to have them. Make a mistake and they'll forgive you. That's what family is about." She trailed off as if thinking about another event. "I don't belong here, Michael. With you. With them. I can't do this anymore."

She turned and fled, leaving him alone with his thoughts. Everything he believed in and worked hard to maintain rose to mock him. His past swam before his eyes, and he tamped down the excruciating pain of failure. His mother's face stared up at him from the camera. She deserved more than this. She deserved more from him.

He pulled out the leather chair and sat down. Slowly, he clicked past all the photos Maggie had taken since she arrived. They were so much more than pretty landscapes. In each shot, she'd reached something elusive, whether it be a color or shape that struck the onlooker. He watched as his four nephews came into focus, a candid glimpse of grinning, messy, mischievous boys as they mashed clay between their fingers. Slowly, he lay down the camera and faced the truth.

He was falling in love with her.

At the same time, she scared the crap out of him. Maggie wasn't the woman he'd ever imagined spending his life with. She twisted everything inside of him until he vibrated at a high pitch, and she made the long line of other women he'd taken to bed fade away into nothingness. She was prickly, hardheaded, honest to a fault, and hid a soft center that melted his heart.

The worst of the whole encounter was his realization that she was right.

He hadn't done his job. Images of his father dying before his eyes tortured him. The guilt of leaving him to pursue his own selfish dreams while his father worked long hours and tried to build a company his children never even believed in.

Emptiness ripped at his gut. But Maggie spoke the truth. Throughout his climb to push the company to the top, he'd refused to see his sisters as equals. In his mind, they reflected the young image of grief-stricken youths in desperate need of protection and stability. Even with his mother's strength, Michael knew it was up to him to provide and assume a leadership role. So he did. He disciplined, advised, and led.

But he never told them good job. He never told them he loved them. He never listened.

He had done each of them a terrible injustice. He refused to allow Julietta any real rewards for stepping in as CEO. She completed all the menial tasks on a day-to-day basis, yet never retained any glory. He kept all the good stuff for himself like a selfish child and never gave his full support.

With Carina, he was so used to her being the baby of the family, he never thought of asking her what she wanted. He ordered, demanded, and expected. Sure, he knew she liked art, but not until Maggie pointed out her talent did he realize she may have a dream of her own, or even need encouragement to pursue something not business oriented.

But the worst, by far, was Venezia. Shame filled him as the admission rose up inside and choked the air from his lungs. Venezia followed her dream to be a stylist, yet he constantly berated her for not taking responsibility for the family business, and he belittled her choice. Now, he realized why. He was jealous—jealous she was able to go after her dream, yet he'd lost his own. Somehow, he needed to let the anger go. He'd always prided himself on making his own decisions, and quitting racing was his choice. Venezia should not have to pay the price for following her dream, or for the loss of his.

And Maggie? She was about to flee. He had no idea how he was going to convince her, or tear down her careful control enough to get under her skin, but damned if he wasn't going to give it his best shot. He would not let her get on that plane until he convinced her to surrender her soul. Then, and only then, could he know if it would work for them.

The shattered pieces of his life lay broken around him. Time to make a decision. First, make it right with his sisters. Second, take a leap of faith. Maggie had the heart and soul of a wounded warrior, and it was time he fought for her.

He needed to find his fake wife and somehow convince her to stay.

Chapter Ten

Maggie lay on the bed and stared up at the ceiling. Her decision was final.

She was getting the hell out of Dodge.

Ever since she stepped foot in the Conte household, she'd lost her balance. She had gotten sucked into family dramas and in a weird way, she'd started to care. That was a no-no. She needed to be able to distance herself from Michael and get used to the knowledge that he wouldn't be around any longer. He would not be hanging around Alexa. She didn't care how he tried to get out of that bargain, she'd make sure he stuck to his word. Anyway, the last thing she needed was to moon over some guy who wanted different things than she.

Didn't he?

Her thoughts whirled and she rolled to her side and groaned. Why was she beginning to doubt herself? Her initial decision to sleep with him and wring him out of her system backfired. One night and she already cared way too much. What if she got attached? What if she got some ridiculous ideas about love and permanence? Sure, he'd give her multiple orgasms and physically she'd be satisfied. But what about her heart? Could her heart handle such a blow?

Nope. Call her a coward, but when Michael returned, she'd be getting on the next plane back home. She'd say her mother got sick. Or come up with a death in the family—some long-lost uncle. Anything to get her far, far away.

A knock sounded on the door. She sat up in immediate dread. "Who is it?"

"Carina. Can I come in?"

"Sure."

The younger girl bounced in and sat next to her on the bed. Maggie smiled at the happy look on her face. For a little while, she had bucked her moodiness and seemed lighthearted. Her makeup was applied with a more subtle hand, and her clothes showed off a bit of her figure, unlike the baggy jeans and T-shirts the girl usually sported. At least Maggie had helped Carina in some way. One item she managed not to screw up.

"How was your evening out?" Maggie asked. "And before you answer, it better be good. I dealt with your cousins last night and I'm still recovering."

Carina laughed and crossed her legs. Her eyes lit with excitement. "Maggie, it was so awesome. I loooooved Sierra; she was supercool. And gorgeous. And the guys were really nice and polite. It was a big group so I never felt uncomfortable and guess what? They said I'd make a great model!"

Maggie smiled. "You would, but I don't know if that's something you'd want to pursue, Carina. Personally, I think you'd do better off with a college education and your art. You're talented."

A blush tinted her cheeks. "Thanks. Yeah, Michael and Mama would probably freak. But it was cool they actually thought I'd be good enough to model. They invited me to their next shoot, and now I have their cell numbers and we're texting back and forth."

"I'm glad you made some new friends."

"Me, too. Can I ask for a favor?"

"As long as it doesn't entail babysitting."

"Can I borrow one of your scarves? Do you have anything ice blue? I want to try on a new outfit and I need a nice accessory." She wrinkled her nose. "Venezia throws a fit when I borrow from her, and Julietta only owns business clothes."

"Sure. I brought some extra in my travel bag. It's in the closet—help yourself."

Carina chattered about the details of her night, and Maggie leaned back on the headboard, relaxing under the ritual of clothes borrowing and girl talk. Carina oohed and aahed over a bunch of her scarves, took two, then paused. "What's this?"

Maggie looked up. Her heart stopped.

Carina held a small fabric-covered book with a bright purple cover. The girl stared at it curiously, then flipped it open.

"No!" Maggie scrambled to the side in an effort to grab it.

"What's the matter? Is this a love spell? Oh, my God, it is. How cool."

Oh. My. God.

The memory of her drunken night slammed into her brain and gave her an instant headache. Yes, she'd supported Alexa when her friend had cast the spell for a man. Yes, Alexa ended up marrying Maggie's brother, and they were happy. But there was no way it had to do with the spell. In fact, Nick was the complete opposite of everything Alexa had originally asked for, but when she pointed that out, Alexa just laughed and said Earth Mother had been right all along.

Alexa forced her to take the book of spells and use it. Maggie had refused at first, but eventually threw it in her bag and forgot about it.

Until that night. When she realized she might never find the right man to marry, never have children, and be alone for the rest of her life. Then she drank too many margaritas, watched a sappy movie, and dug out that violet book. Then proceeded to make a fire in her living room and create the dreaded list.

The qualities she demanded made her squeeze her eyes closed to shut out the memory. Stupid and juvenile. Of course, love spells didn't work, but slipping the paper under the bed seemed like the least she could do after making a frickin' fire and burning the list. She'd never told Alexa, one of the first things she had ever hidden from her best friend. Better to keep the secret in case the news spread.

Anyway, there wasn't a man in the world who contained the qualities she sought. She may as well look up *hero* in the dictionary and wish for Superman to appear outside her condo window.

She totally forgot she'd thrown the book in her travel case in an effort to forget what she had done. Now, the truth of her lunacy mocked her in neon violet. "Carina, it's nothing, really, I forgot it was in there." She laughed, but even to her own ears it sounded fake. "My girlfriend gave it to me as a joke."

Carina skimmed the pages. "Did you do it? The love spell? Is that how you and Michael met?"

Humiliation dragged her down like the sucking tide of an undertow. "No, of course, not. It's just a joke and I forgot to get rid of it."

Carina's eyes widened. "Can I have it?"

Maggie fisted her hands and stared at the book in horror. "What? No, no, it's a silly thing. That stuff doesn't work and your brother will kill me if he sees you with a witchcraft book."

"Not witchcraft. This says you have to list all the qualities you want and need in a mate. Follow the spell and he comes to you." She flipped through the pages while Maggie fought sheer panic. "Wow, it says you have to make a fire to honor Earth Mother. Oh, Maggie, please? I swear I won't tell a soul, it's just supercool."

Maggie's mouth hung open like a guppy. Why hadn't she thrown it out when she had the chance? It was like a bad penny that kept showing up. She was going to kill Alexa for forcing her to take it. Absolutely kill her.

"Maggie? Please?"

With growing anticipation, she stared at the book, as if waiting to see if it would disappear in a cloud of smoke. No such luck. What a rotten day, beginning with a crazy cat. She closed her eyes and hoped this wasn't going to be the biggest mistake of her life. "Okay, fine. But don't tell anyone. You know it's just a joke, right? Tell me you're not thinking of taking this seriously, Carina, or I'll throw it away now."

Carina shook her head and held up her hand. "Promise. I just think it's fun. When I'm done looking at it, I'll get rid of it. Thanks, Maggie!" She bounded out of the room and shut the door behind her.

Maggie rolled over and smashed her face into the pillow.

Enough. She despised pity parties, especially her own.
She'd start packing her bags, line up a plane ticket, and get
out of here.

A knock sounded on the door.

She groaned into the pillow. "Go away!"

"Maggie, I'm coming in."

Michael.

She shot up. Maybe this was for the best. Get the con-
frontation over with. He'd scream at her for messing up his
family life, she'd tell him she was out of here, and they'd
come to some type of arrangement so they can both get
what they want. She smoothed her hair down and took a
deep breath. "Come in."

He entered and shut the door behind him. Her mouth
dried and her stomach fluttered. His presence filled up the
room and crowded out every spare inch with a masculinity
that was a natural part of who he was. Maggie had a crazy
vision of stripping off his clothes and surrendering to him
right here. Right now.

Before she left.

She fought the impulse and remained calm. His dark
eyes seared into hers as if waiting for her to speak. "I sup-
pose you're here to yell."

His lip quirked. "Not this time."

The silence pulsed with an undercurrent of danger.

The sizzling sexual tension lit between them, causing her to scooch back one inch away from him. Just an inch. "Oh. Well, good, because I'm not the in the mood. I've had a crappy day."

"Me, too. I'm about to change that."

She heard a *thump* and realized he'd toed off his shoes. The elegant fabric of his shirt barely contained his broad chest and muscled arms. Maggie curled her fingers to curb the urge to explore each hard angle of his body. She barreled on. "Michael, we have to talk. I want to go home."

One brow lifted but he remained silent. He slowly unraveled his navy-blue tie from the knot, slid it around his neck, and let it drop. "Why?"

Her mouth fell open. "Um, let me think about this. Because this whole trip has been a disaster. Because I'm miserable, and you're miserable, and we're making a mess out of your family. Because I hate lying, and I can't spend one more day pretending to be your loving, dutiful wife. I'll come up with an excuse. Say someone died. A long-lost cousin or uncle so I won't feel guilty. I think we made our intentions known to be married by a priest, and I'm sure we can keep up the ruse until Venezia's wedding."

Michael cocked his head as if listening, then slowly slid the hair tie from his hair. The strands shimmered around his face and fell to his shoulders. The gesture made her thighs clench in agony as wet heat rushed to her center and throbbed. She itched to photograph him—a powerful, dangerous male contained in a civilized suit. God, he was beautiful.

She chattered on with a mad effort to reign in the red-hot want that speared her. "In fact, if you really want me to, I'll come to Venezia's wedding. I gave you my word, and I intend to keep my side of the bargain."

She stared helplessly up at him, certain some type of game was being played but she was not a party to the rules.

A slow smile curved his lips. "Running scared, *la mia tigrotta*?" he drawled. "I'm disappointed. One night together and you already can't handle it?"

She gasped. "You're the one who can't handle the truth, Count. I'm tired of pussyfooting around you like the rest of your family. It's time you wake up and face the way you view your sisters and admit you love control so much you'll do anything to keep it."

"You are correct." His fingers flicked open the first few buttons of his shirt.

She blinked. A swirl of black hair. Deep olive skin. Flat nipples on a mass of muscle. "Huh? What did you say?"

"I said you are correct. I spoke with my sisters and begged for their apology. I agree with everything you said today in the conference room."

Stunned, she just stared as the buttons kept opening. A washboard stomach. An intriguing dark line that disap-peared beneath the buckle of his pants. Her mouth watered and her brain fogged. He untucked the shirt from his pants so it fell completely open.

"What—what the hell are you doing?" she squeaked.

"Taking you to bed." The shirt hit the floor. His hands worked on the belt buckle, then slid it through the loops. Then he undid his zipper.

Her gaze roved greedily over the male perfection before her. He put his hands on his hips. "Come here, Maggie."

Her heart pounded so hard her blood strangled, then pumped madly in an effort to keep up with her hormones. "Huh?"

"Hmm, I should have done this a while ago. Who would've thought you'd ever be speechless?" He snagged her hand and pulled her off the bed.

Dumbstruck by the sexual electricity from the touch of his skin on hers, she allowed herself to be led so she stood before him.

"Let me be clear, *la mia tigrotta*. I'm taking you to bed. I'm going to strip off your clothes, bury myself deep inside you, and make you come so many times the only word from your lips will be my name, begging me to do it all over again." He sank his fingers into her hair and tugged. Then he loomed over her, his eyes hotly promising her every decadent, lustful pleasure she could take. "*Capisce*?"

"I, I don't think, I—"

His mouth stamped over hers.

Her mind may have needed a moment to recover, but her body bloomed and opened under his command. She took every silky stroke of his tongue and demanded more as she dug her nails into his shoulders and hung on. In minutes, her clothes were stripped off.

The sensual taste and smell of him flooded her nostrils. Already, her body grew wet and fiery hot, aching for him to fill her. He growled low in his throat and fit himself quickly with a condom. This time he urged her onto her hands and knees, dragged her thighs apart, and plunged.

She cried out at the delicious sensation of tightness and bucked upward for more. The deep penetration left her nowhere to hide. Maggie panted as she tried to keep something back for herself, but as if he sensed her withdrawal, he reached under and rolled the tips of her nipples between his fingers, slowing his pace. Each deliberate, easy thrust pushed her closer to the edge but didn't give her enough to fly over. She moaned and tried to speed him up.

His warm breath rushed over her ear. "Want something?"

She shivered. "I hate you."

He laughed low. "I love you in this position. You have the most beautiful ass."

He circled his hips and did something that should be illegal. "Michael, please."

"Stay."

She tried to process his words but her body ached and every inch throbbed. "What?"

He nibbled on her ear and caressed her breasts. "Stay with me to the end of the week, *mia amore*. Promise me."

Closer and closer. The orgasm was just out of reach, and she craved him like before, wanted him to pound inside of her and claim her. "Yes. I'll stay."

He murmured in satisfaction, grasped her hips, and gave her everything. The climax came hard and fast, and she shook in the aftermath. He shouted her name and followed, and they sank onto the pillow, Michael holding her close as if he would never let her go.

. . .

Michael stroked her naked back as she stretched into the caress. A deep satisfaction coursed through every cell in his body and reminded him once again that Maggie Ryan finally belonged to him.

Her open, carnal response blew away any other encounter he'd ever had. The warning deep within shimmered inside the locked box, but he refused to spoil the moment by worrying. Somehow, they'd work things out. After the lure of the hunt with a beautiful woman ended in bed, Michael always experienced satisfaction. What blew his mind at the moment was the fierce sense of completion that flowed through his veins. As if he had finally met his other half.

Dios, he must be loco.

Leave it to him to pick a woman who'd make his life a mess. The inner voice whispered the truth in mocking format. She'd also bring a sense of joy and zest and challenge he craved, no matter how hard he fought to settle with an easier woman. It was as if his passion on the race circuit translated to the women he longed for. Wild, untamed, contradictory, and stubborn. He remembered the adrenaline rush of handling such power, riding it around the curves and keeping the vehicle barely under control. Maggie reminded him of the same thrill. She courted the full range of his emotions that were normally locked up and reserved in a civilized manner. His past had finally caught up with him.

And he was happy.

Suddenly, Maggie shot up out of bed. Hair messily falling over one eye, bare-breasted, she gazed in horror at the closed door. "Oh, my God, your mother! Carina! I was loud, I forgot they were in the house."

He chuckled and pulled her back into his arms. "Before I came to your room, Mama said she needed to go into town for some sort of surprise. She took Carina with her, so I knew we'd have a few hours alone."

She let out a relieved breath. "So you had this planned all along." She gave him a mock glare. "I figured you'd come to yell at me for getting involved with your business."

"I planned on yelling afterward."

Her hand snaked out and gave his penis a squeeze. He laughed and pinned her to the mattress with his thigh. On cue, he grew hard and nudged insistently against her moist center. With a mischievous glint, her hand explored, caressing the tip and sliding up and down his shaft. The woman had dangerous hands and may eventually kill him. Still, he'd die a happy man.

"What were you saying?" she purred, alternating between teasing flicks and hard pumping motions.

Michael gritted his teeth.

"Don't play games you can't win, *la mia tigrotta,*" he growled. Then took her lips in a hard, deep kiss. Her musky essence rose to his nostrils as the sweet taste of her flooded his senses.

"I'll win this round, Count," she whispered back. Her tongue ran over his bottom lip and she bit down in a sharp nip. The tiny pain shot straight to his cock and his skin stretched to accommodate.

"I'd show you who's boss right now but I don't have another condom handy."

She guided him one tempting inch.

He paused at her entrance. His head spun like a man with his first woman.

"I'm on the pill, and I'm safe." Her eyes glittered with a mad need that called to him.

With one push, he sank inside her.

They lay side by side, faces close, and he reveled in the

intimacy of watching every expression as he moved inside of her. Her breasts filled his hand, and the berry red of her nipples tempted him to take them in his mouth and suck hard. The scent of sandalwood overtook him, and she met each thrust with an open abandon that fired his blood. He kept the pace slow and easy, not wanting to rush the extreme pleasure of her body flowering open beside him. Her channel squeezed and she gasped as she neared the pinnacle. He clawed for control and tipped his hips to hit the sweet spot, then watched her fall apart.

He swallowed his name from her lips and let himself join her. Then he realized he had called her an endearment he'd never uttered before. A term he saved for the woman who would become his wife. One he'd never used before, even at the height of orgasm.

Mia amore.

My love.

Michael swallowed past the sudden tightness of his throat and held her close.

. . .

"We have to get dressed."

"Hm." Michael ran a hand over her gorgeous curves, enjoying the feel of sleek muscles and silky skin. "In a minute."

"Your mom should be home with Carina. Venezia

wants to go over bridesmaid accessories tonight. And I have to help cook dinner again, damn it."

His body shook with contained laughter, and she gave him a weak punch. "Sorry, *cara,* this whole week was not what either of us expected."

Her voice was whisper soft. "No. It wasn't." A pause. "Michael, what happened with your sisters?"

He turned over to face her, then smoothed cinnamon strands back from her face. "You were right. About everything." Regret loomed but he pushed past, knowing he could only make it right for the future. "I got lost in my role and made a lot of mistakes. After you left, I spoke with my sisters and apologized. I also showed them your photo of Mama and they loved it. We're launching a new campaign based on your photograph."

Her brow shot up. "Are you kidding? That's wonderful."

Michael smiled, tracing the lush outline of her mouth. He cursed her parents, who didn't see the treasure she was and caused her to doubt her ability to love. He realized he'd reached a turning point and needed to force them both to face the truth. Their marriage ruse had veered into something more, and he believed it was too precious to throw away.

Michael grasped her chin and gently forced her to face him. "Listen to me, Maggie. This is important. In a few days, you saw things I'd never even realized. How I treated my sisters and what they really needed from me. You made four little boys feel loved and taken care of, even though it was the first time they ever met you. You respected my mother and made food in her kitchen, which is the most important thing you can ever give her. You gave my little sister a reason to believe in herself again, and believe she is beautiful. You are an amazing woman, Maggie Ryan." He gazed deep into her eyes and told the truth. "Stay with me."

His heart pounded as he waited. She closed her eyes, as if searching for her own answers, then opened her mouth to respond.

"Michael! Are you in there? Come quick; Mama's sick!"

The words she was about to utter died a quick death, and Michael wondered if he'd always regret that moment of interruption. They jumped out of bed, pulled clothes on, and made their way downstairs. Carina stood outside his mother's door. "Where is she?" he asked calmly, trying to mask his worry.

She pressed a hand to her lips and choked out the words. "Dr. Restevo is with her. We went into town and everything was fine, and then she said she felt weak and dizzy. I told her to rest because the sun was hot today, but she insisted I get the doctor." Tears sprung to her eyes. "Maybe I should have taken her to the hospital? I didn't know what to do, Michael."

"Shush, you did everything right." He gathered her in his arms for a quick hug. "Let's wait for a few minutes and see what the doctor says. Perhaps it is nothing. *Va bene*?"

Carina nodded. When he released her, he noticed Maggie took her hand as if it was the most natural gesture in the world. Low murmurings drifted through the closed door, and he tamped down his urge to pace. Finally, Dr. Restevo strolled through.

"*Buon giorno,* Doctor. How is Mama?" Michael asked.

An odd expression crossed the older man's face. Dressed casually in khakis, a white T-shirt, and sneakers, Michael guessed he'd been caught off guard by Carina's call. His black bag fit the standard cliché as his family still believed in home care and door-to-door visits. He peered over his spectacles, his brown eyes concerned.

"Um, a hospital is not necessary at the moment."

Michael waited for more, but the doctor remained silent, shifting from foot to foot. He averted his gaze. Michael curbed his impatience but Carina burst out in front of them. "What's wrong with her? Did she have a heart attack? Why aren't you telling us something—is it very bad?"

The doctor ran a hand past his receding hairline and coughed. "No heart attack. She needs to rest; that's it."

"Was it the heat? Her medication? Anything we need to do?" Michael asked.

Dr. Restevo shook his head and edged past him. "Keep her in bed today. Plenty of liquids. This happens sometimes, no need to worry." The older man paused and suddenly clasped Michael's shoulder in a death grip. "Remember one thing, Michael. No stress. Whatever your mother asks for, just give it to her. Capisce?"

"But—"

The doctor dropped his hand, gave Carina a quick kiss on the cheek, and studied Maggie. Eyes narrowed, he drank in her figure, as if studying for a quiz, then patted her cheek. "Congratulations on your marriage, *signora bella*. Welcome to the family." Then with a little smile, he hurried out the door and left them.

"Oh, thank goodness. It was probably just the long walk and the heat," Carina said. "I'll go get her some water and juice." His sister left and his knees weakened with a rush of relief. Without a word, Maggie stepped into his arms and held him close.

A deep sense of peace settled within his soul. He breathed in the sweet smell of her strawberry shampoo and allowed himself the luxury of leaning on another person. He was so used to shouldering the burden on his own, the sheer pleasure of having someone comfort him shook him to the core. Was this how it would be if Maggie was in his life permanently? She was strong enough to hold up her own end, and he'd never have to worry about keeping things from her. She'd be a true partner in every sense of the word. Michael held her until his breathing returned to normal, then gently released her.

His voice sounded ragged. "Thank you."

She quirked a brow. "For what, Count? Not being a pain in your ass for a minute or two?"

Her cheekiness made him laugh. He reached out and rubbed a thumb over that luscious lower lip. "For being there." She retreated behind her wall of defense, but now he knew the move well and developed the proper block. This time, he decided to give her space. "I'm going to check on her. Be right back."

He walked into the bedroom and sat beside the bed. The familiar scent and sight of his mother's room wrapped around him, reminding him of his youth. The same king-size bed with the heavily carved cherrywood headboard. The cheerful yellow on the walls and the spill of vivid green plants and bright red geraniums in her window box. The room led to a private balcony, and he remembered many nights cuddling on his mother's lap while she rocked in her chair and counted the stars. Now, the powerhouse of a woman lay against the plump pillows with her eyes half-closed.

He took her hand and brought it to his lips. "Mama. How do you feel?"

She gave a small smile. "Silly weak heart. Quite annoying. Your papa and I used to hike in our spare time and climb mountains. Don't get old."

He smiled back at her usual phrase. "Carina's bringing you liquids and I want you to stay in bed. No baking. No stress. Doctor's orders."

She let out a *humph.* "Baking relaxes me. But I will stay in bed, Michael." Her eyes sparkled with a bit of humor. "At least today."

"Mama—"

A quick knock on the door made him turn. Carina stood behind a tall man dressed in the standard black with a stiff white collar and a cross around his neck. His face was heavily wrinkled, but his vivid blue eyes held a glint that lit up the room. A leather Bible was clutched in his hand as he moved forward and held his arms out.

"Father Richard!" Michael rose and hugged the man.

The priest had given his family religious education lessons for many years and was grief stricken when Michael decided not to be a priest. He had an idea Father Richard dreamed of leaving him his legacy, but with the first discovery of the naked female form, Michael was a goner.

"What are you doing here?" Michael stiffened in sudden alarm. "Wait—*Dios,* you're not here thinking she needs last rites, are you?"

Father Richard's booming laugh rang out through the room. He pressed a kiss to his mother's forehead. "Of course not, Michael. Your mama will outlive all of us if my instincts are right. Didn't she tell you?"

Michael glanced back and forth between his mother and the priest. "No, I'm sorry, Father. Is this about Venezia's wedding? She's not here at the moment but should be home later this afternoon."

"Wait! Let me get Maggie; she needs to hear this." Carina dragged Maggie into the room and made the introductions.

Maggie furrowed her brow in confusion as she murmured a greeting to the priest.

Carina jumped up and down in bubbling excitement. "Mama, can I tell them? Please?"

His mother nodded.

"Mama and I went into town to get Father Richard. We have a big surprise for you."

A sense of doom beat through Michael, as if he were watching a horror movie and the deafening music was swarming to a crescendo during the final murder. "What surprise?"

Carina paused for dramatic effect. "Father Richard can marry you in Italy! Right now! Venezia and Julietta will be here any moment. Michael, we got approval for you to marry Maggie. We're having a wedding!"

The words slammed into his brain like a mean left hook. Maggie stood in perfect stillness, those cat-green eyes wide with a mixture of horror and shock.

Porca vacca. He was screwed.

Chapter Eleven

Maggie stared at the priest like he'd arrived to perform an exorcism. The room fell quiet, and Carina
seemed anxious over their complete nonexcitement. In
fact, at another time and place in her life, this may be
hilarious. Almost like one of the comic sitcoms she loved
where stupid situations happened in the comfort of her
living room.

No way. She was *not* going to marry Michael Conte.

A crazed laugh bubbled from her lips. Enough was
enough. She waited for Michael to explain the truth. He'd
never go through with it. Hell, she was his own worst nightmare come to life, even though they had great sex and he'd
said some sweet things. In the cold light of morning, he'd
lose interest and move on for his search for a proper wife.

One who was better suited to him and his family. Someone like Alexa.

Carina finally spoke. "Um, guys? Aren't you excited? We're going to have a wedding."

Since her fake husband seemed dumbstruck—with the emphasis on dumb—she decided to be the rational one. Maggie took a deep breath. "Listen, everyone. We have something important to tell you. You see, Michael and I—"

"Wait!" Michael's roar choked off her words. Her eyes practically bugged out of her skull as he calmly walked over, took her hand, and faced his family. "What Maggie means to say is, we never expected to have the ceremony take place so soon. Maggie had her heart set on inviting our cousins and uncles to the celebration." His laugh came out hollow and fake. "How did the approval go so fast? I mean, Father Richard, I figured you'd want Maggie and me to go through some classes first before blessing our union."

Father Richard, in his godlike presence, sensed no evil lies in the vicinity and smiled warmly. "Well, of course, that is the standard, Michael. You know the church takes a while to approve a marriage, but you have been under my care since you were young. As soon as your mother knew you were flying back home, she contacted me and we pushed the paperwork through. You are a count, and royalty does have some assets."

Mama Conte struggled to sit up. She sipped at the water and handed the glass back to Father Richard. When she spoke, her voice was threaded with weakness. Odd, because even when she was tired, his mother snapped out her words with a strength in complete contradiction to the frail vision before him. God, maybe she was really, really sick. "I understand, my son. And I do not wish to take away your wishes, but I'm afraid I will not be up for a big party. I feel so weak. The doctor will be back tomorrow, and he said if I am still this way, he may choose to take me to the hospital for tests."

Her brown eyes held a glint of determination. "I ask you two to do this for me. Recite your vows on the back terrace so I can be certain your union is complete."

Carina seemed relieved at their concerns and went back to nonstop chatter. "See, there's nothing to worry about. I know we'd rather do a big party, but if you're flying back next week, Mama decided it's more important to have the religious ceremony immediately." She clapped her hands together. "Maggie, I got a dress for you! I hope you like it; I snuck in your closet and got your size, and I have it in my room. Let's get you dressed! The girls should be here any moment. Michael, you should wear that gorgeous tux you left here from the last time. La Dolce Famiglia delivered a chocolate cannoli cream cake, and I have a few bottles of champagne chilling. This is going to be so much fun!"

The scene blurred before Maggie. Her heart sped up, and sweat pricked her skin. The breath lodged in her throat and refused to emerge. She tried her normal fighting tactics, but a part of her understood she was too late. She was crashing fast, and this may be one of her most embarrassing moments of all time.

Suddenly, Michael's gaze sharpened on her face. As if he sensed her impending collapse, he made a quick excuse, then dragged her out of the room. Maggie shuddered as the waves of adrenaline surged through her and stole her sanity. They reached the bedroom, and Michael guided her to the bed, pushing her head down between her knees. The instinct to fight the fear of losing control made her reaction worse. She clenched her fists and gasped for air. She was about to scream in helplessness when Michael's strong hands and voice shredded through the fog and commanded her attention.

"Listen to me, Maggie. Breathe. Slow and steady. You will be all right; I have you and I won't let anything happen to you. Give up your control and let yourself go." His hands rubbed her back in gentle motions, and his fingers interlaced with hers in a show of strength. She focused on his voice and clung to the solid weight of his words. She gave in to the feelings twisting inside of her and finally, her lungs clutched air. The clock ticked, and her heart slowed, allowing the breath to release back into her body. All the while, Michael kept talking to her, low nonsense that soothed her and brought her from the brink. Finally, she lifted her head.

He pressed his forehead against hers and cupped her

cheeks. "Better, *cara*?" His fathomless onyx eyes drilled into hers with worry and a deeper emotion she didn't recognize.

Maggie nodded. Emotion surged, a strange mixture of tenderness and need she never experienced. Too afraid to speak, she reveled in the stroke of his hand down her cheek and the warm rush of breath over her lips.

"Let me get you some water. Stay there and just relax. We will work this out."

He left the room and came back and gave her tiny sips of cold, fresh water that trickled down her raw throat. A calmness settled over her. She was safe. Somehow, some way, she trusted him. First with her body.

Now her heart.

"I guess the thought of marrying me wasn't very tasteful," he said dryly.

She sputtered a laugh. "Didn't mean to hit your ego, Count. Just something about legally marrying my fake husband in front of his family threw me for a second."

He sighed and dragged his hands over his face. "This is very bad."

"You think? I feel like your mother is the hitman from the movie *The Marrying Man*. Remember when the mobster made them get married because they had sex?" She moaned. "We never should have gone to bed together. Somehow, we're being punished. We have to tell your mother the truth."

She waited for his nod, but instead he shot her a strange look. "I do not know this movie, and my family is not Mafia."

She rolled her eyes. "Well, duh! Why do I feel like you're not on the same page as me?"

"What page?"

Lord, sometimes she forgot how many American expressions he didn't understand. "Never mind. Why aren't you horrified?"

"I am! I'm just thinking of all the angles. Look, *cara,* my mother is sick. The doctor said to avoid all stress and give her anything she asks for. If I tell her the truth now, she may end up having a heart attack."

Maggie's heart lurched at the thought of being responsible for Mama Conte. She nibbled at her lower lip. "Michael, what are you asking me?"

His gaze drilled into hers. Each word struck her like nails driven into her proverbial coffin. "I want you to marry me." He paused. "For real."

She jumped up from the bed. "What? We can't do this. Are you crazy? We'll be legally married. When we get back to the States, we'll have to go through an annulment or divorce or something. Oh, my God, this is insane. How is this happening? I'm trapped in a frickin' romance novel!"

"Calm down." He crossed the room and snagged her hands. "Listen to me, Maggie. I will take care of everything. No one else has to know. We'll say our vows, have a party, and leave for home. I'll take care of all the paperwork and expenses. It will be discreet. I'm asking you to do this for my mother, for my family. I know I ask too much, but I'm asking anyway."

The world tilted. Michael waited for her answer, his face calm as if he had asked her for a dinner date rather than a marriage vow. Pushing past all the screaming thoughts blurring in her mind, she reached deep for an answer.

His mother was sick. Yes, she'd made a bargain for a fake marriage, but telling the truth at this point could be a complete disaster. His sisters would feel betrayed and heartbroken. Venezia wouldn't be able to marry, and who knows what type of drama could ensue? Would it be so bad to say some vows and make it legal? It was just a piece of paper. Nothing would change, and it wasn't like anyone had to know. She had no one back home—no lover or family she cared about other than Nick and Alexa. Maybe the whole thing could work. If she married him now, she could hop on a plane tomorrow, hitch it back to New York, and pretend the whole thing never happened.

Yeah. She was in the land of denial.

He'd owe her big-time, and she'd be sure he stayed far away from Alexa from now on. One tiny sacrifice to make in the big scheme of things. They were just silly words from a book. A holy book, sure, but still man-made. Right? Meant nothing.

Mia amore.

The term rattled her to the core and she trembled. Who was she kidding? He asked her to stay. Acted as if he cared about her beyond the physical sex. If she agreed, in some crazy way she'd allow herself to fall completely for him and end up smashed. He was already getting so close to the truth of her past, and she swore no one would ever feel sorry for her. Vowed all those years ago no one would ever know.

There was one way, though, to make sure she never got hurt. "I'll do it."

He moved toward her but she shook her head. "On one condition, Count. Stop pushing me. We finish this ruse for the rest of the week and go our separate ways. No more sleeping together. No more pretending this is more than it is."

His eyes delved into hers and swirled with an array of emotions. "This is what you ask from me?"

Silly tears threatened but she ruthlessly shoved them back and tilted her chin. Then lied. "Yes. This is what I want."

"I am sorry you feel this way, *cara,*" he whispered. Regret and something more, something dangerous, shone in his face. "*Va bene.*"

Maggie yanked her hands from his, strode across the room, and threw open the door. "Carina, get up here and help me get that wedding gown on. And uncork the champagne."

A loud whoop and clapping drifted up the stairs. Michael nodded, then walked past her without another word.

Her throat tightened as she prepared for the biggest show of her life and tried to pretend she didn't feel so empty.

•••

The sun exploded in burnt-orange radiance over the horizon. Maggie stood before the priest on the back terrace. In a few hours Michael's sisters had transformed the yard into a simple elegance that took her breath away. Colorful roses burst from hanging baskets amid paper lanterns casting an intimate glow along the walkway. His mother sat propped up on cushions in her chair, an elegant handmaid quilt tossed over her lap. His sisters flaunted a variety of colorful dresses with tiny bouquets of white lilies as they walked before her, but it wasn't until she gazed upon her soon-to-be-real husband that Maggie realized her life was about to change.

He was dressed in a dark tux that emphasized the wide breadth of his shoulders and chest, his hair tied back, and the carved features of his face softened as he stared at her with admiration. The sheer white dress skimmed over her figure, dipping low in the front and hugging the full length of her arms. A small train spread out behind her. Michael took her hand and placed a kiss in her palm. Tingles shot up her arm, and a tiny smile quirked his full lips as he sensed the connection. He kept her hand tucked in his arm as if afraid she'd flee. The priest faced them and began the ceremony. The words mingled and blurred in a rush, until she began to recite her vows.

For better or worse . . .

In sickness and in health . . .

To honor and respect . . .

Till death do us part . . .

Birds chirped in the trees. Dante threw a disgusted look at her as he perched beside her, licking his paw and waiting for the embarrassing scene to be over. The wind blew warm and soft, mocking her words and carrying them far over the hills. A deep silence settled over the courtyard as the Conte family waited.

"I do."

The kiss was feather light, but when he lifted his head, she sucked in her breath at the satisfaction gleaming within onyx depths. She didn't have time to think about it, because she was thrust into his arms and given champagne while the truth vibrated through every nerve ending in her body.

She loved him.

She was in love with Michael Conte. For real.

Venezia squealed with excitement and held Dominick's hand. "I'm so happy! Now, we have another surprise for you. We're sending you to our second home in Lake Como for a honeymoon night. You need some privacy without worrying about your family sleeping downstairs." Her eyes sparkled, and she handed the keys to Michael. "Leave now and we won't expect you back till tomorrow night."

Michael frowned and glanced toward his mother. "I thought we rented it out for the season? And I don't feel comfortable leaving her before I confirm she's okay."

Somehow, the woman's sharp sense of hearing kicked in. She shot her son a look that should have withered him on the spot. "Oh, you will go, Michael and Margherita. The house is empty for the next month, so you might as well take advantage. The girls will take care of me and call immediately if anything changes. You will not rob me of the satisfaction of giving you a honeymoon night."

Unbelievably, heat rushed to Maggie's cheeks. She'd gone skinny-dipping, handled naked men on her job, and watched Alexa give birth to her niece without a hiccup of shyness. Now, the very idea of sleeping with her husband with his mother's staunch approval caused her to blush. What the hell?

Venezia whispered something to Dominick and then tugged Maggie off to the side. Her eyes, so like her brother's, shone with an inner light that took Maggie's breath away. The woman interlaced their fingers and gently kissed her hand. "Thank you, Maggie."

"For what?"

Her face grew serious. "For what you did. I know you probably dreamed of your own wedding with Michael in the future, and I also suspect Michael rushed this engagement for me. You've changed him. When he came to apologize to me, he admitted he never realized how he acted until you told him. I can only hope you know how much you mean to this family. You've given me a gift—the opportunity to marry Dominick this summer—and I'll never forget it. I'm so glad you belong to us now."

As Venezia hugged her, a part of Maggie's soul broke off. The oozing pain of deceit and longing swallowed her whole, but she managed to fight it back with the long years of practice in being alone.

. . .

Within the hour, she found herself tucked neatly in Michael's Alfa Romeo, racing down the narrow, twisting roads heading toward the lake. He'd changed into faded jeans and a casual black shirt. His hair blew loose around his face, occasionally masking his expression from her sight and adding that pirate sexiness that appealed to her baser side. Her tummy fluttered and her panties grew damp. She shifted in her seat and pulled her mind from the gutter.

"What are we going to do?" she asked bluntly. "Have you even thought this whole thing through? Are we going to tell Alexa and my brother? What if your family visits the States? What about Venezia's wedding?"

He gave a deep sigh as if she worried about nonsensical items instead of a marriage. "Let's not worry about that now, *cara*. I think we need a night alone to work out some things between us." His pointed look held a smoldering undertone of lust. She fought a shiver. Damn him for controlling her with sex. She'd always been the one in charge, and that's the way she liked it. Maybe it was time to turn the tables.

"Sorry, silly female that I am. Why worry about such things as vows to God and divorce? Let's have some fun. Oh, I know a great subject to talk about. Your mother told me you used to race cars."

His hands clenched on the steering wheel. Bull's-eye. Guilt pricked her conscience as he seemed to struggle with his words. "She told you, huh? We never talk about that anymore," he murmured. "I raced when I was young. My papa got sick, and it was time to head the family business, so I gave it up. End of story."

He seemed calm, but the sudden distance in his demeanor told her emotions simmered beneath the surface. She softened her voice. "You were good. You could've gone pro."

"Probably. We'll never know."

The wind whipped her hair and the scenery whizzed by. "Do you resent having to give it up?" she asked curiously. "You never wanted to run La Dolce Famiglia, did you, Michael?"

His profile reminded her of carved granite. A muscle worked in his jaw. "Does it matter?" he asked. "I did what I had to do. For my family. I have no regrets."

Her heart squeezed and broke open. Without thought, she slid her hand across the seat and grasped his. He threw her a startled look. "Yes, it matters. Have you ever even recognized and mourned the loss of something you loved? Not your father. Your dream. You were getting close to something you'd always wanted and suddenly it was ripped away from you. I'd be severely pissed off."

She got a chuckle from him but he kept his gaze on the road. "My papa and I had a difficult relationship," he admitted. "He looked upon my racing as a dangerous, selfish hobby. Eventually, he pushed me to choose—my career or the family bakery. I chose the circuit, so he told me to leave. I packed my stuff, went on the road, and tried making myself a name. But when I got the call that he had a heart attack, and saw him so frail and sick in the hospital, I realized my wishes weren't as important as I originally thought." He shrugged. "I realized sometimes others have to come first. As Papa once told me, a real man makes decisions for everyone, not just himself. I owed it to everyone to make the business work, and I did. In a way, I have no regrets."

She stared at him a long time "Do you miss it?"

He tilted his head as if considering her question. Then shot her a grin. "Hell, yes. I miss racing every day."

Dear God, this man was going to break her apart. Not only was he honest, he never viewed his self-sacrifice in any negative manner. How many men had she dated who whined about anything that didn't please them or fit perfectly into their own wants or needs? No, Michael held a core of beliefs she'd never experienced with another lover. "Your family is lucky to have you," she whispered.

He didn't answer. Just squeezed her hand as if he'd never let her go.

They reached the vacation home a few hours later. Maggie inwardly laughed at the Contes' version of a rental. The elaborate mansion held its own helicopter pad, lagoon, gardens, and hot tubs. Ivy climbed over the massive brick walls and matching clock tower surrounded by jungle greens and elaborate gardens. The cobblestone path led up a massive staircase where an open terrace held comfortable rocking chairs and was connected to a full bar. Polished marble, brightly colored mosaic tiles, and rich chocolate browns and gold made up the color scheme. A warm breeze flew through the rooms from the open windows, and the scents of lilac and citrus flooded her senses.

Her heels clicked on the gleaming tile as Michael grabbed a bottle of wine and two glasses from the bar, then led her upstairs. One door opened up to a huge bedroom with a king-size platform bed. The balcony doors were opened as if they were expected and the room was already prepared. A full bouquet of bloodred roses sat on the high table, serving as the centerpiece of the room. She walked over the rich Oriental carpet, admiring the carefully placed antiques and fine white lace curtains. Then she realized her husband stood to the side, hip propped up against the bureau, studying her from across the room.

Maggie swallowed. Suddenly, a rush of pure terror overtook her. This whole thing was too much—the bed, the wedding, and her realization of her true feelings for her count. The ground broke beneath her and she scrambled for footing. Her nails curled into her fists in an urge to grab for leverage. Damned if she'd let her voice shake like a virginal bride. She chided herself for this type of behavior and straightened her spine.

"Do you want to go to dinner?" she asked.

"No."

The blood thickened in her veins. His lip quirked upward in a half smile, as if he sensed her sudden awkwardness.

She stuck her chin out and refused to break his gaze. "Do you want to go for a walk in the gardens?"

"No."

"Take a swim?"

"Nope."

She crossed her arms in front of her chest to hide the

obvious thrust of her nipples. "Well, what do you want to do? Just stand there making googly eyes at me?"

"No. I want to make love to my wife."

Grief ripped through her. *His wife.* God, how she wanted it to be real.

"Don't say that," she hissed. Maggie grabbed on gratefully to the anger that burned in her blood. "I'm not really your wife and we both know it. You promised to leave me alone. No sex."

He closed the distance and took her in his arms. The concern and tenderness on his face broke her in two. "*La mia tigrotta,* what is wrong? I would never do anything you didn't want." He stroked her hair back from her face and tipped her chin up.

"This is a lie." She blinked back blinding tears, enraged at her weakness before him. "*We're* a lie."

His breath rushed over her lips and he kissed her gently, slipping his tongue inside to tenderly mate. She longed to fight him but her body weakened under each hot stroke and his musky scent. She opened for him and gave back, digging her fingers into his shoulders as every carved muscle pressed against her curves.

Slowly, he lifted his head. Inky dark eyes seethed with a blistering heat that seared through her and crashed every ounce of resistance. "No, Maggie," he said fiercely. "This is not a lie anymore. We are not a lie. I want to make love to you, my wife. Right now. Will you let me?"

His honor came first, and Maggie knew only a shake of her head would force him to his own separate corner. Dear God, what was wrong with her? Why did she want this man so much after only a few hours of being in his arms? He'd destroy her.

He waited for her decision.

Her body and mind warred, but deep inside, the tiny voice triumphed. Take what you can get now and you'll have the memories. She'd survived much worse. But she didn't think she could survive pushing him away tonight.

She dragged his mouth to hers. He kissed her completely, his tongue tangling with hers as he carried her to the bed. Each movement melted into the next as he stripped off her clothes and explored every part of her body with hands and mouth and tongue. She moaned as he brought her to the brink, stopped, then stripped off his own clothes and started again. She writhed and begged until finally he parted her thighs and paused at her entrance.

As if sensing her innate fear, he immediately rolled her to the side without question, grabbed her hips, and pulled her down onto his shaft.

He filled every aching crevice and she cried out and began moving, frantic for release. His hands rubbed her breasts, flicking the tips, and with one final scrape against her clit she exploded into a thousand pieces.

He cried out her name as they rode out the orgasm,

until she collapsed on top of his chest. His arms came around her and he whispered in her ear. "This is real."

Maggie didn't answer. Her heart wept, and her lips trembled to burst out the words inside of her, screaming to be free. *I love you.* But the taunting whisper reminded her of the only truth she'd ever known. *Not forever. No one could love you forever.*

So she said nothing. Just closed her eyes and slept.

. . .

Michael sat beside the bed with two flutes filled with champagne, watching her sleep. Odd that only yesterday, he'd claimed her for the first time. Usually, once he slept with a woman he cared about, the edge of need dulled a bit more at each encounter, each day, until nothing was left but a lukewarm friendship they both couldn't do anything with. But now, looking down at his new wife, a sense of excitement and rightness coursed through his blood. The same exact feeling he'd embraced on the track, the call of the unknown with a deep knowledge he was meant to drive a race car.

Maggie was meant to be his.

He knew this now. Accepted it. Realized he needed to make some careful moves if he was ever going to convince her they could have a real marriage. Funny, how love seemed this distant, magical thing in the future until you wanted it so bad, you actually pretended feelings were there that never were.

Now he knew. All along, he'd been waiting for Maggie Ryan.

He'd sensed the connection that night of their blind date. Her wit and kick-ass sexuality pummeled him like a sucker punch. She fascinated him on every level, but the lure of something deeper and more permanent sang in his blood, so he'd frozen in fear. He knew once he made love to her he'd never want to let her go. And she was everything he believed he didn't want in a wife. He sensed she'd stomp his heart to tiny pieces, and he'd never recover.

He'd thought of her many times throughout the year, but always pushed her image to the back of his mind, convincing himself they would be an impossible couple. Now, it seemed every step led straight to Rome.

She was his soul mate.

He just needed to convince her.

But in order to do that, he needed to break down some walls. Michael took a deep breath at the task ahead. He'd been thinking of the right course of action to take, but it was a risky move. He wanted to reach her on a deeper level, and her constant unease with him taking control in bed told him she owned secrets that needed to be told. Could she ever trust him enough to share? Could she ever completely surrender?

He was about to find out.

She opened her eyes.

He smiled at that sleepy, satisfied look as she stretched against the pillows. The sheet fell and offered him the tempting sight of her perfect breasts. She grinned. "See anything you like?"

She'd put him in an early grave, but he'd go to heaven with a smile on his face. He shook his head and handed her the glass of champagne. "The letter *C* stands for all the items needed in life," she said. "Coffee, chocolate, and champagne." She sighed with contentment and took another drink.

Michael leaned back in the antique floral chair and smirked. "Aren't you missing the best letter of all?"

"What's that?"

"S. For sex."

Her grin grew wider and more satisfied. His erection rose to full staff and he shifted in the chair. "Oh, Count, when are you going to learn all the American words?" she drawled. "*C* is also for climax."

He burst out in laughter and shook his head. "*Cara,* you are amazing. Both in and out of bed."

"I try." She sipped her champagne, but Michael sensed her guard already solidifying. He needed to move at a steady pace and keep her off balance.

"Maggie, do you like being in control?"

"Is that a bad thing?"

He kept his gaze steady but she refused to lift her

head. "Not at all. You're a strong woman and you wouldn't have made it this far in life without such a quality. I just wondered how you felt about being dominated in bed."

She gasped and her head shot up. "Why? Do you like domination?" She shuddered. "I'm not into that sub stuff, Count. I've read those BDSM novels but whips just don't do it for me."

Dios, he was nuts about her. "No, *cara,* I'm not into pain, either. It seems you prefer to control the lovemaking, which is fine, but I wonder if you've ever truly surrendered."

She narrowed her eyes. "I surrender every time I climax. What are you getting at?"

He went to the bathroom, tugged two of the sashes from the luxurious white robes, and returned to the bed.

"What are you doing?" she asked. "Getting kinky?"

He sat beside her. "Do you trust me, Maggie?"

Wariness skated over her features. "Why?"

"Do you?"

She hesitated. "Yes. I do trust you."

Relief coursed through him at the raw honesty in her voice. "Thank you. I'm asking you to let me do something to you."

"What?"

"Tie you up."

A strangled laugh escaped her lips, but it lacked humor. "Tell me you're joking. Can't we just have regular sex?"

"Yes. But I want more with you. I want to give you so much pleasure you explode. I want you to be able to let go, on your own terms. I'm asking you to trust me enough to surrender your control for tonight. If you get uncomfortable, tell me to stop and I will. Will you do this for me?"

She sat up and stared at the ties, biting down hard on her lip. "I don't know if I can give up control," she admitted.

"I think you can." A smile touched his lips as he dangled the ties out in a teasing gesture meant to calm her nerves. "We can have some fun. I always dreamed of tying up my wife. You can make my fantasy come true."

He waited patiently while she thought the scenario out. Emotions warred and fought for dominance. Finally, she nodded. "I'll try." She blew out an annoyed breath. "But only because you have some bondage fetish I think you need to get out of your system."

He laughed. With deliberate motions, he tied her wrists together over her head with one sash, and with the other, he wrapped them around the post by the headboard. She tugged, and he made sure there was plenty of slack so she wouldn't feel trapped. Just enough to allow her the freedom to let go. His arousal simmered at her naked body.

"Now what?" She blew the hair out of her face and frowned.

Michael grinned at her cranky expression, straddled her, and looked down.

All humor left him in a rush. She was gorgeous—all sleek curves and muscles. Slowly, he leaned over and kissed her deep, plunging into her mouth, thrusting his tongue in and out in a precursor of what he planned to do to her. When he released her lips, she breathed hard, and her eyes misted with arousal.

He took his time. He nibbled and sucked on her nipples and let his hands drift over her belly, her hips, then slide behind her to cup her ass and spread her legs wider. His fingers paused on the nub begging for his touch, then plunged into her channel.

She cried out and pulled at her ties. He pushed her higher, using two fingers to sink into her wet heat while his thumb flicked at her clit. Every muscle beneath him quivered with anticipation, and she writhed on the bed.

"Damn you, untie me! I want to touch you."

"Not yet, *cara*. I am having too much fun with my fantasy."

She cursed him and he laughed, dipped his head, and tasted her.

She came hard. Her scream ripped from her throat, and he allowed her to ride out the wave. When she surfaced, her flushed skin trembled helplessly underneath him. He pushed her thighs wider apart and drove his penis in with one solid thrust.

He gritted his teeth and prayed for control. Her channel clenched him in a tight vise, and spasms shook her body like ministorms. He filled her completely and pure pleasure exploded within him. Slowly, he pressed her down into the mattress.

"Michael." Her glazed eyes suddenly shone in panic, and she bucked beneath him, tugging at the restraints with a frantic motion. "Don't."

The rawness of her fear made him second-guess himself. "Look at me, *mia amore*. Look into my eyes and see who I am."

Her focus sharpened as she gazed deeply into his eyes. Her pupils dilated in recognition, and inch by inch her muscles relaxed, allowing him further access. Tears swam in her eyes. He kissed her tenderly, his thumb wiping away the tear that trickled down her face.

"I love you, Maggie. It's never been Alexa, and it never will be. I'm in love with you."

He moved. Each motion claimed her for himself, told her of his emotions and need for her to belong to him. The last of the fight eased from her body and she matched him thrust for thrust, her heels digging into his back as they climbed higher and higher. She exploded beneath him and he let himself go. The unbearable pleasure wrecked him, overtook him, and threw him over the edge. When the storm finally passed, Michael realized his life would never be the same.

And he didn't want it to be.

. . .

He loved her.

The words echoed over and over in her head. Sometimes as beautiful as opera. Sometimes with a cackle of merriment and mocking. Either way, she needed to deal with it, but Lord knows she was too freaked out at the moment.

She flexed her now freed hands. He held her with more tenderness than a man had ever shown her. His lovemaking seemed less about kink and more about giving her everything, and asking for the same.

She swallowed past the words bubbling up on her lips and remained silent. Just three simple words, but they were the most difficult words she could think of to utter. His sweat-dampened skin pressed against hers, solid and real. He'd given her a gift that had no price. Trust. Somehow, with her being tied up and forced to surrender, she learned to trust another human being.

He dropped a gentle kiss to her tangled hair. "Thank you for giving me your trust. I want to know all of you, *cara,* but I can wait."

His patience rattled her foundation. Why did he seek more than her body? His confession he never loved Alexa rang clean and true. Perhaps she'd always sensed the truth but didn't want to lose her final obstacle. Now there was nowhere to run, yet she couldn't say those three words he needed.

Maggie closed her eyes and gave him the only other gift she had left. Her truth.

"I was sixteen. I was crushing majorly on the cliché of all clichés—the quarterback of the football team. Of course, he barely noticed me, but I did all the usual girly things to gain his attention. One day, he came over and talked to me. Days later, he asked me out. I was giddy and believed we'd finally be boyfriend and girlfriend."

His hand stopped stroking her hair. Slowly, he turned to face her in bed. She felt his gaze caress her, but she stared up at the ceiling as the events unwound before her vision.

"I made myself up with lots of makeup. Short skirt, lots of cleavage showing the little I had. I had no one to chaperone me at the time, so I came and went as I pleased with no rules.

"He took me to a movie, then back to the school at the football field. We sat on the grass and looked up at the moon. I was so happy. Until he pushed me down on the ground and stuck his hand up my shirt. You see, I was all talk and no action. I'd never dated a guy before, never even had a crazy make-out session. I let him do some things because I thought it was the right thing to do. Until he pulled down my skirt."

She gulped a breath, and his hand clasped hers. He waited in silence as she struggled, but his warmth slowly seeped into her skin. "He raped me. Afterward, he rolled away, stood up, and said he was disappointed. Told me I'd been looking for it with my clothes and my attitude. That if I told anyone, I'd be the laughingstock of the school. I got my clothes on and he took me home. When he got to my house, he told me thanks for the good time. Let's do it again.

"I got out of the car and my mother was watching television in the living room. I went straight over to her and told her the whole story."

The events of that horrible night rolled over her, but this time, someone lay beside her. This time, someone cared enough to listen.

"My mother laughed and told me I got what I asked for. Said to get on birth control, get smarter, and deal with it. Then she walked away from me." Maggie ripped her gaze away from the blank ceiling and turned toward him. "I didn't know what to do. Felt like I could go insane. I took the next few days off, then went back to school. And when I passed him in the hall, I just nodded a hello. The pregnancy test came back negative. I got on birth control. And suddenly, I realized I had two paths before me and I needed to choose.

"I could hide my sexuality behind baggy clothes and never feel comfortable being physical with a boy again. Or I could push past it and own my own stuff. Somehow, I realized I could get pleasure from sex, but it would be up to me to set the terms. I'd be sure something like that would never happen again."

Her heart pounded on the verge of an attack. "I decided I wouldn't let that bastard take away who I was. I dressed the way I wanted, and I controlled who I had sex with from that time on. When I wanted, where I wanted, and how I wanted. But sometimes, when a man is on top of me, something flashes back to that time and I panic. I hate it, but I can't seem to control that part of my memory. Until now."

Michael reached out and tucked her head against his chest. Strength and heat and safety wound its way through her with a seamless grace that took her breath away. "I am so sorry, *cara*. I didn't know. If I had, I wouldn't have pushed in such a way."

She shook her head hard. "No, I'm glad you did. Now, I'm not afraid."

He sucked in a breath, and she realized he trembled beneath her. Slowly, she raised her head to look into his face.

Fierce pride and raw fury shimmered in his eyes. His hands were as gentle as a butterfly as he stroked the hair back from her face. "For someone to hurt you like this makes me question what is fair and right in this world. But you, *mia amore*, took such an event and gained strength. You made your life on your own terms with no one to help. You humble me."

She bit her lip and lowered her head back on his chest. His words echoed in the silence of the room and exploded the last brick of the wall guarding her heart. He didn't comment on the tear that fell upon his chest.

That made Maggie love him even more.

Chapter Twelve

Two days later, Maggie lounged on the back terrace, sipping a glass of wine and stroking Dante. He lay on the table, basking in the heat of the sun, grunting softly. He flipped over and exposed his massive belly, his favorite place to be scratched. Every time her hand got tired she'd stop, but then he'd hiss at her in pure menace that she now knew was completely fake.

"You're such a drama king," she admonished.

Those huge green eyes stared at her with implacable demand and crankiness. She let out an impatient sigh and put down her glass. She raked her nails lightly over his belly and he went back to purring so loudly he sounded like a chain saw. "Fine, fine, here, happy now?"

God, she hated cats.

Of course, like Dante, she was a big fat liar. This feline had worked its way under her skin. A cheap thrill skated through her that the stray wouldn't let anyone touch him except for her. In a wacky way, she felt as if they belonged to each other. Two stray, bad-ass loners who didn't know how to handle people.

What was she going to do?

Michael loved her. Ever since his shattering admission and her shattering confession, they'd silently agreed not to discuss the topic further. Maggie wanted to believe him, craved the ability to say the words back, but something held her prisoner.

Her past.

The sunlight struck the two-carat diamond on her ring finger and shimmered in mockery.

She needed to make a decision soon. She agreed to stay a few days longer while they made sure Mama Conte was okay, and they could get Venezia's wedding plans solidified.

She had never told anyone except her mother about the rape. Her mother's betrayal killed a trust deep inside of her, and Michael brought it back to life. Goose bumps lifted her arms at the memory of his hands and mouth and tongue on every part of her body without the ability to do anything but surrender. Damn, now she knew why that bondage stuff was so widely read.

Dante leered as if he knew her thoughts, kicked her

hand away, and stretched into a different position. "Yeah, I bet you're a male stud, knocking up all the helpless females around town," she pointed out to him. "Take some responsibility for your actions, buddy. I think I need to take you to the vet and get you fixed."

"Are you talking to the cat?"

Maggie turned her head and fought a blush. Carina stood with her arms crossed, laughing at her. "Of course not," she denied hotly. "You're hearing things."

She snickered. "Yeah, sure. Hi, Dante." She took a few steps closer, her hand held out, a low, soothing tone wrapping around the cat. He watched her slow approach and Maggie and Carina held their breath.

With a disgusted hiss, he jumped up, swished his tail, and disappeared into the bushes. Carina's mouth dropped open. Maggie hid her satisfied expression and sipped her wine. "Why doesn't he like me?" she whined. "I love animals. I feed him. You insult him and he adores you."

Maggie shrugged. "Men are fickle. What's going on?"

"We're going into town to look at flowers. Wanna come?"

Maggie wrinkled her nose. "Boring. I'll pass."

Carina giggled. "I know, I'm not a flower kind of girl myself, but since you're still new to the family, you can get out of these things." She let out a sigh. "Fine, be a brat. I'll see you a bit later. Mama's resting but doing fine." A confused expression flitted over her face. "It's really weird, too.

As soon as you guys left, she had all this energy, was back to her old self, and seemed fine. The doctor came again and said the whole thing must have been a false alarm."

"Huh. Weird, but at least she's better."

"Yeah, you're right. See you later."

Carina left and Maggie sat for a while longer, basking in the heat and the silence. She needed to find Michael. With the house empty, it was time they talked. She drained the last of her wine for liquid courage and went inside the house.

She peeked through some of the rooms, then caught his deep voice from the study. She stopped outside the door and paused before knocking. Maybe she'd wait outside until—

"No, Max, she didn't marry me for my money. She makes enough on her own. You are like an overprotective mama, *mia amico*."

He paused, then spoke with a coldness that gave her a chill. "You did what? Hiring a private detective to check on her background is unacceptable. Yes, I know about her past. She is unlike her parents. *Merda,* do not challenge me on this; she is my wife now."

More silence.

"No, I don't think children will happen for a while—she needs some time. She is not the typical woman I wanted to marry but things change. I can wait." Maggie heard his footsteps back and forth. "This is my decision and I no longer want to discuss it. I will make this work."

The conversation went on a bit longer while she hid in the corridor. Humiliation burned until her skin actually prickled. Max didn't believe she was good enough for his best friend. What had the detective told him? That her parents were a joke and she had no experience with a healthy relationship? Within minutes of meeting her, Max realized the truth she'd been desperately trying to hide.

She was only a shell of a woman. Michael deserved more. He needed someone with an open heart and no complications. A woman his family didn't have to train; one who loved cats and children and cooking.

Not a woman like her. One with a crappy past, a bruised heart, and an inability to love.

She backed up slowly as the panic attack threatened. Turned. Then she heard him.

"Ah, *la mia tigrotta,* would you like to go for a walk with me? It is a beautiful evening."

His musical, rich voice caressed her skin and tempted her to forget.

The truth slammed through her.

She couldn't pretend anymore. Not with him. Not with herself.

Maggie stared up at her husband and made the only decision she could.

"Michael, I'm going home."

He blinked and reached out, but she jerked back. He

frowned. "What's the matter, Maggie? Did something happen?"

"I want to go home alone."

"Is this about us?" He grabbed her arm and leaned in. "Are you running scared because I confessed my feelings? I know we didn't talk about it right away, but I thought I'd give you some time."

She yanked her arm away and sneered. "Don't do me any favors, Count. Let's just say I'm sick of the lies, and I want my life back. Not this fake life. This fake marriage." She flung her hands up and encompassed the room. "This is all bullshit! We've been playing a part, pretending to be married, then forced into a real marriage when there's no way it'll work. We're too different. I don't want this!" she cried out. "I don't want overbearing sisters, and stray cats, and forced baking lessons! I don't want to feel strangled all the time under the weight of responsibility. I like being free and making my own choices. So it's time we both wake up and stop playing at a damn movie of the week."

A muscle ticked in his jaw. The anger swirled with pain and only enraged her further. "Did my words mean nothing to you?" he asked furiously. "I told you I loved you. Did that mean nothing?"

She stuck out her chin. Met his gaze dead-on. "Your words meant nothing."

She turned on her heel to leave. He made a move to stop her but she spit like Dante and bared her teeth.

"Leave me alone; can't you see I don't want this anymore? I don't want you or this awful lifestyle your real wife would inherit! Have some pride, for God's sake."

This time, he let her go.

She raced down the hall, seeking shelter to lick her wounds before her speedy departure. She'd walk into town, leave her belongings, and get them at a later date. Other than her camera, everything else was replaceable. Better to get out now before she faced his sisters. Michael could come up with some excuse.

With leaden feet, she grabbed her camera, purse, and cell phone. She made some quick calls and left the only home that ever made her feel like she belonged. The only home that ever made her feel loved.

Maggie didn't look back.

• • •

"What's going on?"

Maggie sat in the living room and stared at her best friend. Alexa rocked the baby on one hip, the standard drool cloth tossed over her shoulder, while Lily babbled and squealed as she stared at the puppy playing by her mother's feet. The small golden ball of fur pawed at her slipper-clad toes and scampered back and forth every time Alexa moved away.

Old Yeller, the ugly hound Alexa convinced Nick to

keep more than a year ago, lay in the small patch of sun leaking through the window and watched the puppy with an air of disapproval. The familiar blue and orange Mets bandanna wrapped around his neck gave off a distinguished appearance unheard of for a once mangy stray.

Maggie tried to avoid the subject. "I can't believe you got a puppy. Nick hates messes."

Alexa let out an impatient breath and danced out of the fur ball's reach. "Oh, I didn't do it this time. Nick was coming home from the waterfront and found Simba in the woods, crying. Bruises all over the poor thing's body. Must have been thrown out of a moving car."

Maggie winced. "I can't believe he didn't take it to the shelter. What have you done to my brother?"

Alexa laughed and bounced in time to the hip-hop music streaming from the surround-sound speakers. Simba growled in delight and tried to keep up with the moves. Lily giggled. "First he took the dog to the vet, then brought it home while demanding I don't get attached. He said he'd put an ad in the paper and find the dog a home." She shrugged. "So I let him. After a week, the ad disappeared and we never spoke about it again. He says hello to the puppy before me when he gets home from work."

Longing washed through Maggie. She missed that stupid cat and the way he'd roll over and demand his belly be scratched. She missed Carina's bouncy eagerness, and Julietta's crisp business attitude, and Venezia's dramatic outbursts. She missed Michael's mother's quiet insistence in the kitchen, the smell of baking, and drinking coffee on the terrace.

She missed her husband.

Maggie concentrated on breathing and struggled through the raw pain. One day at a time. She'd be okay; she was a survivor. But who knew surviving was so much less than living?

"Well, you can thank him properly because I got you a present." Maggie tossed her friend the silky red negligee. "No details, please. Still too weird for you to shag my brother."

Alexa laughed and examined the gorgeous piece of lace and silk in one hand. "Thanks, babe, it's just what we needed tonight. Besides a babysitter."

"I'll take her one night this week so you can have a date night. I'm not going on any other trips for a while."

Maggie flexed her hands. Her naked ring finger flashed in mockery, and she hurriedly clasped her hands in her lap.

Alexa studied her for a long while. Her voice was soft and comforting when she finally spoke. "Maggie, you have to tell me the truth. What's going on?"

She shrugged. "Went to Italy. Saw Michael. Back now. Nothing else to tell."

"Michael came to see me."

Her head shot up and she gasped. "What? What did he tell you?"

Alexa marched over to the playpen, placed Lily in, kicked Simba gently off her leg, and joined her on the couch. Her blue eyes held a mixture of sympathy and support. "Michael told me everything, Maggie. About going to Italy and pretending to be his wife. About the priest making it real. And how he confessed his feelings to you but you ran away and threw them back in his face."

Literal red blazed before her eyes from the sheer lies he'd uttered. She trembled and tried to speak rationally. "He didn't give you the whole story, Alexa."

"Then why don't you?" Hurt shimmered in her face. "You're my best friend."

Maggie grabbed her hands and held tight. The tears threatened, then held. "I'm so sorry. I had a plan, but the whole thing misfired and now it's a mess. I made Michael a bargain—I'd pretend to be his wife if he promised to stay away from you. I know he has deep feelings, and I was worried about you and Nick. He agreed, but when we got to Italy, things got complicated."

"I cannot believe you are still stuck on this idea. There's never been anything between us but friendship."

"I know that now."

"What happened? You started to fall for him?"

Maggie nodded. "At first I thought it was just sex. But then his family sucked me in, and the stupid cat, and then we had more sex and I began to get crazy ideas about a relationship between us. He told me he loved me."

Alexa squeezed Maggie's fingers. "And what did you say?"

"Nothing. I couldn't say anything, because I didn't really believe him. I was going to talk about it, but then I heard him on the phone with his friend Max." She took a breath. "He didn't believe I was good enough for Michael. Thought we were a terrible match, and he's right."

Alexa gasped. "When have you ever listened to anyone's opinion?"

Maggie shook her head stubbornly. "I heard the conversation. I'm not right for him—I'm not the type of woman he needs. He wants a big family with pets and constant trips to Italy. He wants a nice, solid wife with a respectable career and a sweet manner. We fight. And I hate all those things."

"Oh, Maggie." Alexa gripped Maggie's hands as tears filled her eyes. "My dear friend, don't you know you *are* all those things? When are you finally going to believe it? Just your loyalty toward Nick and me and your willingness to protect us tells me you were meant to have a family of your own. Michael is a complicated man—something not many other women see or even know is there. But you do. You challenge him, and push him, and make him feel things more intensely. When he came to tell me everything, his heart was broken. He believes you don't love him, can never love him, and he's destroyed."

Maggie fought tears. God, the idea of Michael hurt

tore her to shreds. She loved him so fiercely, yet she knew Alexa couldn't see the truth.

She needed so much more. Funny how she never believed she was worth the demand before. But Michael had changed her. In allowing herself to fall in love with him, she knew she'd always need to be with a man who felt the same way. Anything else may break her.

"I'm sorry, Al. I want to move on with my life and I never want to talk about Michael Conte again. If you're truly my friend, you'll do this for me." Her voice broke. "Please."

Alexa let out an annoyed breath. "But—"

"Please."

She pressed her lips together. Then nodded. "Okay. I just want you to be happy, Maggie."

The bleakness of her future descended on her like a cloud, and she forced a smile to her lips. "I'll be okay. Now, let's talk about something else."

The rest of the hours passed and for a little while, Maggie pretended everything was back to normal.

• • •

Michael sat behind his desk and stared at his notes on the opening ceremony. In two days, his dream for his family and La Dolce Famiglia would finally come true. The first chain of bakeries would be revealed Friday night in a lavish presentation and party to rival all others.

The weather should hold, promising a beautiful crisp spring day with lots of sun. The bakery was prepared to fling open its doors with a variety of desserts, special coffees, and fresh breads. The downtown waterfront was a dream for a few investors who saw a vision like no other.

This should be the happiest week of his life.

Instead, grief wracked his body and tortured his heart. He decided to tell Alexa the truth in an effort to see if there was a way to reach Maggie. How her words had shred him, and her speedy departure only confirmed her harsh confession. She didn't want him. Didn't love him. And didn't want the life he could offer her.

The night had been a mess. He'd spun a crazy tale of a sick uncle and had to play the proper part to convince his mother and sisters everything was okay. He left the next day and had his driver deliver the luggage she left behind. Michael pressed his fingers against his aching temple. *Dios,* what a mess. He'd finally fallen in love, and the woman didn't even want him. How would he ever get over her?

Her image taunted him nonstop. The way she surrendered in his arms and shattered with climax. The way she bullied him, and laughed with him, and challenged him at every step. The tenderness she showed his family, and the way she catered to Dante, though she swore she disliked him. Contradictory and loving to a fault, she was meant to be his. He never confessed his past to other women. No woman had ever dug deep enough to even bother to ask about his dreams. But Maggie understood, acknowledged, and supported him.

A deep grief beat within his heart, and needing to drown it, he quickly reached for the bottle of cognac and poured himself a glass. The burning liquid slid down his throat with ease and exploded in his belly. Maybe if he got rip-roaring drunk, he could finally sleep without images of her naked and open beneath him.

His cell rang. He muttered a curse and looked at the ID. Paused a moment. Then hit the button. "Alexa? Is everything okay?"

He listened for a long time as she spoke. Suddenly, the jagged pieces slid together and fit. His heart sped up, and he stood from his chair as his friend detailed the conversation. A plan formed, and he knew what he needed to do.

It would be his last stand, but she was worth fighting for.

He only hoped it would be enough.

. . .

Maggie stood in the crowd near Alexa and watched the ceremony take place. Her luggage had arrived on her doorstep yesterday. A simple note came attached to the handle in his elegant scrawl.

I will adhere to our bargain and file the necessary papers to dissolve the marriage.

She ignored the disappointment and concentrated on the satisfaction that her family would be left alone. The emptiness in her gut drove her to reach for the phone and set up some jobs overseas. She needed to get out of New York and keep busy. She'd arrive in London by the end of the week. Maybe she needed lots of distance to heal.

Distinguished sailboats and water ferries cut their way gracefully through the water, lending to the perfect backdrop of the buildings. The designs all seemed to flow with the majestic mountains and water, the lines fluid and sleek and low, enhancing rather than blocking nature's view. Limestone lent a cool, fresh air to the spa, and the lush gardens snuck around each of the buildings set up with benches, sculptures, and trickling fountains. The sushi restaurant boasted an ancient Japanese tearoom, and the bamboo walls and gorgeous red silks blended in a visual feast of the senses. Bright murals had been painted on the old brick walls that once housed a broken-down train station. Fully restored, the waterfront now reminded her of what creativity, TLC, and a little money could accomplish.

La Dolce Famiglia was the final store to be revealed. A sprawling cloth with the logo imprinted on it covered the building, the ropes ready to drop at the sign from Michael. The crowd stirred with excitement, and the band struck up with dramatic flourish.

Alexa hooted and hollered when Nick cut the red ribbon, and Maggie joined in as pride rushed through her.

Nick had worked hard and believed in his vision to transform the waterfront into something beautiful. He believed in his dreams. Maybe it was time she did the same. She may not get the man she loved, but she had the ability to change her career for a deeper satisfaction. After flipping through the photos she'd taken in Bergamo, an inner calling to shoot something more meaningful rose within her. Usually she ignored such instincts. This time, she decided to explore her need to capture some of the beauty in the world with her own unique vision. She planned day trips around her regular shoots, and made arrangements to meet with some magazine editors in England she knew to discuss some new options for her work.

Michael stepped up to the raised podium. Her heart tripped. Every cell in her body screamed for the right to smooth back his hair, touch his hard cheek, and revel in this moment with him. Dressed in an elegant charcoal suit with a purple tie, he took up the entire stage with his presence and immediately quieted the crowd. His dark good looks and sexy brooding stare made the women around her giggle and chatter. Maggie fought the primitive instinct to tell them to back off. Instead, she remained silent.

"Ladies and gentlemen," he said into the mic, "I'm pleased to be with you to finally reveal the culmination of a family dream. My family built their first bakery in Bergamo, Italy, with pastries cooked out of my mama's kitchen. With a lot of hard work, the Contes opened stores throughout Milan, and always dreamed of coming to America to share our recipes. That dream is finally here, and I thank all of you for sharing it with us."

People clapped and roared. He went on to thank Nick and Dreamscape Enterprises, his business partners, and a variety of other members who helped along the way. Then he paused. Looked out into the crowd. And stabbed her with his gaze.

Maggie caught her breath.

His eyes seethed with emotion. He spoke as if they were alone, each word drilling into her mind and her heart with a deliberate intimacy that made shivers run down her spine. "Family is very important to me. This is something I believe in. The name of La Dolce Famiglia is a sign of my beliefs and my pride in what I hold dear. In what I love above nothing else."

Her palms grew damp as she stood rooted to the ground, transfixed by his voice and his eyes and his presence.

"I have now discovered a new type of family. I have fallen in love with an incredible woman, one who made me believe in happily ever after. One who cracked my world open and made me whole. But, alas, she does not believe me. Words are not enough to convince her that I need her in my life. That she makes me whole. Therefore, I am proud to reveal my new bakery, and a new chain to open in America, where I have met the woman I want to be my wife."

With a nod, the ropes tugged, then released.

The elaborate scrolling sign with bold letters proudly displayed the name.

La Dolce Maggie.

The blood pumped through her veins, and the world blurred, tilted, and held. She blinked and turned her head toward Alexa, who fiercely held her arms and gave her a tiny shake.

"Don't you understand, Maggie?" she asked with tears shining in her bright blue eyes. "He loves you. It was always you—but you have to be brave enough to reach for it. You have to believe you're worth it. That's what you told me the day Nick confessed his love for me, remember? If you love someone, you fight for them, again and again. My best friend is not a coward. You deserve this. You deserve love."

Like a vampire coming back to life after a deep sleep, suddenly she saw every color and shape slide into sharp focus. Her senses exploded, and she began walking through the crowds, making her way to the stage, where Michael waited for her.

He met her halfway. She studied his beautiful face, the full curve of his lip, the shadowed stubble over his chin, the crooked nose, the seething heat in his onyx eyes. He cupped her face between large, hard hands and pressed his forehead against hers. His breath rushed warm over her mouth.

"My Maggie, *mia amore,* I love you. I want to live with you, grow old, and have *bambinos* with you. You wrecked me. Completely. I could never settle for another woman because I'd be bored out of my mind. Don't you understand? I don't want the typical wife you think would make me happy, because you were meant for me, all of you. Your sarcasm, and wit, and sexiness, and honesty. You belong with me, and I won't give up until I finally convince you. *Capisce*?"

She choked back a sob and reached for him.

His lips came down on hers and he kissed her deeply, as the roar of approval from the crowds echoed in her ears. Her heart expanded in her chest and settled. A sense of peace and homecoming flooded through her, and she finally believed.

"I love you, Michael Conte," she whispered fiercely when his lips released hers. "And I want it all. With you, your family, your bakeries, everything. I've always loved you, but I was too afraid to take it."

He kissed her again. Michael grabbed her and lifted her high, laughing in joy. She stood wrapped up in the tight circle of his arms, finally complete.

With her own home and happy ending.

Epilogue

"**M**aggie, hurry up! The movers are here!"

She grumbled under her breath and looked once more upon the empty rooms of her condo, making sure she hadn't missed anything. Moving into a mansion wasn't easy. Hell, they'd already fought over placement of things and room arrangements. She licked her lips when she thought of all the lovely ways they had made up, also. Many rooms had been christened.

Fortunately, there were many more to go.

"Coming!" she screamed.

With one last glance at the bare mattress still lying on her bed, she paused as a memory took hold. Maggie walked over to the bed and stuck her hand underneath the mattress.

The list.

The love spell.

She gazed at the white ledger paper and unfolded it to look at her list. Thank God, Michael hadn't seen it; she would've died of humiliation. Shaking her head at the ridiculousness of her actions, she glanced down at the list of items she had requested Earth Mother provide her in her husband. The qualities blurred together as her gaze slid over the paper.

A man with a sense of loyalty.

A man with a sense of family.

A man who is a good lover.

A man who can be my friend.

A man who can challenge me.

A man I can confess my secrets to.

A man I can trust.

A man with confidence.

A man with an open heart.

A man who will fight for me.

A man who can love me exactly as I am.

Maggie caught her breath. She reread the list, an odd sense of foreboding washing over her. Drunk, defenses down, and lonely; the qualities on this list would never have been composed in her rational mind. No, every item cried out for someone who could complete her.

Michael. Earth Mother had sent her Michael Conte.

The diamond ring shot icy glimmers of light as she carefully folded up the paper and crumbled it in her hand.

Ridiculous. She was getting herself spooked. There was no such thing as Earth Mother. The perfect man and love spells didn't exist.

Right?

Warily, she decided to throw out the book of spells. Where had she put that purple book?

Carina.

When they'd returned home from the waterfront the evening of their reconciliation, Maggie was shocked to find Carina on Michael's doorstep. The best part was the massive ball of black fur she held against her chest.

As soon as Dante spotted Maggie, he'd jumped out of Carina's arms and into hers like he belonged there. Carina confessed that once she'd told Dante she wanted to take him to see Maggie, he walked right into the cat carrier like he understood. And maybe he had.

Her family complete, Maggie realized what it meant to fully belong to others and swore she'd never forget it. Still, she didn't like the idea of her new sister holding on to a book of spells that may actually work.

She nibbled on her bottom lip and wondered if she should say something.

Nah, what were the odds? It was a silly little thing, and Carina would probably read it, get a laugh, and throw it away.

Maggie shook her head and left the room and her old life behind her.

Acknowledgments

Since *The Marriage Bargain* hit the *New York Times* and *USA Today* bestseller lists, I have been overwhelmed by the amazing support of readers and my fellow writers. There are just too many to thank here, but every time I need a laugh, or to share a good or bad moment, you are there. Here's the short list: Wendy S. Marcus, Aimee Carson, Megan Mulry, Janet Lane Walters, Liz Matis, Barbara T. Wallace, Abbi Wilder, and Julia Brooks. Shout-out to Tiffany Reisz for being my deadline buddy!

To the fabulous crew I met and celebrated with at RT and RWA 2012. All the Harlequin authors were amazing and fun and there are too many to name here personally! Special shout-out goes to Megan Mulry for drinking champagne with me when I discovered I hit the *Times;* Cat

Schield and Barbara Longley for hanging with us at the gangster ball; Katee Roberts for her energy and humor; Caridad Pinerio for being so sweet at the book signing; and Catherine Bybee for talking shop. I can't wait to do it again!

Finally, to the amazing Entangled crew who blow me away with their talent and efficiency, and my new Gallery Books team who welcomed me with open arms and amazed me with their skills—you rock!

Keep reading for an exclusive sneak peek of

searching for beautiful

Book Three in *New York Times*
bestselling author Jennifer Probst's
Searching For series

On sale from Gallery/Pocket Books
in May 2015!

one

She had to get out of here.

Genevieve MacKenzie bent at the waist and tried to gulp in air. The filmy, delicate veil brushed her face like a dozen fingers bent on tickle torture. Panic clawed at her gut, and she reached up and ripped off the pearl-encrusted lace, placed her hands on her knees, and prayed for sanity.

She was getting married. Right now. In five minutes. Her family stood outside the door, excited and chattering as they waited for her to emerge in all her pristine white glory. David posed at the front of the church in his tux, with the priest and his best man flanking his side. She imagined his beautifully tousled golden hair, killer smile, and sparkling green eyes. Perfect, as usual. While she was getting dressed, a delivery had arrived at the house. Two dozen white roses with just the faintest tinge of pink in the centers. The card read: *I cannot wait until you are finally mine.*

Her bridal party sighed with pleasure. Her twin sister, Isabella, rolled her eyes and clutched her neck in mockery of gagging to death. She'd been quietly shushed by the others while everyone held their breath, hoping she'd remain manageable until at least after the ceremony. It had been a rocky road between the sisters, so that Izzy even bothered to don a bridesmaid dress was a miracle. Gen's best friend, Kate, hurriedly put the roses in water until they stood straight and proud in the center of the dining room table amid a group of giggling, excited women. Her sister Alexa teased her husband about not receiving a thing on her big day, which brought on a tirade of groaning from Nick and her dad whining about how reality television had given women false expectations of real romance.

Gen kept smiling, murmured the correct responses, and held the card in a death grip. Then she ran to the bathroom, trying desperately not to vomit.

Not the best reaction for a bride-to-be. Of course, she chalked it up to nerves, ignored her nausea, and got her ass into the stretch limo. She nodded and responded to her chattering bridal party. As the limousine gobbled up the miles and sped toward the church, her brain clicked over the final details, worrying if she missed anything. David hated sloppiness of any sort, and with almost three hundred guests, it was an important enough event to guarantee press and some high-society attendees. She'd wanted a wedding planner, but David insisted on keeping it private and personal. Of course she agreed; it would be nice to say they did it all themselves instead of relying on a stranger. Exhaustion beat into her bones, but Gen pushed it back. Yes, she'd done absolutely everything, triple-checking each detail for the past few days nonstop.

From the apricot bridesmaid dresses in silk so light the fabric shimmered, to the exquisite ribbon-wrapped orchids, the bridal party was breathtaking. The venue had been almost impossible to secure without the right contacts on just a year's notice. The castle in Tarrytown boasted stunning gardens, soaring architecture with vaulted ceilings, a banquet hall to rival Buckingham Palace, and French cuisine. Sure, she would've rather be married at Mohonk Mountain House near her parents in a more relaxed, fun atmosphere, but at least David agreed to the church ceremony. And she'd won the argument insisting Izzy stay in the wedding. David may not approve of her, but Gen stood her ground, and now her entire family was by her side.

The limo pulled in. She ducked her head against the flash of photographers, and Kate helped her with the massive pearl-encrusted train spilling onto the sidewalk. The Vera Wang gown was ridiculously pricey and reminded her of someone else, but it was the stuff princesses and brides were made of. Lace, tulle, diamonds, and pearls. Too bad she couldn't breathe.

She kept it together in the back room of the church while her mother cried, straightened her veil, and told her she'd never been more proud. Alexa beamed with joy, and her beautiful niece, Lily, looked like a fairy princess with her basket of petals and mini ballroom dress to match the bride's. Her other niece, Taylor, glowed in her junior bridal dress, a delicate pale pink exactly like the center of the roses. Gina, her sister-in-law, winked and announced the bride needed a moment alone before walking down the aisle. Gen almost sagged with relief, and finally the door shut. Blessed silence filled the room.

Everything was perfect, just like it should be.

Perfect. Like David always wanted it.

Gen panted and tried to get herself together. The murmur of voices and organ music drifted from the door. She stumbled to the gorgeously painted stained-glass window of Madonna and child and yanked on the knob. Stuck. Dizziness threatened. Crapola, she needed air, right now. Her French manicured fingers wrapped around the old-fashioned handle and pulled frantically. Light exploded off the pristine diamond weighing down her knuckle. Finally, a few inches opened up and she bent her head toward the gap, sucking in hot air. Why oh why did she have to wait until now to completely freak out? Maybe all the wedding stress had finally gotten to her. She'd open the door, walk down the aisle with her head held high, and say her vows. She loved David. Who wouldn't? He treated her like a queen, told her every day how much she meant to him, and pushed her to be better. Always better. They'd be the envied power couple of their time—surgeons who saved lives, attended charity functions, and changed the world. They were madly in love.

I can't wait until you are finally mine.

A shiver crept down her spine. She looked down at the flawless three-carat diamond ring that shimmered around her finger. A symbol of ownership. Once she committed herself, it would truly be forever. He'd never let her go.

Run.

The inner voice that had been squashed for

so long in fear of retaliation rose up from her gut and screamed one last word. Gen clutched at the windowsill. Ridiculous. She couldn't run.

Right? People only did that in the movies. Besides, she couldn't do that to David.

Run.

The past two years with David taught her to sift through her rioting emotions and connect with the core of rationality that hid in every person's center. Her fiancé despised messiness, impulse, and decisions based on emotion. He cited death and destruction time and again, until she'd finally managed to quiet that crazy voice that had once sung in freedom, slightly off-key but always joyous. Gen figured she'd beaten it back so hard, in fear and determination, that she'd never hear from it again. But of course, with her lousy luck, it had taken this moment of all moments to reassert its independence and general brattiness.

Run before it's too late.

Her brain spun in a mad rush. Not much time left. Once her family came in, it was over. They'd calm her down, term it bridal jitters, and escort her down the aisle. She'd marry David. And she'd never be the same again.

Which would be good, right? She wanted marriage. Forever. Commitment. With David.

Gen looked behind at the closed door. The action she took in the next few seconds would set her on a course that would change the rest of her life. She didn't have time to go over the checks and balances, advantages and disadvantages, and make a neat statistical chart. Instead, she dug deep into her gut that had served her well when faced with a child bleeding on her table: life-and-death decisions that even David couldn't make her stop because it made up the center of her soul. A future surgeon. A woman. A survivor.

Run.

Gen didn't waste another moment.

Breathing hard, heart pounding, she shoved the crank around and around until it wouldn't budge another inch. The window gaped halfway open. The judging eyes of baby Jesus beamed down at her. She could do this. For the first time it paid to be Hobbit size. Gen stuck her upper body through the window, leaned forward, and wriggled her way to freedom.

two

Wolfe lit up the cigarette and looked around guiltily. Damn, this one vice killed him every time. Sawyer would get pissed, and Julietta would do that disappointed stare thing she nailed so well. But they were still in Italy, miles away, and would never know. They might not be his legal stepparents, but they'd saved him, given him a new life, and he loved them like they were his own blood. Just one cigarette and he'd throw away the rest of the pack.

The smoke hit his lungs and immediately calmed his nerves. No one would catch him anyway; the ceremony was about to start. He should be up front and center with the rest of Gen's family, with a big grin on his face as he watched his best friend commit herself to an asshole. And he would. In a few minutes. Right now, he wanted a beat of silence and a smoke before he had to fake his way through the rest of the evening and pretend he was ecstatic.

Guilt nipped at him. He was such a jerk. After all, David Riscetti was perfect for Gen, and just about worthy enough to marry her. Wasn't the guy's fault Wolfe couldn't get rid of that nagging instinct something was off. Wolfe used to catch him looking at Gen with such possessive pride, like he was appraising a racehorse rather than a capable, independent woman. And the way he ordered her around pissed him off, too. But Gen never said she didn't like it, and only had nice things to say about him. Hell, she loved him enough to get hitched, so who was he to judge? Wolfe knew nothing about relationships.

If he delved deep and played therapist, he was probably irritated Gen replaced him. For almost five years, they'd hung out together at bars, watched movies, and did general best-friend stuff. There wasn't a woman in the world who didn't want money, favors, or sex from him. Except Gen. Hell, the moment they'd met something clicked between them. She was as genuine and real as Julietta and the rest of the women in his adopted family. They had just liked each other from the get-go, and when the hell does that ever happen?

Of course, David frowned upon their relationship from day one, and over the past year, Gen made more excuses not to see him in order to soothe her fiancé.

Whatever. He needed to get over it.

Wolfe held back a whiny sigh. The church bells rang once. Twice. The limos were parked at the curb, and a few reporters lingered on the steps. Guess the surgeon was a big shot in the news because no one else pulled in such a crowd. He moved backward a few feet, not in the mood to meet and greet any latecomers. The crooked pavement and shaded archways shielded him from any prying observers. He enjoyed the last of his cigarette, pulled at the confines of his tuxedo, and tried not to scrape the polished sole of his dress shoes. Even after working in the corporate and modeling worlds, he always craved his workout clothes and still felt like he was an intruder in his own body in suits. Or designer underwear that cost more than someone's yearly salary. Who would've thought? Scrambling for food and shelter one day. At the top of *Fortune*'s up-and-coming millionaires the next, all at twenty-fucking-six years old.

He beat back the nasty thoughts that threatened to swamp him and got his head back in the game. It was Gen's wedding day and he needed to be there for her. Not smoking like a chump and playing self-pity games. Wolfe crushed the butt under his heel, adjusted his cuffs, and turned.

"Holy shit."

He stared in shock at the sight before him.

The bride lay in a tangle of limbs, sprawled out on the pavement. The white cloud of lace and dozens of pearly jewels floated around her in a swarm of glory. His heart stopped, stuttered, and kicked back into gear. Jesus, she was gorgeous. Gen had always been an attractive female by all standards, but now she looked as delicate as a doll perched on a wedding cake. She must've ripped off her veil because her elaborate twist hairdo lay drunkenly to the side with pins sticking out. The humidity kicked her curls into gear, and already they were springing wild, refusing to be tamed. Snapping blue eyes glared at him, framed in black liner and some sparkly shadow. She never wore makeup. But today, those stunning navy eyes dominated her heart-shaped face with a sultry, sexy air he rarely spotted from her. Four-inch stiletto diamond-encrusted heels stuck out from her balloon hoop gown. Wolfe caught the flash of white lace garters and curved, muscled legs before she flipped the skirt back down and huffed out a breath. "Are you smoking on my damn wedding day? You told me you quit. Julietta's going to kill you."

He fought past his lack of speech and wondered if this was a hallucination. "Not if you don't tell her."

She sniffed. "You wish. I don't want you to die of lung cancer. Don't just stand there gaping. Help me up, I can barely move in this thing."

And then she was just Gen again. His best friend, a general pain in the ass, and the most precious person in the world to him.

Wolfe moved fast and pulled her up. "Are you okay? Did you fall out the window?"

She rebalanced herself on those ridiculous heels and waved her hand in the air. "Yeah, I'm fine. My hips got stuck but I managed."

She dusted off her pristine white dress as if jumping out of church windows were a normal occurrence. Damn, she was a hell of a woman. "Umm, babe? Are you pulling a runaway bride thing? Or did you just want to confirm the fire exit worked?"

Her ballsy humor faded from her face. She tilted her chin up, and her lower lip trembled. "I'm in trouble. Will you help me?"

He kept his face calm even though his palms sweat. Something bad had happened, but right now she needed his head in the game. "We ditching the groom?"

"Yeah."

Wolfe decided to play it like a big adventure. "Cool. I got you covered. Lose the shoes."

She kicked off the killer stilettos. "Are there reporters out there?"

"No worries, this is a piece of cake. But we gotta move now. Take my hand."

She placed her small hand in his and squeezed. Wolfe swore that even if he had to fight the whole Taliban, he was getting her out of here and to someplace safe. Discussion was for later. "My car is parked down the street so we're good. Follow me."

He led her down the back steps, behind the rectory, and maneuvered through a perfectly formed line of flowering bushes. She paused in flight, wincing at the chips of mulch and gravel. "Ouch."

"You're such a girl. Here, you're going too slow." Wolfe heaved her up into his arms in a tumble of satin and lace and cut through some weeping willow trees.

"I can't believe you parked so far away. That means you were late. Some best friend you are."

"Be glad I was late. I'm saving your ass now."

She gave a humph. He walked faster, sensing chaos and a complete breakdown not too far behind. If he didn't get her out in time and anyone caught them leaving, it would be a virtual shitstorm. He ducked under a low-hanging branch, tracked through the backyard of a Cape Cod behind the church, and took a hard right. She stayed silent, and Wolfe bet he had two minutes before her crazy impulsive decision hit her and she said she'd go back.

But if something made her run, it was too important to ignore. The hell he'd take her back.

Finally, he spotted his black Mercedes convertible. He fished the keys out of his pocket, hit the alarm, and opened the door. "In."

Another lower lip tremble. "Wolfe, maybe I'm wrong. Maybe I should go back."

"Do you want to marry him, Gen? Deep down, in your gut, where it counts?"

Her teeth sank into her lower lip. Shame and fear and humiliation etched out the lines of her face. Her voice broke on the word "No."

He nodded and calmly pushed her in the seat. "Then you're doing the right thing and we'll work it out. I promise."

She swallowed. Returned his nod. And slid into the car.

Wolfe wasted no time. He revved the engine and did a three-point turn, going out the back way and speeding away from the church like it was a devil's sanctuary and their souls were at risk.

When they hit the open road and no one seemed to be following, he glanced over. She slumped in the seat, her hair hanging halfway down her neck, her graceful profile carved in stone. She stared out the window as if she was watching her life dissipate behind her. And in a way, it was.

Knowing what she needed the most right now, Wolfe hit the speaker system and Guns N' Roses blasted out, hard and loud and raw. He didn't speak.

Just drove.

WANT MORE JENNIFER PROBST?

Check out the first two installments in her sizzling new **Searching For series**

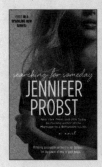 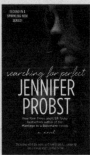

And look for the next two books in the series, **Coming spring/summer 2015!**